Defining Moments:

Black and White

Defining Moments:

Black and White

Ben Burgess Jr.

www.urbanbooks.net

Urban Books, LLC
300 Farmingdale Road, NY-Route 109
Farmingdale, NY 11735

ISBN 13: 978-1-64556-045-6
ISBN 10: 1-64556-045-7

First Trade Paperback Printing May 2020
Printed in the United States of America

10 9 8 7 6 5 4 3 2 1

Distributed by Kensington Publishing Corp.
Submit Orders to:
Customer Service
400 Hahn Road
Westminster, MD 21157-4627
Phone: 1-800-733-3000
Fax: 1-800-659-2436

Defining Moments:

Black and White

by

Ben Burgess Jr.

Chapter 1

Ebony

Ground Zero

"You heard that?" I asked my partner, Rashida.

"Yup, sounded like shots, Ebony."

"Hit the lights. Let's check it out."

"Units, be advised, I'm getting numerous callers stating they've heard gunshots on the corner of Fourteenth Street and Tenth Avenue," the radio dispatcher said.

I grabbed my radio, keyed the microphone, and responded, "Sixth Precinct Sergeant, Central. Show me responding. I'm two blocks away."

"Sergeant, be advised: I'm now being told by various callers that this is a 10-13. Officers need immediate assistance. Callers are stating that two cops and two unidentified males have been shot. Are there units to back the sergeant and confirm?"

Every unit in the area agreed to back me up. Rashida's light-skinned complexion reddened, and her dreads swayed as she stepped on the gas and weaved through traffic.

We got to the corner and rushed out of the car. Two of my cops, Officers Mendez and Mahoney, were holding a man at gunpoint. He had blood on his hands, wore a black T-shirt, and jeans.

"Drop your weapon and get on the ground with your hands on your head," Mendez yelled.

Mahoney slowly moved in closer to the man with his gun pointed directly at the man's chest.

"This is fucked-up. I didn't do it. I found them like that," the man at gunpoint yelled.

"I'm not going to tell you again. Drop the gun and get on the ground now," Mendez yelled.

The man dropped the gun but put up a hell of a fight, swinging wildly at Mahoney when he moved in. Mahoney grabbed his arm and wrestled him facedown to the pavement. Rashida kicked the gun from out of the man's reach while Mendez, Mahoney, and I fought and struggled to cuff him. My knee was on the man's lower back while Rashida held his other arm for Mahoney to cuff. The man winced in pain as Mahoney tightened and locked the cuffs.

"Fuck you, pigs! I didn't kill anybody. I want a fucking lawyer," the perp said, squirming while Mendez frisked him before raising him up off the ground.

He hocked up the phlegm in his throat, turned his head, spat, and kicked at Mendez and Mahoney as they struggled to put him in the backseat of their marked car.

Winded, I asked Mendez, "Where are the cops Central said were shot?"

"Once we pulled up, we saw this guy holding a gun with blood all over him. He bolted, and we chased after him. We didn't get to look for the other cops."

"I'm on it. Handle things with this guy."

Rashida and I ran around the corner. I scanned the area, and my eyes landed on a patrol car riddled with bullets on the corner of Gansevoot and Washington Streets. My heartbeat sped up. People were crowding around two men lying on the sidewalk in front of the Allouche Art Gallery.

"I'll check on the men on the ground," Rashida said, sprinting toward them.

Several shots were in the car doors, windows, and windshield. Gomez slumped against the driver's-side door. His eyes were open and glazed over, but he wasn't blinking. Roberts was shaking and holding his throat. I opened the driver's-side door and gasped when I saw Gomez's bullet-riddled body and a gunshot wound in the middle of his forehead. He was gone.

I moved toward the passenger side and opened the door, and Roberts fell to the concrete, gasping, grunting, and holding his neck. His bloody hands were covering a wound where he was hit in the throat, straining to breathe.

"Fuck," I yelled.

Rashida came over to me.

"Both of the guys across the street were shot and killed—"

"Gomez and Roberts are hurt."

Rashida stared at Gomez.

"Boss . . . Gomez is—"

"I know, but we have to try. We can't let both of them die out here."

My trembling hands reached to key in my radio. "Central, I need you to rush buses to this location now. We have confirmed four men shot. Two unidentified males and two officers. I repeat, two officers have been shot."

I was nervous, but I needed to keep my composure. Panic was on Roberts's face. Tears streamed from his eyes as he looked at me, and his legs kicked frantically as he fought to live.

"You're going to be OK. Don't give up on me, Roberts. Stay with me," I shouted.

I couldn't wait for the ambulance. I had to get Gomez and Roberts to a hospital ASAP.

"Fuck it. Rashida, let's go. Grab Gomez. We'll throw them both in the back of the car and drive them to Bellevue. We don't have time to wait for the bus."

Rashida nodded and helped me put Roberts and Gomez in the back of our patrol car.

More units arrived at the scene. I rushed over and immediately started delegating tasks. I pointed to the first group and said, "I need you to wait for EMS to take care of the victims across the street."

I faced the other group. "I need you to search for witnesses and cameras in the area that might've caught this guy killing everyone."

Everyone dispersed to handle their assignments. I hurried back to my car.

We screeched away from the corner, swerving in and out of traffic. At some places, Rashida drove on the sidewalk to avoid traffic and make it to the hospital as fast as possible. I turned to the backseat. Roberts's movements were gradually slowing down. Gomez's glassy, lifeless eyes were staring back at me. I didn't want to believe it, but he was dead. I sighed and focused my attention on Roberts.

"Stay with me, OK? We're going to get you some help. We're almost there."

I keyed the microphone on my radio and said, "Sixth Precinct Sergeant."

"Sergeant, proceed."

"Central, please contact Bellevue and advise them that I'm taking the two injured officers to the hospital myself. The officers are badly injured, and we're losing time waiting for the ambulance."

"10-4, Sergeant. I'm putting in the notification now."

Once we pulled up to the hospital, the staff hurried outside with gurneys and equipment and rushed the officers inside. Blood covered my uniform and trembling hands. Rashida and I exchanged scared looks as we watched the hospital staff frantically work on Gomez and Roberts. My cell phone buzzed with a call from my commanding officer.

"Williams, where are you?" Inspector Phillips asked.

I brought him up to speed with all the details on the scene.

"Jesus, I'm on my way. Are you all right?"

"I'm good. I just hope the paramedics can save them. Once everything is cleared up, I'll head back and take care of everything at the scene—"

"Everything at the scene is under control. I sent Captain Wallace there. I want you to make sure you're all right. You saw a lot tonight. You can't help anyone else if your head's not focused."

"Honestly, I'm good."

"Keep me posted on Roberts and Gomez's conditions if anything changes before I get there."

"Yes, sir."

I ended the call. The hospital staff looked up at me and shook their heads with saddened expressions. I knew it was too late. They both had passed.

Chapter 2

Ben

The Token

I gradually opened my eyes and gathered my bearings as I heard my cell phone buzzing. I felt around the nightstand for my phone and grabbed it. The neon red digits on my cable box read two forty-three in the morning. Becky was sound asleep in my arms, nuzzled against my chest as I answered my cell phone.

"Hello," I said groggily.

"Ben, I need you to wake up, buddy."

I squinted to read the name of the person that was crazy enough to call me this early in the morning. My eyes bulged. I sat up when I realized it was Tim, one of the partners from my law firm.

"Good morning, sir."

"Ben, we need you to come to the firm ASAP. An important case just came in, and it could define your career in a very positive way if you pull out a win."

"What's going on?"

"I don't have time to get into all the particulars. Hurry. The other partners and I will brief you when you get here."

"I'm on my way now, sir."

He ended the call.

I tried to ease out of bed without waking Becky. I tossed the covers off and draped my legs over the side of the bed. Becky stirred and rolled over next to me, her hard pink nipples exposed. She stretched and yawned.

"What time is it?" she asked.

"Almost three."

"What's going on? What do they want now?"

Becky was used to seeing me jump whenever the partners called.

"I gotta go. A big case came in, and they want me to handle it."

"Ugh, it's so early."

"I know. Get some sleep, baby. I'll call you once things calm down."

"Since I'm up now, wanna have a quickie before you go in? You'll be more relaxed for work."

"Rain check."

Rebecca sulked and buried her face in the pillow.

Seeing her lying there naked was tempting, but I didn't want to start something I couldn't finish. After I showered and got dressed, I rushed toward the door.

"Don't work too hard, babe. Call me when you get a free minute during the day," she said, adjusting my tie.

"I will. I promise."

I gave her a quick kiss and ran out the door of our brownstone. Since it was early in the morning, I figured the commute from Fort Green, Brooklyn, to the firm in Midtown Manhattan shouldn't take more than fifteen minutes.

I was a junior associate at one of the biggest law firms in New York—Wayne, Rothstein, and Lincoln. I was also the only African American associate. Many at the firm felt that I was only hired because of affirmative action. Working in a prestigious law firm came with loads of responsibilities, and being the only black associate, I had to work twice as hard as the other associates just to be seen for who I was and what I was capable of.

I spent eight years grinding, busting my ass night in and night out, sometimes working eighteen hours a day so I'd be taken seriously and earn the respect of the partners. I sacrificed, missing important events, special milestones, and anniversaries with Becky and my family to take on every assignment the partners asked of me. I wanted to make a name for myself and rise in the firm, with one goal: making partner. I did everything possible to be close to flawless in my work. I'd seen firsthand how different things were when a white associate made a mistake and when I, their token black guy, made one. One fuckup would erase all the positive things I'd done and bring me back to square one.

With all my hard work, the partners often had me serve as the first chair, along with the senior partners on some of the most critical and newsworthy cases handled by the firm. If what Tim said was true, this case had to be huge and might be what I needed to push the firm to make me a partner finally.

I turned on the radio and flipped to the go-to news station in NY, 1010 Wins, to get an idea of what I was going in for as I sped to the firm.

The top news was about a rapper named "Co-Kayne" who was arrested for killing a pair of cops and a gay couple. The police found him standing over the couple's bodies, holding the murder weapon and covered in their blood. I prayed that wasn't the case I was handling, but I was sure that it probably was. Other trending news was about an NBA player, Johnny Alfieri, who was scheduled to turn himself in to the police after a stripper made claims that he raped her.

***

I pulled up to the firm and parked my BMW 750 in the parking lot underneath the building. Bill, another associate who had a winning record as good as mine, pulled his Range Rover into a spot close to me. The guy exuded confidence. He was a brown-haired, blue-eyed pretty boy that joked and laughed with the partners regularly. They playfully teased him about his black girlfriend, and, when they thought I was out of earshot, shared stories with him about the times they fucked black women. He had lots of photos with his girlfriend all over his office, but I kept very few personal things in mine. I heard how the other partners dogged black women. I didn't want them to have animosity toward me because I was dating a white one. I kept my private life private.

To most of the people of color around the firm, Bill gave the appearance of being "down." If you closed your eyes and heard him speak, he even sounded "black." Every morning, he greeted and hugged the firm's only black secretary, Mrs. Wilson, but I knew it was all for show. While he might've had her and most of the minorities around the office fooled, I saw through his façade. He was just another bigot that hid it well.

"You're here early," I said as we walked toward the elevator.

"Yeah, Francis said he and the other partners needed me to come in for a case ASAP."

"Me too. Tim called me. I wonder why they needed both of us."

Bill's cell phone buzzed on our way up to the office. He pulled it out of his pants pocket and answered it.

"Hey, babe, I had to come into work early. What's up?" he said.

His eyes widened. "Oh my God. Are you OK?"

He looked shaken and alarmed by the call.

"Fuck it, where are you? I'll come to you. It doesn't matter if I'm at the firm. I'll explain to the partners I have a family emergency. Babe . . . You say you're all right, but I can hear in your voice you're shaken up. All right, I'll calm down, but as soon as I handle things here, I'll call you. I love you, babe. See you soon."

He ended the call.

"You all right?" I asked.

"My girl is a sergeant for NYPD in Manhattan. Some rapper went crazy and killed two cops she worked with and two other guys around a club on Washington Street. The cops died right after she rushed them to the hospital."

"I heard about that on the radio on the way here. Sorry about your girl."

"Yeah. Thanks."

There was an awkward silence for a minute.

"I wonder if that's the case they want us to handle," I said.

"I hope not. It'll be a conflict of interest for me."

We took the elevator to the twenty-first floor, walked down the hall to the conference room, and saw the three partners of the law firm, Richard Wayne, Tim Rothstein, and Francis Lincoln, sitting at the head of the long mahogany conference table.

"All right, gentlemen, have a seat," Richard said. "We're pressed for time, so we need to move fast. I'm going to be talking quickly, so I suggest both of you take notes."

I nodded and took out my legal pad.

"The firm picked up two clients with very difficult cases. One of the clients is the rapper Co-Kayne that allegedly killed two cops and a gay couple. Our other client is an NBA player that allegedly raped a stripper at a gentlemen's club."

I knew he was worried about these cases. His face was as red as his bloodshot eyes. Richard slid a file over to me.

"Ben, we want you to handle the rapper case. You're going to be the first chair, and Tim will be second to help advise and oversee everything."

He slid another file over to Bill.

"Bill, you'll handle the ball player. The district attorney's office sent us a video from the gentlemen's club incident. It's pretty clear and detailed and doesn't look good for our client. We'll discuss that later after we go over Ben's case."

Richard faced me. "I'll start with your case first, Ben, because I need you to head to the 6th Precinct right after I brief you. Co-Kayne, whose real name is Reginald Brown, was found with the couple's blood on him and the gun in his hand when the cops caught him. His record label spokesman told us four witnesses saw him arguing with the gay couple inside the club, and he screamed he'd 'fucking kill their faggot asses' an hour before they were killed."

I shook my head.

"It gets worse. The club has a video of him throwing his drink in one of the victim's faces. Later on, the video shows the couple leaving the club, and three minutes later, Reggie stumbles out drunk, headed in the direction of the couple. He has a rap sheet full of drug and assault charges, and his music is full of homophobic lyrics."

"Great," I said sarcastically.

"Luckily, he lawyered up quickly, and we advised him not to say anything to the detectives until we send representation for him."

"Co-Kayne only wanted a 'brotha' to represent him, so we knew you'd be perfect for this case," Francis said.

"Excuse me for asking, but am I perfect because you think I'm capable of winning or because I'm the only black associate at the firm?"

Francis chuckled and said, "Both."

"Well, Ben, we get the best of both worlds with you," Tim said. "You appeal to our black and other minority clients, but you don't act all 'ghetto,' so you're a good asset to have."

The partners laughed.

I didn't.

They saw a disparity in the way I dressed, talked, and acted. To them, I was black but tolerable. They made jokes all the time about how, in their eyes, I didn't "act black enough." I didn't want to do or say anything that would prevent me from making a partner, so most of the time, I laughed them off and let it slide, but deep down, their words tore me up inside. Since I was a kid, I never felt "black" enough when I was around my own people. When I played sports with other black kids, they'd often say things like "you talk white" or tease me for not understanding slang. My parents were respected judges. We lived in Brookville, Long Island, a mostly white upper-class neighborhood. I went to the prestigious Portledge Private School my entire childhood and grew up around mostly whites.

Richard leaned back in his burgundy executive chair, inhaling and exhaling deeply.

"We have nothing but confidence in you, Ben. These cases are important to the firm. It's a lot to ask of the two of you to win both of these cases, but as an added incentive for the two of you to get a win, whoever does the best will be strongly considered for a partnership with this firm."

My ears perked up when I heard the mention of "making partner." Bill and I looked at each other. I knew what this was. They weren't giving me this case because of my hard work. I got it by default because I was black.

If this case would be the one to boost my career and promote me to partner, I'd do everything legally possible to win, even though this case felt more like a suicide mission. Bill's case seemed more winnable, and I bet the partners were rooting for him because he was white, but I wouldn't let that discourage me from trying to win my case.

"All right, Ben, rush down to the 6th Precinct. Keep Tim posted on everything."

"Yes, sir."

I gathered my things and watched the partners smiling and laughing with Bill while they got the video ready for his case. I rushed out the door. I knew they had him pegged as the next partner, but I was determined to win my case.

Chapter 3

Billy

Sex, Lies, and Videos

"Whew, Ben's going to have his hands full with that case," Richard laughed.

"Yours is no walk in the park either, but be thankful that thug wanted a 'brotha' for a lawyer," Francis said. "Your chances of winning this case are way better than Ben's."

The partners laughed while I put on an unsure grin.

The truth was, Ben was going to be strong competition. Some of my best strengths were that I was good at reading and understanding people. I could usually connect with anyone, especially trial juries, and that had helped me become a successful lawyer. Ben was a meticulous lawyer with a great eye for detail. He saw all the small things that most lawyers missed. He worked his ass off, but I needed this partnership, I was sure, more than he did.

The partners mentioned awhile back that Ben grew up pampered and well off with both of his parents, who were successful judges. I didn't have that luxury then, and I damn sure didn't have it now. I grew up with just my mom and me in a poor, single-parent home. It was hard for us because, to this day, my mom still battled multiple sclerosis, deteriorating daily from it.

I made decent money, but becoming a partner would give me a big enough salary to easily cover all my bills, the financial ability to put my mom in a comfortable, assisted-living place full-time, and the flexibility to plan my proposal to my girl Ebony. The ring I'd bought for her had been sitting in my desk drawer for months. I looked at it every day, but I hadn't popped the question yet because I had nowhere near enough money to give her the wedding she deserved.

A large projection screen descended from the ceiling. Francis operated the laptop on the conference table while Richard continued to talk.

"Now we're lucky. The surveillance video had audio. After the NYPD vice unit raided the strip club two years ago, the owner, Jerrod, swore he'd run a legit business without prostitution. He had high-definition cameras installed throughout the club with audio capabilities as an attempt to stop the strippers from sleeping with the customers. He's willing to testify on our client's behalf."

"What's the name of the strip club?" I asked.

"J's Gentlemen's Quarters," Francis answered.

"We'll play the video so you can see what we're dealing with here," Richard said.

The video started with Johnny sitting in the corner of the strip club directly under the camera. Since he was so close to it, we could see and hear their conversation. The video showed the stripper, Sophia, saunter over to Johnny. He pulled out a wad of money and waved it at her. Sophia smiled, climbed into his lap, and straddled him.

"Damn, ma, how much?" he asked.

"It depends on what you're looking for."

"You know what I want."

"Uh, we don't do that here anymore. Are you a cop?"

"You don't know who I am?"

"Should I?"

"Fuck, yeah. I'm Johnny Alfieri, the best white boy playin' in the NBA."

"Sorry, I don't watch sports. Look, I can give you a private lap dance, but that's about it."

"The only type of lap dance I want from you involves you riding my lap with neither of us wearing clothes." He laughed. She didn't. "You really gonna lose out on making all this money?" He pointed to all of the scantily clad women walking around the strip club.

"Just name your price. Come on. I'm sure none of these other women here would turn down making this easy money."

She looked like she was questioning whether she should.

"All right, get a VIP room, and we'll fuck in there. No anal and no leaving marks. I want my money up front before we do anything," she said, standing up.

Johnny smiled. "*That's* what I'm talking about."

A devilish grin grew on his face as he slapped her on the ass and watched her walk away.

The video went to the next camera, where Sophia met up with Johnny in the VIP room.

She got undressed.

Johnny started fondling her breasts, and Sophia looked uncomfortable. "Wait . . . I don't want to do this. I'm sorry. I can't," Sophia said, gathering her clothes. She tried to leave, but Johnny blocked her path and grabbed her hand.

"Bitch, I already told you I'm not a cop, and I'm about to pay you good money."

She ripped her hand from his grip, shoved past him, and rushed toward the door. Johnny grabbed her by the arm and slammed her against the wall. She winced and held the back of her head in pain. He placed his hands flat against the wall on both sides of her and said, "I *always* get what I want, and you're gonna give me what I want."

Johnny fumbled with his belt, pulled down his jeans, grabbed Sophia by the nape of her neck, and shoved her on the black leather couch. With his pants dropped to his ankles, he grabbed Sophia by her hair and held her head down, forcing his dick into her mouth until she coughed and gagged. Tears streamed down her face as she woefully sucked him.

"Don't act like you don't like this shit. I know you want this money," Johnny said.

He stopped her, stood up, and maneuvered her until she was bent over. Sophia attempted to loosen herself from his grasp, but he wrenched her arm, forcing her to comply. Then he slid into her without protection.

"There we go. Tell me you like it," he said.

"I like it," she repeated.

He had an expression of shock at first, but then he seemed to enjoy it as he pumped into her. "Tell me you want this dick."

"You know I want it, daddy. Give it to me."

Sophia's grunts and moans seemed to excite him. Johnny quickened his pace and smacked her ass cheeks. Sophia winced with each slap but continued to encourage him to keep fucking her.

"Come for me, daddy. I want you to come," Sophia begged.

Johnny moaned, pulled out of her, and came on her back. He laughed. "See, I knew you'd like it."

He threw the money against her forehead, adjusted his clothes, and walked out. Sophia picked up the money and wrapped her arms around her naked body. At first, it looked as if she were laughing, but it immediately turned into weeping. The video cut off.

"Now, you see our dilemma. If this goes to trial, we need to convince the jury that Sophia wanted that money, and those crocodile tears at the end were just her disappointment in her own life—not because she felt raped."

"What is he saying? Does he think he raped her?" I asked.

"He's a dumb jock who can barely spell his name. He's impressionable. You can tell him he raped her, and the dumb son of a bitch would probably believe he did. You heard her. She wanted him to come inside her. She told him she wanted it and loved it. She's a whore, and we need to convey that message to the jury if this goes to trial. We're all counting on you, Billy."

"What's the woman's name?" I asked.

"Sophia Winters, but her stripper name is Sapphire," Francis said.

The partners chuckled.

"She's just some dumb stripper that's disappointed after fucking a rich client. He didn't whisk her away and give her a happily-ever-after fantasy life like the whore Julia Roberts played in *Pretty Woman*," Francis said.

I turned to Richard. "You keep saying *if* this goes to trial. What do you mean by *if?*"

"We had an anonymous friend of the firm reach out to her to set up a meeting for later on today after Johnny turns himself in and goes through arraignment," Richard said.

"Who's the friend?" I asked.

"That's not important," Francis said.

"How did you manage to set up a meeting with her?" I asked.

"We had our 'friend' tell her to hear us out, that there has to be an agreement we can come to that would suit both parties regarding this 'misunderstanding,'" Richard said.

"She bought that?"

"Our friend said she'd hear us out."

"Take her some place low-key, talk to her, and let's settle this bullshit out of court," Francis added.

"With all due respect, sir, talking to her after Alfieri turns himself in is tampering with a witness. I could get disbarred for that. The firm could get prosecuted for it too."

"That's why no one needs to know about it," Francis said. "We want everything done discreetly, so it doesn't come back to any of us. Bill, one of your biggest strengths is your charm. We need you to charm her into dropping this rape charge. Start cordial, and if she makes this go to trial, we'll play dirty and dig deep into her past. From the information we gathered so far, she was caught in that raid at the strip club and arrested for prostitution. Explain to her that we'll paint her like the whore of Babylon if she doesn't fall in line. Everyone knows this case is bullshit. A sane person would jump at settling and drop the charges. Draw up an ironclad confidentiality provision. Alfieri is willing to pay up to $10 million to make her go away, but start at $2 million and slowly work your way up if she's greedy. She needs to understand that it would be better for everyone if she just takes the money, signs the release and confidentiality agreements, and goes on about her life."

A deal like this was highly unethical and illegal, but if I could win this case without even going to trial, it was something I had to consider strongly. I needed this partnership, and this was my shot, but morally, I didn't feel right about going this route when I knew it was wrong, and I had so much to lose.

"If I convince her to take the money, is the partnership mine?" I asked.

Richard smiled. "We'd all highly consider it. Get this done for us, Bill. We need it resolved immediately."

"I got this. I won't let you down."

"I know you won't," Richard said. "Look, Alfieri is on his way here. Talk with him a bit and then go with him to the precinct so he can turn himself in. We'll make some calls to get him through Central Booking quickly and into arraignment. Most likely, he'll get bail, and then you can meet up with Francis to talk to the whore."

"I'm on it."

I stared out my office window, waiting for Johnny to arrive. The paparazzi was parked in front of our building, waiting to get a shot of Johnny walking in. A sleek, black limo pulled up in front of the firm. The doors opened, and Johnny Alfieri stepped out, followed by two older white men. Johnny quickly walked past the media and avoided answering questions. I made my way to the elevator to meet him downstairs.

"Good morning. I'm Bill O'Neil. I'm going to be representing you, Mr. Alfieri."

"Cool, just make sure you clear me of this shit, yo," Johnny said.

He was about six foot six, blond with blue eyes, and had a cocky air about him. He wore a bandanna, with a long, white T-shirt and sagging baggy jeans.

A thin man wearing a gray suit, in his midthirties, with his black hair pulled back into a long ponytail, extended his hand to me.

"Please excuse his rudeness. Hi, I'm Johnny's agent, Paul Marshall, and this is his publicist, Greg Goldman," he said, pointing to another man.

I shook hands with the three of them.

Greg was tall too, about six foot four, stocky, with military-short, dirty-blond hair.

"Yo, your boss, Richard, said somethin' about payin' this bitch off and sweepin' this shit under the rug. How quickly can we do that shit, yo?" Johnny asked.

I was annoyed with him already. He was trying way too hard to sound "street." I'd Googled him before he came here and found out he grew up in East Hills, a wealthy town on Long Island, and he went to private schools as a kid. There was nothing "street" about him.

"Mr. Alfieri, let's talk in the conference room first before we get into that," I said.

I took Johnny, Greg, and Paul upstairs to our floor.

"Do you two mind if I talk to Mr. Alfieri privately before we all discuss the strategy for this case?" I asked Paul and Greg.

They both agreed and sat in the lobby while I talked to Johnny in the conference room.

"Yo, so we gonna talk to this chick or what?" Johnny asked.

The firm had made a mistake telling him we would do some shit like that. I didn't want him blabbing to anyone about the illegal tactic the firm was using, so I made sure to word my comment in a way that let him know we'd handle it without incriminating the firm.

"Under the law, an attorney can't attempt to alter or prevent the testimony of a witness in a criminal or civil proceeding. The firm is going to do everything in its power to relay the message to her that we want this resolved out of court."

"Fuck that, yo. I'll go back to the club and talk to the bitch myself."

"No. Under no circumstances should you ever go back to that club. Everything will get handled, I promise, but in the meantime, can you explain to me what exactly happened that night?" I asked.

"Did you see the video?"

"I did, but I want to hear your side of the story to understand things better."

He sighed. "I'll be straight wit' you, homie. I wanted a pretty piece of ass, and I heard that club was known for their strippers fucking the clientele. I offered to pay her to fuck me in the VIP room, and she said yes. At first, she was feisty because she thought I was a cop, but I calmed her down, and it was cool. We handled our business, then I paid her and went on my way."

It was almost humorous that he said she was "feisty." He never mentioned her crying or fighting with him.

"Did she make any indication that might've suggested she didn't want to have sex with you?"

"As I said, she was feisty at first, but after I calmed her down, she was begging me to fuck her. She wanted it. Now, she's actin' like a fucking victim so she can get famous. I didn't rape that bitch."

He didn't avert his eyes from me. His voice was even-keeled. His body language indicated that he was telling the truth, but I wanted him to confirm it one more time.

"So, you're certain you didn't rape Sophia Winters."

"Whatever the bitch's name is, I swear on my life I didn't rape her."

"All right. We already arranged with the 47th Precinct that you'll turn yourself in. Once you're there, they'll process you and bring you to Central Booking. The partners of my firm pulled some strings to expedite your process with the court to get you seen by the judge as soon as possible."

"How are we going to end this?"

"If everything works out as planned, she'll sign a non-disclosure agreement, drop the charges, and this whole thing will be over."

"Yeah, offer her the cash. I know that bitch will jump all over the deal. She's a money-grubbing ho, just like the rest of them."

The way he talked about her, he never made her sound like a person. He only referred to her with derogatory names, which made me question if he were a racist, an asshole, or both.

"Mr. Alfieri—"

"Just call me Johnny."

"OK, Johnny. If things don't work out, and we go to trial, you have to make a habit of calling her by her name. Since you've been here, you've called her a 'bitch' and a 'ho' several times in our brief conversation. That won't fly in front of a jury."

"A'ight. I see whatcha talkin' about."

I brought Paul and Greg into the conference room and shared the plan with them. Everyone seemed optimistic and felt we could get things settled smoothly.

Johnny, Paul, Greg, and I rushed to the limo to head to the precinct but were bombarded by reporters.

"Mr. Alfieri, did you rape that stripper?"

"Do you think this tarnishes your image to your African American fans?"

"Yo, I didn't rape that . . . woman," Johnny said, catching himself.

"Come on, Johnny, don't make any more comments," I said.

He nodded and got in the limo.

The paparazzi gathered around the limo snapping pictures and knocking for Johnny to lower the window so they could ask more questions. I hated media attention with cases. I've had high-profile cases in the past that went well, but being front and center for all of the world to see made me feel exposed. I preferred to keep a low profile and not be all over the cover of newspapers.

We pulled away from the firm, and I was confident I could end this before it even got to trial.

Chapter 4

Ben

Oreos

After rushing through morning traffic, I arrived at the 6th Precinct. There was a media circus in front of the precinct already. All the attention from the press was a little intimidating, but I've had high-profile cases like this before and relished it. The bigger this case got, the bigger the reward would be if I were able to pull out a win. There'd be no way the firm wouldn't bring me in as a partner.

I took a deep breath, exhaled slowly, avoided responding to the numerous reporters' questions, and rushed inside.

In the lobby was a sitting area along the side wall filled with people waiting to report their problems to a young white officer with a clipboard standing in front of them. The dark-skinned brotha with the sergeant's badge sat behind a huge wooden desk in the middle of the room, filling out paperwork. Above the desk were numerous closed-circuit monitors that displayed the cells and all the various areas around the precinct.

I walked up to the desk, flashed my business card, and spoke to the sergeant. His name badge read Sergeant St. Clair.

"Good morning, sir, I'm Ben Turner. I'm representing Mr. Reginald Brown. I was told he was being detained here."

He grunted. "Yeah, we got him. That's your client's publicist and manager sitting down over there," he said, pointing to a short, heavyset, balding white man and a thin, blond woman with glasses.

"Give me a minute, and I'll have my detectives set up a room so you can talk to your client," he said.

I nodded.

Sergeant St. Clair lowered his voice and said, "Look, brotha, I know you got a hard job just like me, but that guy killed four people, two of whom were cops. Think about *that* before you defend a murderer."

I nodded, although there was no doubt in my mind I was going to be defending Co-Kayne for this case.

I signaled to the people the sergeant mentioned.

"Are you Co-Kayne's lawyer?" the blond woman asked.

"Yes, I'm Ben Turner. Have you seen him?"

The heavyset man cut in. "No. These bastards said we couldn't talk to him at all because he's under arrest. He used his phone call to contact us, and we reached out to your firm. I'm Bernie, his manager. This is Jessica, his publicist."

We shook hands.

"I'm so sick of this asshole always getting into shit," Bernie said. "I purposely got him bodyguards to stop him from fighting and keep him out of trouble, but he sneaks away from them and goes and does this shit."

His nostrils flared as he continued. "Do you know how many damn times I've been woken up in the middle of the fucking night to bail that drunken dumbass out of jail? Too many. I always have to clean his messes when he fucks up. This time, I might not be able to fix this clusterfuck for his sorry ass."

"I'm going to do everything possible to help him get through this," I assured them.

"Thank you, Ben," Jessica said.

"You tell him this: If he doesn't want to spend the rest of his fucking life in prison, he'll shut up and listen for once and do everything you ask of him," Bernie said. "He's in enough shit, and the last person he needs to piss off is you, who's here to save his stupid ass. You have to be firm with him, or he won't respect you. If he acts up, call him by his real name, Reginald. That'll fix him."

"You ready? I'm going to escort you to your client now," an officer said, cutting short my conversation with Bernie and Jessica. I nodded.

We walked up one flight of stairs to the second floor and stood in front of the detective's office. The officer knocked on the door.

"The detectives will help you from here," he said before heading back downstairs.

A balding black man wearing a blue suit opened the door. "You're Co-Kayne's lawyer?"

"Yeah."

"Follow me."

We walked to a steel door with a small Plexiglas window. The detective with me opened the door to a small, gray room. Half of the wall on my left was glass, but I was sure it was a two-way mirror. Co-Kayne was sitting at a metal desk in the middle of the cramped room. He was brown-skinned, with long cornrows, and was wearing a pair of blue sweatpants and a sweatshirt. I was sure they gave him whatever clothes they could find around the precinct because they were keeping his clothes for evidence. I took a seat across from him at the metal desk.

"Wait a minute. Hold up. Who's this?" Co-Kayne asked the detective. His breath still reeked of liquor.

"It's your lawyer, jerk-off," the detective snidely answered before slamming the door behind him.

"Hi, I'm Ben Turner. I'm going to be representing you," I said, extending my hand.

Co-Kayne batted my hand away and said, "Nah, I told Bernie I wanted a brotha, and he gets me some prep-school Oreo to defend me."

I exhaled and rolled my eyes at his comment. Oreo. I hated being called that. It meant I was black on the outside but acted as if I were white.

"Did the detectives read you your Miranda rights before questioning you?" I asked.

"Yeah, but I didn't tell them shit."

"Good."

"Ben Turner. You even got a white-ass name. What kind of Uncle Tom shit is that?"

"Reginald—" I said.

"Don't call me by my government name."

Bernie said it would piss him off. It was my subtle way of getting him back for calling me an Oreo. "Can I call you Reggie?"

"Whatever."

"I come from Wayne, Rothstein, and Lincoln, the best criminal defense law firm in New York—"

"I don't care where you come from. I want a black man as my lawyer, and you're not what I'm looking for."

"Well, I'm the best chance you have of not doing life in prison, so you can either accept me as your lawyer or rot in a cell for the rest of your life. Your choice."

Reggie sucked his teeth and looked at me. "You walk around with your Ivy League education and nice suits and look at me like I'm just some poor, stupid, street nigga."

I glared at him.

"You know why I think you're a sellout? Because I can tell you're the type that doesn't live around other blacks," Reggie said.

"You don't know anything about me."

"And you don't know shit about me, either, but I bet as soon as you walked through those precinct doors, you already believed you knew all you needed to about me. You're not a real black man. I told your firm I wanted a real nigga."

"You're right," I said. "I'm nobody's 'nigga,' and to degrade me because I don't meet your standard of 'blackness' is sad and ignorant. We're both running the same race and jumping over the same hurdles, but instead of helping to lift me up, fellow black man, you'd rather drag and put me down. Now, are we going to go over your case or not?"

Reggie smirked. "You don't like me, do you?"

"I don't know why you insist on thinking I have a problem with you, but it's not my job to like or not like you. My job is to keep you out of prison, and that's what I plan on doing."

"Well, I didn't do it. I didn't kill anybody."

"OK."

"I'm serious."

"OK."

"Be straight with me. You think I did it, don't you?"

"You said you didn't, so as your attorney, I'm taking your word, and I'm giving you the benefit of the doubt," I said.

"Stop giving me the bullshit lawyer answers. Do you think I killed those people?"

I took a long breath and exhaled through my nostrils before answering him. "I don't know. Honestly, you have a lot of evidence against your innocence. You have an extensive rap sheet of assaults with weapons and previous convictions dating back to when you were a juvenile, which shows a history of violence. Before the murders, you argued with the victims in the club, which shows a motive and places you at the scene. A lot of your songs encourage violence toward gays, and on top of all that, you were found with the gay couple's blood on your clothes. You were also holding the murder weapon when the cops arrested you. It's asking a lot of me to believe you had nothing to do with their deaths, but I'm going to do my best to try to convince the jury that you're innocent."

"If you can't even convince yourself, how do you expect to convince a jury?" Reggie asked. "I knew having an Uncle Tom-ass nigga like you was going to put me back in prison."

"Explain it to me then. Help me understand what happened."

He sighed. I opened my briefcase and checked my notes as he went on.

"I was in the club drinking and dancing when these two dudes came up to me and told me they recognized me. They told me I was cute and wanted to take me home with them. People were watching us. I couldn't have that shit leaking out to the media that faggots were hitting on me in clubs. My fans would think I'm about that life, and that's bad for business, so I flipped out on them. I was drunk. I didn't mean it when I said I'd fucking kill them."

"According to witnesses, you said you'd 'kill their faggot asses.'"

"Whatever. Anyway, between the paparazzi and my security team always following me around like my fucking shadow, I snuck out of the club to go down the block to clear my head and smoke a cigarette alone without a million people in my face."

I watched and studied his mannerisms to see if he was lying to me, but so far, he seemed genuine.

"When I got to the corner, I heard gunshots. I ducked down because I didn't know where the shit come from. I stood up to head back to the club, but some guy dressed in black slammed into me. We collided so hard that both of us were on the ground, and he dropped his gun. Blood was all over him, and some of it got on me. Without thinking, I stupidly picked up the gun, and it was still warm. The guy stood up and balled up his fist like he was gonna swing on me. Before he decided to go all crazy on me, I raised the gun to his face, and he ran off. I looked to my right and saw two bodies on the ground. I walked up to them, and it was the gay guys I argued with earlier in the club. The cops came, and it hit me that I was still holding the fucking gun and standing over the bodies. I know how it must've looked, and I know how the cops are, so before they killed my ass for some shit I didn't do, I got the fuck outta there."

"Then what happened?"

"What do you think? I couldn't outrun them, and I didn't want to get shot in the back, so I stopped running."

I pulled a pen and a pad from my briefcase and quickly scribbled down notes.

"What you writing down?" Reggie asked.

"Your story so I can go over it later."

"You think I'm lying, huh?"

"I don't think anything yet. I'm just gathering all the facts."

"Yeah, right. You think I'm stupid and don't see this shit?"

"See what?"

"The silent judgment you have for me."

"And you don't have your thoughts about me?" I asked. "You think because I don't live in the projects, I'm oblivious to how black people are viewed in this world."

Reggie laughed at me.

"Stop laughing."

He kept laughing at me.

"Stop laughing, or I'll walk out of this precinct right now, and you're on your own."

Reggie shut up and stared at me after hearing my empty threat. I glared at him and said, "I make a choice every day to not be another angry black guy like you. You think I don't see when salespeople and security guards watch my every move when I'm shopping, or when I'm getting pulled over by the police because I drive a nice car? There are a million things daily I have to choose to let go, so I'm not consumed by anger."

Reggie clapped and smiled. "I'm fucking with you. I don't want a bitch for my lawyer. I needed to know you're tough enough to handle this shit."

"I'm not here to play mind games with you. I'm here to defend you. Now, I'm assuming from what you told me, that we're pleading not guilty, correct?"

"Yeah, I didn't do shit."

"Good."

There was a solid knock on the door before it swung open.

Detectives came in, stood Reggie up, and checked his handcuffs and leg shackles.

"Sorry to cut this short, but we're ready to transport him to Central Booking now," one said.

I nodded and faced Reggie. "Don't say anything to anyone."

"This isn't my first time being locked up. I know the drill," he replied.

"I'll see you at the arraignment."

We walked outside, and a sea of reporters, spectators, fans, and protesters stood outside the precinct. The press snapped pictures and shoved microphones in Reggie's face and mine.

"Co-Kayne, what caused you to go on a murderous rampage and kill those people?"

"Do you hate gays?"

"Were you beaten by the police after killing two officers?"

"Were you influenced by drugs and alcohol?"

Reggie didn't answer. He kept his head down as the cops waved off the reporters. The protestors, press, and spectators parted to allow the detectives to put Reggie in the back of the unmarked Chevy Impala.

Reggie looked defeated as he was being taken to Central Booking. I guessed reality was starting to hit him.

Thousands of people stood outside the court building on Centre Street in Manhattan. Some were fans, and some were protestors angry that he'd killed a gay couple. In an attempt to limit the amount of time the unwanted crowds spent surrounding the building, the court had pushed his arraignment to be earlier.

I called the firm and briefed Tim on everything Reggie told me. I let him know I was waiting on the arraignment, and Reggie planned on pleading not guilty. Then I called my best friend, Gabby, and made plans to get coffee with her as soon as I got out of court.

Quietly, I sat on the benches in the courtroom and waited for Reggie's case to be called. I reflected on everything he had said to me at the precinct, and it brought back old feelings I thought I'd buried and healed from. It bothered me that he and other people in my race believed I wasn't "black enough." My thoughts drifted back to my childhood.

Every year around Thanksgiving, my dad took my cousin, Simone, and me to his old neighborhood, the Edenwald Houses in the Bronx. We were forced to stand in the schoolyard of PS 112 and hand out turkeys and food to the community. Simone was more like a sister than a cousin to me. She lived with us and was raised by my parents for most of her life. Simone's mom, my aunt Joan, was a junkie prostitute and was constantly getting arrested. Since she was always in and out of jail and unfit to be a mother, the courts gave my parents custody of Simone.

"Dad, do we have to go there?" I'd asked.

"Yeah, Uncle Curtis, do we have to?" Simone added.

"Yes, we have to and stop asking," Dad replied. "It's important to give back to the community."

The last place either of us wanted to be on a Saturday was Dad's old neighborhood.

"Those people are mean. I hate going there," Simone said.

"Me too," Mom mumbled.

"You're not helping, Maybelline," Dad said.

"I don't understand the reasoning of going to the ghetto and giving those ungrateful people food for Thanksgiving. They just take your free food and talk behind your back every year."

"Those 'people' are 'our people,'" Dad said. "I wouldn't be the man I am today if it weren't for my old neighborhood, and when you say things like that, you sound no better than the white people who say that blacks just mooch off the system. Yes, some of them are ungrateful, but a lot of them aren't. We're bringing hope to some of these kids, and it's important to me. Besides, it's good to toughen up our kids and make them appreciate the lives they have."

Mom sighed. "I guess."

***

"*This is a good thing you're doing, Curtis,*" *Officer Watson said.*

"*Yeah, if no one else says it today, thank you for this,*" *Officer Buckley added.*

Officers Watson and Buckley were the community affairs officers for the 47th Precinct. They acted as security and helped hand out the food my dad gave away to the community every year.

"*Thanks, guys,*" *Dad said.* "*I used to live here. I know what it's like to think this is all life has to offer. If I inspire at least one person or give someone just a glimmer of hope today, I did my job, and it'll hopefully spark a change.*"

I saw my mom roll her eyes.

"*What? You don't agree with what Dad's saying?*" *I asked.*

"*Hell no,*" *she said.* "*This neighborhood is a graveyard, full of dead hopes and buried dreams.*" *She pointed.* "*You see those women sitting there on the bench? Those old gossip hounds have been sitting there on those same benches since your father was a little boy. They haven't gotten any better or worse. They just sit there like they've done all their lives—stagnant.*"

"*Come here, son,*" *Dad said.*

I walked over to my father, who was organizing items in the truck.

"*This is the rare occasion when I'm going to tell you to ignore your mother. Your mom and I lived here together when we first got married, but she doesn't have a deep-rooted history here like I do. In any community with impoverished people, you're going to have crime and drugs. It's easy to get pulled into the negativity and become a product of your environment, but it's important to remember that not everyone is the same. There's* some bad in this neighborhood, but there's a lot of good too. We're out here today giving hope to people so they can see that the good can outshine the bad. Do you understand?"

I nodded, and he smiled.

"Good. Now help me unload this truck."

"You're a good man, Mr. Turner," a senior woman told my father.

"Thank you, ma'am. Enjoy your Thanksgiving."

Dad had Simone and me handing out bags of food to go with the people's turkeys.

"Can I have one?"

Dad quickly turned around. "Joan?"

"Yeah, it's me."

Her clothes looked dirty and tattered. She was noticeably pregnant.

Dad hopped off the truck and hugged her.

"Simone, come say hi to your mom."

Simone scrunched up her nose and looked embarrassed. "Nah, I don't want to."

Joan sucked her teeth. "Fuck you, then. I don't want to talk to your stupid ass either, little bitch." She turned back to my father. "Can I just get my food now?"

"In a minute . . . Who's the father for this one?" Dad asked.

"The same one as the last one, Silky."

"No mother in their right mind would name their son Silky. What's his real name?"

"Why? You gonna get your cop friends to look him up? I'm not tellin' you shit."

"If you want this food, you will."

She sighed. "You ain't shit, Curtis. His name is Sammy Miller. Are you happy now? Gimme my shit so I can go on with my business," she said, sticking out her dirty hand.

"You look like you're about to have this baby any day," Dad said. "Are you still using?"

"That's none of your business. All I want is my fucking turkey, come on."

"I know you're not working at the job I got you at Payless. The manager told me you quit after a week."

"I didn't want to be a slave to that damn chump change. I make more in two hours on the street than what I made in two weeks working there."

"It's called honest work, Joan." Dad shook his head. "Your phone is cut off, and the last I heard, you were evicted from your apartment. Why don't you stay with us for a while?"

"Curtis—" Mom snapped.

Dad held up a hand to stop her. Mom sighed and shook her head.

"I don't need your help, and I don't want your fucking pity," Joan said.

"You heard her, Curtis," Mom said. "You can't save anyone who doesn't want to be saved. Leave her be."

"Listen to your wife," Joan said. "I'm doing fine. We're barely even blood."

"You're my sister—"

"I'm your half sister. Your cheatin'-ass daddy fucked my momma, and I was the result of it. We were never supposed to be a family. I was a mistake, and our sperm donor of a father made that clear by never being in my life."

"It doesn't matter how it happened. You're still my sister, and he cared about you," Dad said.

"Sure, he did."

"Before he died, he told me everything. He wanted me to correct what he never had a chance to."

"It's too late for all that."

Simone was scowling at Aunt Joan.

"Stop staring at me, you little bitch. I should've swallowed you."

"Joan! That's your daughter," Mom yelled.

"I don't like her lookin' at me like I'm a piece of shit."

"Ben, take Simone and go play basketball while I talk to your aunt Joan for a bit," Dad said, handing me a basketball from the truck.

We left them talking and went to the courts.

"I hate her," Simone said.

"She's not bad. She's just on that stuff," I said. "Dad said once she cleans up, she'll be good."

"Uncle Curtis always sees the good in people, but she's not good. She's an evil witch, and I never want to be like her."

I was in the middle of a jump shot when someone pushed me from behind. I hit the ground hard. I hopped up and turned around with my fist balled. It was JJ, a heavyset kid around my age who tormented me every year at this event. He was laughing with a bunch of other boys.

"What are you going to do about it, pussy?"

I glared at him and didn't respond.

"What are you doing on our courts, punk?" JJ asked.

"First off, I'm not a punk, and second, my family is handing out food for Thanksgiving, like they do every year. I'm just shooting around with my cousin."

JJ stepped up, got in my face, and shoved me again. "Yeah, your punk-ass father is tryin'a win Brownie points in the hood by handing out scraps again."

"You and everyone else are taking them too, so what does that say about you?"

"Oooooh," the boys behind him said.

"Yeah, we take your father's free shit, but he still gets no love here," JJ said. "You and your family think you're saints for coming around here once a year and treating us like charity cases. Everyone knows your family uses this shit as a tax write-off. Your pops is an Uncle Tom. He doesn't care about us, and we don't give a shit about him. Once y'all leave, we laugh at his sellout ass."

I hated JJ because I knew he was telling the truth. I figured most of the people at this event were only mooching off my dad but didn't really care about him.

"Shut up, you ugly, black monkey, before I tell Uncle Curtis not to give your bum-ass family any food," Simone said.

"Before I tell Uncle Curtis not to give your family food," he mocked. "Listen to you talkin' all proper and shit. You sound like a white girl. Mind your own business before I pay your momma five dollars to suck my dick."

His friends laughed. Simone looked embarrassed, and JJ noticed.

"Yeah, my dad said the whole hood fucked your mom in the ass for twenty bucks. How much you charging?"

Simone cried and ran over to my mom. I watched Mom storm over to my dad and yell at him. More kids joined the growing group around JJ and me.

Our bickering and shoving drew the attention of the grownups. JJ's dad walked over to us and egged us on.

"Boys, that's enough," Dad said, separating us.

"What's the matter, Curtis?" JJ's dad asked. "Your boy too soft to fight his own battles?"

"I see you still haven't changed, Jamel. You're still the same bully you were as a kid, and now, I see you're training your son to follow in your footsteps."

"Whatever, nigga. I can't help that your boy is too soft to survive around here."

Dad patted me on the shoulder and fired back, "He's tough. I just don't want him to beat your kid's ass in front of all his friends."

"Get the fuck outta here with that bullshit." JJ's dad turned to the cops. "What do ya say, Officers? Can y'all let the boys fight a fair one for two minutes?"

Dad nodded in agreement with the officers.

"You sure, Curtis?" Officer Buckley asked.

"Absolutely," Dad said.

"Officer Watson and I are going to finish packing up the truck. When we get back, whatever business that needed to be taken care of needs to be over with. You got two minutes until we get back."

"That's all the time we need," Dad said.

I looked up in terror at my father. He faced me.

"Are you crazy, Dad? I'm not fighting him," I said.

"Look, son, you've been training to box for two years now. I got you into boxing so you'd know how to defend yourself if the time ever came. Well, the time is here, son. People like JJ will keep picking on you unless you stand up for yourself. You can take this kid. Win or lose, you have to stand up for yourself."

"Curtis, you done coaxing that pussy into fighting?" JJ's dad asked.

"You ready for him to whoop your son's ass?" Dad fired back.

"Now, don't anyone get involved in their fight, or you'll answer to me, y'all hear?" JJ's dad said to the crowd.

"Yeah," was heard throughout the sea of people.

JJ balled up his fists as his father pushed him toward me. My heart pounded in my chest. I slowly raised my fists as we faced off in the middle of the street, circling each other. JJ threw a wild haymaker that I sidestepped. I didn't want to fight him, but I didn't want to get picked on anymore, either. JJ hit me with a quick jab and right hook that staggered me. The crowd cheered him on and heckled me.

"Kick this Oreo's ass, JJ," someone in the crowd shouted.

He moved in to throw a right cross, but I ducked and hit him with four good hooks to his ribs. His breathing doubled. He wheezed and charged toward me, swinging wildly, but I dodged his punches and swept his foot. JJ stumbled onto the concrete, scraping his face. I turned him over, mounted him, and rained down blows. I thought about all the things he and his friends said about my dad. I thought about all the times I came here, and he and the other kids made Simone and me feel like we weren't black enough because we didn't live in this neighborhood, and I kept swinging.

Tears streamed down my face. Blood poured from his nose and mouth as I hit him repeatedly with haymakers and elbows. My knuckles were raw, the blood from his face dripping down my fists. I was crying hysterically when my father dragged me off him. JJ was rocking back and forth in pain.

Officer Watson touched my shoulder.

"All right, everyone, the show is over," Officer Buckley said.

The look on the crowd's faces showed they were disappointed that the cops were stopping the fight.

JJ's legs wobbled as his dad yanked him up off the ground by his Mets T-shirt and popped him upside the head with his palm.

"I can't believe you lost to that punk. I'ma beat your ass myself when you get home. I raised you to be tougher than that," his dad said.

I wiped my tears with my shirt and walked with my dad back to our SUV. Mom yelled at him the entire ride home, and after that day, Dad never took any of us with

him to the old neighborhood when he gave back to the
community.

Reggie reminded me of those kids from the old neighborhood who used to heckle me. He showed me that the
internal battle I struggled with every day and thought I
could handle was real and slowly eating at me. To him
and most of the other black people I'd met, I was an Oreo.
It didn't matter how dark my skin was. Reggie reminded
me of how most of the world viewed me: a sellout. An
Uncle Tom. A disgrace to my race.

I was instantly pulled back to the present when I heard
Reggie's case being called in the courtroom. It took two
hours before his case came up.

"Docket number seven-five-three—Reginald Brown,"
the court officer called.

Reggie stood up with his head high. "It's Co-Kayne."

There were a few chuckles and some low cheers in the
audience.

"Order," the judge demanded. "Mr. Brown, curb your
attempt at humor. You're in enough trouble."

"I didn't do shit."

The judge ignored Reggie's statement and went on
with the arraignment. "Will the prosecution present the
case?"

"Your Honor, Mr. Brown is being charged with possession of a loaded weapon, four counts of murder in the
first degree, menacing in the second degree, and resisting
arrest," District Attorney Daniel Torres said.

The firm had had cases against Torres in the past. He
was a stickler for asking for the maximum amount of
prison time. He was tall, around six-three, and thin. He

was clean-shaven and had a deep, powerful voice that grabbed your attention.

DA Torres told the judge in detail what Reggie was being accused of.

"How does the defendant plead?" the judge asked Reggie.

"What do you think? Not guilty. I already told you I didn't do shit," Reggie said.

More laughter came from the audience.

"Order! Based on the evidence that was presented by the state of New York in this arraignment, it is the ruling of this court that there is probable cause to believe that, on November 16, 2017, the defendant, Reginald Brown, committed four counts of first-degree murder causing the death of Michael Santiago, Alexander Graves, Officer Ricardo Gomez, and Officer Kenneth Roberts. Due to the severity of these heinous charges, the defendant will be remanded to await prosecution."

Reggie sucked his teeth and reluctantly placed his hands behind his back as the court officers reached to cuff him.

"Stay strong," I said. "I'm going to do everything in my power to help you beat this thing."

Reggie shook his head. "My life is over, man."

He dropped his head and trudged slowly as the court officers escorted him out of the courtroom.

Chapter 5

Bill

Ugly

"The court will set bail for Mr. Alfieri at $10,000," the judge ordered.

"Thank you, Your Honor," I said.

"All they want is ten grand? That's chump change, yo," Johnny said, adjusting his tie. "So, you're gonna talk to this bitch now?"

"Lower your voice. Don't say things like that to anyone. As your attorney, I can't speak to her, but I told you it'd be taken care of."

"Cool, get that shit done, yo. I want this shit wrapped up quickly, a'ight?"

I shook my head and resisted rolling my eyes at his comment as we handled his bail. Then I texted Francis about Johnny making bail and his court date as we walked out of the courtroom and out of the building.

He texted me back.

Francis: Go to the Bronx Zoo ASAP. Sophia on her way there.

Me: The zoo?

Francis: It's a crowded location that's in public, but no one will realize what you two are talking about. Keep your conversation brief, get her to sign, and get the fuck out of there.

Me: Sure thing.

I placed my phone back in my pants pocket and told Johnny, "Everything is set. Rest up, relax, and I'll keep you posted."

"End it," he said, entering his limo while photographers snapped pictures and reporters shoved microphones in his face.

I waved him off and headed to the zoo, hoping I could do what he asked of me.

"You waiting here for Sophia?" a beautiful woman asked.

Sophia was about five-eight, with a flawless, mahogany complexion, full lips, and jet-black, shoulder-length hair. She was beautiful in the video, but she was even more stunning in person. She had an amazing figure, so I was sure she made decent money stripping.

"Yes. It's nice to meet you, Ms. Winters," I said, greeting her with a grin as we sat on a bench at the zoo.

I sent a quick text to Francis.

Me: She's here.

Francis: I'm busy overseeing other cases. You're going to have to go at it alone. I have faith in you, Billy. Get this settled . . . partner.

"I always figure lawyers like you were slimy. How fitting that we're meeting in front of the reptile exhibit."

I laughed off her clear insult to me and my profession.

"Smooth not telling me who you are. Anyway, my manager, Jerrod, at the club, said to meet you here. Why are we at the zoo?" Sophia asked.

I now knew who the firm's "friend" was. The partners had already talked to Jerrod about testifying against her. I guessed he wanted her to end this before she brought more trouble to his club.

"It's a nice day—" I said.

"Let's cut the bullshit. What do you want? Jerrod said I should hear you out, so I'm here."

"I'll cut to the chase, Ms. Winters. Mr. Alfieri believes this is all a big misunderstanding. I asked you here to see if we can work something out that'll be beneficial to all of us and save a lot of time."

"By 'beneficial,' you mean he's offering me money. How much are you talking?" she asked.

"Mr. Alfieri is willing to offer you $2 million to settle things."

She laughed. "This should show you that he's guilty. I don't want his fucking money," Sophia said.

"What?"

"I said I don't want his money. That motherfucker raped me, and he's not gonna pay his way out of this. I know everyone thinks I'm some bitter groupie that's out to extort him. People expect me to take the money and disappear, but I don't want nothing but to see him rot in prison so he can never rape another woman again. He and all these other celebrities need to know they're not above the law."

"Sophia, you should consider this deal. A long, drawn-out trial might not paint you in the best of lights. It's terrible what you're saying he did, but you know what can easily help you forget about the incident? Money. We can negotiate more money and make you a *very* rich woman."

I hated the way I sounded. This wasn't me. I felt slimy, phony. I couldn't believe the bullshit that was spewing out of my mouth. I was ashamed of myself.

"Nope. As far as I'm concerned, we're done here. Sure, taking his money would make me rich, but it would only give him the green light to rape more black women. I want him to rot in prison. I'm gonna be his *last* victim."

I knew the media would eat up Sophia's brave story of not wanting anything from Johnny but justice. There was no doubt: she'd make shitloads of money doing interviews going that route.

"Let your douche-bag client know I'll see his ass in court. Tell him, don't drop the soap when he goes to prison."

I sighed and nodded. "I'm sorry we couldn't work this out. Please, if you do change your mind, let Jerrod know. I hope you'll reconsider and put more thought into settling this misunderstanding."

"Nah, there's nothing to think about. I want justice."

Sophia stood up. I wished her well, and we walked our separate ways. Then I immediately called Richard.

"We have a problem with the Alfieri case," I said.

"Bill, please tell me you got the stripper to sign the papers," Richard said.

"Unfortunately, no. She's standing firm with her accusations. She said she doesn't want Johnny's money. All she wants is to make sure he goes to prison for what he's done and never rapes another woman again. She wants the world to see that just because he's a celebrity, it doesn't make him above the law. Those were her words."

"I was hoping this would've been open and shut, and she'd be smart enough to take the fucking money, but now we'll show her no mercy," Richard said. "All over the news, I see clips of her using this incident to make herself famous. By the end of this trial, I want her to be *infamous*. Billy, I need the world to see her for the whore she is. Dig up every nasty detail about her past."

I sighed. "I understand, sir."

"Good. Handle it and keep Francis and me posted."

He ended the call, and like clockwork, Francis called me.

"Tell me you have good news for me," he said.

"I wish I could."

"What happened?"

I filled him in on what went down.

"We got some strategizing to do, but it's no biggie. Right now, his public image is crucial. We'll do a charity event. We'll surround him with some smiling black and Hispanic kids from the hood. We'll have him hand out a few basketballs, sign some autographs, and he'll be like the Messiah to those people."

I realized this was going to be an ugly battle, and it was already turning me ugly.

Chapter 6

Ben

History

"All right, Mom, I gotta go. I'm here at the restaurant," I said, sticking a finger in my ear to drown out the noise.

I rushed to end the conversation with my mom after she made several comparisons between Becky and Gabby. I'd initially called to tell my parents about the case, but somehow, the conversation had evolved into a lecture. She made it clear that she preferred for me to be with Gabby instead. I said goodbye to her, then shot a quick text to Becky, explaining that I was going to get coffee with Gabby and Terrence. I wished her a good day, and I couldn't wait to tell her about my case later. I sent out another text to Terrence, letting him know what coffee shop to meet Gabby and me at. Then I walked into The Bean on Second Avenue in Manhattan. It was a nice, quaint coffee shop on the Lower East Side.

My eyes darted around the crowded room as I scanned it for Gabby. I spotted her. She waved me over, and I weaved through the crowd to get to our table. She was wearing a black pencil skirt that clung to her curves. She wore subtle makeup on her flawless brown skin, and her eyebrows were done to perfection. Gabby was an all-around gorgeous woman. Her beauty and intelligence had always attracted me to her. She was one of my best friends. There was a time when I was in love with her and wanted more than a friendship, but I didn't have the same feelings now that I had when we were younger.

Gabby handled mergers and acquisitions law for Akerman LLP, another huge New York law firm.

"Hey," I said, greeting her with a hug and a kiss on the cheek.

"What's up, Big Head?"

I smiled at her childhood nickname for me. "Terrence is on his way here too," I said.

"Ugh, why did you invite that punk?"

I rolled my eyes.

"What are you going to eat?" she asked.

"Nothing. I'm just going to get coffee. Becky and I have dinner plans tonight with her parents."

"Ugh, hearing her name is blasphemy to me."

"Anyway, the partners at my firm assigned me the murder case for that rapper, Co-Kayne. If I can pull off a miracle and get him cleared, they'll consider making me a partner."

"Wow, you think you can win?" she asked.

"It seems damn near impossible, but I need this win. I'll find an angle. It doesn't stop there, though. Remember that white guy at my firm, Bill, the one I told you is dating a sista?"

She rolled her eyes. "Yeah."

"Well, my firm is also handling that basketball player's rape case, and they assigned it to him. Since both of our cases are legal nightmares, the partners figured the odds of both of us winning were slim to none, so they gave him the same agreement—that whichever one of us got the best results would get the partnership."

I gave her more details about my case.

"So, you're competing against a white guy?" Gabby said. "You better hope you win. You know as well as I do the partners are rooting for you to fail."

"I feel that way too, but I need this partnership. I see how chummy they are with him, and I know they have him pegged to win, but they're going to be highly disappointed when I pull off a win with this case."

"Well, at least you have a positive mind-set. Did you tell your little white girlfriend the news yet?" The bitterness in her tone rose.

I sighed. "No, I didn't tell Becky yet. I didn't even tell my parents. You're the first person I'm explaining it to after I handled everything."

I knew she'd enjoyed having that little victory.

"Ugh, you're not the only sellout here," she said, pointing at an interracial couple.

"Don't start with that today."

"It's becoming a fucking epidemic. It's not enough that white people run the world. Now they have to take all the successful black men."

"I see brothers hitting on you all the time, and you always make an excuse for why they aren't good enough."

"I'm saving myself for you," she said, playfully punching me in the arm.

"It's a little too late for that, don't you think?"

"Nope, I don't believe that. Eventually, you'll come to your senses, see the truth about your snowflake, and drop her."

"*You* pushed me away, remember?" I said. "I met Becky because you snubbed me."

"We all make mistakes. I've waited years to correct this one. You want your usual coffee order?"

"Yeah."

"Hold our table. I'll get it."

I nodded and stared at her as she got in line. There was no doubt Gabby loved me, but I questioned if it was based on romance or if it was competitiveness because she couldn't have me. Before I dated Becky, Gabby only viewed me as a friend. Once I made things official with Becky and stopped chasing after Gabby, she wanted to be in a relationship with me.

My mind drifted back to my childhood and how my drama with Gabby led me to date Becky.

I went to private school all of my adolescent life. My parents adamantly pushed me to befriend minorities whenever possible. I figured it was their way of helping me not to forget who I was. Growing up, my best friend was Terrence. Terrence's parents were successful African American bankers. Not too many of us black kids were in school. The number of minority students was in the single digits, including Terrence and me, which didn't leave me with a lot of options when it came to looking at girls my parents would approve of, but that changed when I met Gabby.

I had eyes for Gabrielle Thomas since sixth grade. Even back then, I was drawn to her. To me, she was the smartest and prettiest girl I'd ever seen. I remembered when I would write love letters to her, and she would correct them and hand them back to me. My mom would laugh and say, "Oh, she's just playing hard to get. She'll come around." I was determined to get her to like me.

Her parents were both successful, one a professor at Columbia and the other an orthopedic surgeon for Winthrop Hospital. Her family lived two blocks away from me, and since her mom and dad were both successful black people, our parents hit it off and became good friends. They hung out at our house often. Gabby idolized my mom, and once she expressed interest in becoming a lawyer, my mom took Gabby under her wing and mentored her.

I was a whipped puppy around Gabby. I canceled plans with Terrence if she asked, and brought her along to play video games, study, and watch TV with us whenever she wanted me to.

My infatuation grew the older I got. She had boyfriends growing up, and I had my fair share of girlfriends, but I didn't take them seriously. I viewed them as practice for when I finally convinced Gabby that we were meant to be together. I'd wanted to say fuck it and move on, to find a girl who appreciated me, but every time I felt like I was close to getting over her, she showed me the sensitive side that I knew she hid under all her toughness, and it sucked me back in to wanting her.

Growing up, when her boyfriends broke her heart, I dropped whatever I was doing and comforted her. I was there for her through so many heartbreaks. I played on the basketball team and ran track, even though I hated running so that I could bond and be closer to her since she enjoyed those sports as well. We confided in each other and trusted each other with our dreams, fears, and secrets, but no matter how close we were, she never took me out of the friend zone.

Our senior year, Gabby promised she'd be my date to the prom, but reneged and took some other guy she met online named Tyshaun, or her nickname for him, "Freaky Ty." That hurt. I remembered my mom comforting me and saying, "Baby, she'll come around. She's going through a selfish phase right now."

"Selfish phase or not, it's time to let her go, son," my dad said.

"Oh, hush, Curtis. I put you through the same shit when you were courting me," Mom replied.

"You never did anything this selfish. Gabby promised our son she'd be his date and broke it off to go with another guy without any remorse. That's blatantly disrespectful." Dad turned to me. "Move on."

I ended up not going to my school's prom, but Mom wouldn't drop it. She told me I'd regret missing the experience and forced me to go to another school's prom. Mom played matchmaker with a woman from our church named Jonna. She and her daughter Erica matched me up with their good friend Lynn. Lynn was gorgeous, and while I thought there could be a connection there, she was still hung up on her ex-boyfriend, so the relationship was over before it started.

When it was time for college, my parents wanted me to follow in their footsteps and go to a historically black college, preferably Howard University in Washington, D.C., where they met and were alumni, but in my heart, I truly believed Gabby was my soul mate. I didn't want to risk losing out on dating her one day, so against their wishes, I applied to Columbia to go to college with Gabby.

We studied, worked out, and hung out together all the time. I was around her more than her loser boyfriend. In my mind, she loved me too, but she was trying to be a good girl and stay loyal to Tyshaun.

Sophomore year, I felt my chance had finally come when he dumped her.

Terrence and I were headed to Equinox Gym to work out and play basketball when my cell phone rang.

"Hold up. It's Gabby," I said.

"Don't answer it. We got plans already, and once you talk to her, I know she's going to fuck everything up," Terrence said.

"I'll be quick."

"How are you so pussy whipped and didn't get the pussy yet?" Terrence laughed.

"Shut up, punk." I laughed too.

I answered my cell phone. "What's up, Gabby?"

Gabby spoke so fast that the words sounded like gibberish.

"Slow down. What happened?"

"Tyshaun broke up with me for some cheerleader he's fucking at his school," she cried.

"Damn, I'm sorry."

"I need you right now. Can we hang out?"

"Hold on, OK?"

I muted my phone. Terrence threw up his hands.

"C'mon, man, she always does this shit, and you go running whenever she calls," he said.

"It's not like that. Tyshaun broke up with her—"

"So? Tell her she needs to use this time to reflect on what she did to fuck her relationship up. We got plans," he said.

I shook my head. "She needs me."

"No, she doesn't. I should've known you were gonna drop everything for her. She's going to give you DSB."

"What? DSB?"

"Deadly sperm build-up, bro. Tell her if she's going to ruin your plans, she can at least let you fuck, so you don't suffer from blue balls."

"You got jokes."

We laughed.

"Don't worry about it, Ben. Take care of your girl. I hope you finally get her."

I mouthed, "Thank you," and unmuted the phone as he waved and headed out. "Gabby, I want to take you out on a date."

"I just asked you to hang out, Big Head."

"Nah, I don't mean hanging out like you do with Terrence and me. I mean you and me on a real date. Can we do that tonight?"

There was a long pause before she said, "Sure."

I picked up Gabby and took her to Frames Bowling Lounge on Ninth Avenue in Manhattan. I figured we'd do something fun to take her mind off Ty.

"Thanks for taking me out, Big Head," Gabby said.

I smiled. "I always have your back. You know that."

"I know."

We laughed, bowled, and had a good time, but I noticed her facial expression changing during one of our games.

"What's the matter?" I asked.

"I just saw Ty walk in here with what I'm guessing is the bitch he left me for."

I looked around. "Where is he?"

"He spotted me, winked, and left." She looked hurt by the encounter.

"Do you want to go somewhere else? I don't mind."

"Nah, I'm fine here. Fuck him."

I grabbed her hand and held it in mine. I listened to her vent and let her get the anger out of her system. I wined and dined Gabby to show her my intentions were for us to become more than friends finally, but as the night went on, our date felt more like she was only with me out of familiarity and comfort rather than attraction and love.

We went back to my house.

"I'm cold," Gabby said.

I lay on my bed staring at the ceiling, disappointed that our date didn't go the way I'd wanted, while Gabby dug into my closet and pulled out my rumpled Columbia University sweatshirt.

"What's wrong? Why are you pouting?"

"I'm not pouting. You wouldn't understand."

"I know you like me, Ben—"

"So, give me a chance."

"Maybe one day . . . Look, I'm going to shower. When I come back, I expect you to have nothing on."

"Wait—what? Are you serious?"

"With the kind of day I had, I need a good fuck. Can you give me that, or do I have to find someone else?"

"No, no. I can handle it . . . I mean you," I stammered.

Gabby smirked and winked at me. "We'll see."

I heard the shower turn on, so I swiftly dimmed the lights in my bedroom and lit candles. I stripped off my clothes and sucked on one of the Listerine strips I kept inside my nightstand. I was anxious and as hard as a rock. I'd waited for this opportunity for so long. I wanted everything to be perfect. I needed Gabby to realize I was the perfect guy for her.

Gabby came out of my bathroom, and her towel slipped off her wet hourglass figure and fell to the floor. She stood in front of me naked.

"You ready?" she asked, her voice a hoarse whisper.

I walked up to her. I saw there was doubt in her eyes, but I needed her to be comfortable and understand that this moment wouldn't hurt our friendship—it would evolve our relationship into something more, something better.

I rubbed my hands down her curves and eased Gabby onto my bed, laying her gently on her back. She widened her legs for me. I wasted no time bathing her treasure with my tongue. She moaned, twisted, and turned, pulling the back of my head and pushing my tongue deeper inside her. I sucked on her clit with a steady rhythm. She moaned loudly and tossed her head back against a pillow. Her thighs shook in my hands; her breathing came out in quick pants.

"Oh shit, Ty," she groaned.

I pulled my mouth off her. "I'm not him."

"Sorry . . . Oh fuck. Don't stop, Ben."

I slipped two fingers inside her, which caused her to scream out, "Oh shit."

I pumped them in and out of her in a rapid rhythm to draw her mind off Tyshaun and have it focused on only me.

Then I leaned over and pulled out a condom from my nightstand. I opened that packet and rolled it onto my throbbing erection.

Gabby grabbed my cock and guided it inside her.

I wanted to savor this moment, to lock this memory and sensation of being emotionally and physically connected to her forever.

I stared into her eyes. "You all right?"

"Yeah."

"You don't seem like you're into this. Do you want me to stop?"

"Stop talking. I'm fine. Don't ruin the mood. Keep going."

The sex wasn't how I envisioned our first time together would be. It felt forced and meaningless . . . like she was doing me a favor instead of sharing an emotional experience with me. We went through the motions and sexed in different positions, but seeing her stare down at her fingernails and, at one point, drift off with a blank stare, as if she were thinking of someone else, proved her heart wasn't in it. I was just a rebound.

When it was over, she rolled on her side and wrapped her naked body in my bedsheet. I placed my hand on her shoulder, but she shrugged it off and stared, unblinking, at the wall. The silence was deafening. I tried to ease the tension by being heartfelt and honest.

"This meant something to me, Gabby. This wasn't just a fuck. I want us to be more than a fling. I hope this'll be the start of a future for us together."

Gabby stood up and searched for her clothes. She grabbed them off the floor and dressed. "I'm sorry, Ben. This was a mistake . . ."

"What? Why was this a mistake?"

"I can't do this. You're a great guy . . . You know I care about you a lot, but I don't love you, and I don't think I'll ever see you like that. I'm sorry."

She left without saying so much as a goodbye.

I spent the rest of my night staring at the ceiling, praying I didn't lose my best friend for good.

I glanced at the screen on my cell phone for any communication from Gabby. Nothing. After our intimate night, I didn't see Gabby for over a week. She didn't return my texts or calls and wouldn't answer the door whenever I stopped by her apartment. It drove me crazy knowing that she was avoiding me. It made me question if she got off by knowing she could control me, and if my feelings for her were one-sided. Was it just me that felt our night was special? I moped around everywhere, disappointed, feeling embarrassed, heartbroken, and lonely. Finally, I got out of bed, put on some workout clothes, and went for a run. Even that couldn't get my mind off her.

Growing up, my dad taught me to be constructive. He taught me never to let stress cause me to do things that would bring me further down and hurt me. I followed his advice and realized it was easier to shield myself from the pain of heartache if I resorted to what I always did when I was upset: drown myself in work and not be distracted by women.

I told Terrence about the latest drama between Gabby and me.

"Damn, brother. She left right after the sex? Were you that bad?" he asked.

"Shuddup," I said.

"I've been telling you to stop chasing that girl since junior high. Maybe now you'll listen."

I shook my head.

"Ben, you pretty much worship the ground she walks on. You're too available. Look, Gabby's hot and all, but she treats you like shit because she knows you'll always chase after her. Once she sees you've backed off a bit and stopped being so thirsty and desperate, she'll respect you and give you a chance."

Terrence gave me more words of advice but didn't bother to try to convince me to party and chase women with him. He was used to my recluse act whenever Gabby hurt me, so he gave me time to be by myself.

It was Friday night, and while most guys my age were partying with their friends and chasing women, I was sitting in the university library studying my law books. I had nothing but time on my hands since my life mostly revolved around Gabby. With her not around, I had no life. I tried to convince myself that this was all for the best, that I didn't need a woman clouding my goal of being a great lawyer, but the truth was that I was miserable.

I was sitting at one of the tables reading my law books and taking notes when a curvy blonde approached my table.

"Do you mind if I sit here?"

I gave her a quick scan. She was wearing tight blue jeans and a white V-neck shirt spilling with cleavage. She was hot . . . for a white girl, I thought at the time, but I didn't need any distractions.

I purposely looked around at the nearly empty library, where there were plenty of deserted tables, and hoped she'd get the hint. After a few seconds of her staring at me and waiting for an answer, I shrugged and said, "Sure."

I checked her out as she got situated. She had deep blue eyes, thick lips, a beach tan complexion, and curvy hips that flowed into toned, thick legs. She was nice to look at, but she was disruptive. She kept mumbling as she read, fidgeting in her chair, and digging in her purse.

I tried to avoid eye contact and focus on my books, but she randomly broke into tears. She was drawing a lot of attention. The few people in the library were whispering, pointing, and snickering at her. It wasn't any of my business, and I knew I should avoid getting involved, but I felt sorry for her.

"Excuse me, are you OK?" I asked.

"No. I'm such a loser."

Her eyes were red and swollen. I didn't know what I should say, but I couldn't leave her alone after she said that. I figured I'd calm her down, convince her to go home, and go back to studying once she was gone. I stood up and put a hand on her shoulder.

"You're not a loser. You're probably stressed because of midterms."

"It's not just that," she said, wiping her eyes.

I pulled out the chair next to her and sat down. She pressed her face into my chest and sobbed quietly. I awkwardly patted her back.

"It's OK. What's wrong?"

"Where do I start? My parents think I'm a useless, helpless, talentless moron. My boyfriend broke up with me and told me I'm a decent fuck and good eye candy, but I'm too dumb to be marriage material. Maybe he and my parents are right. I mean, I'm doing terrible in all of my classes."

"Don't think about yourself like that," I said. "The first part of success is having confidence in your abilities. You just need the proper motivation. Use your ex's negative words and your feelings toward your parents as strength to prove them wrong. Trust me, I have similar stress, and I'm here doing the same thing."

She smiled. "Thanks. I feel a little better," she said, dabbing her eyes with a napkin from her purse.

"I'm glad I could help," I said, nodding and turning to head back to my chair.

"Wait, what's your name?"

"Ben Turner."

"Rebecca Preston, but please call me Becky. It's nice to meet you."

"Nice to meet you too."

We shook hands.

After a good two hours of studying, I rubbed my eyes and stretched. I looked up and noticed the outline of Becky's huge breasts and protruding nipples in her tight V-neck shirt as she yawned and stretched. The two of us made eye contact before I could look away. I checked to see if she was still staring at me. She gave me a warm smile and said, "My eyes are shot."

"Yeah, mine too. I think that's it for me tonight."

She ran her fingers through her honey-blond hair and bit her lip. "Are you hungry?"

"Somewhat, but I might just get something from the vending machine. Do you want anything?"

"I was wondering, since we're both calling it quits, maybe we could get a quick bite to eat."

"What did you have in mind?" I asked.

"I don't know. Somewhere we can sit around, maybe get a drink or two, and get to know each other. I'm sorry. I didn't even ask. Is there anyone special in your life?"

"Nah. No one special in my life. I could use a drink . . . sure."

I figured what the hell. I wasn't doing anything tonight, and nothing was going to come out of just getting a meal together.

"Great," she said, touching my shoulder.

Applebee's was crowded. I was about to suggest going somewhere else, but Becky had already given her name to the hostess. We made small talk, mostly about our classes and majors, and in minutes, we were seated. Luckily for me, they sat us near the TV so I could catch the Knicks game.

The sounds of laughter, cheering, and talking caused us to speak louder so we could hear each other.

I glanced at my phone, making sure I hadn't missed a call or text from Gabby, but there was nothing.

"So, let's get to know each other," Becky said.

"What do you want to know?"

"Well, for starters, what's your favorite book?"

"That's an interesting icebreaker question," I said, as I toyed with the straw in my soda.

"Yup. I love seeing how other people think and view the world. So, which book is your favorite?"

"I don't know. I guess if I had to pick one, I'd say Great Expectations. I've read it a million times."

"True, it's definitely a classic, but why that book? What makes it so special?"

"It's fitting to my life. I'm like the main character, Pip, an idiot who wastes his time trying to build himself up to chase after a woman who doesn't want him."

Becky's openness with sharing her painful experience with her ex, Dennis, made me feel comfortable enough to share my history with Gabby. Becky made me feel comfortable enough that I wasn't my usual guarded self. After I finished telling her about Gabby, I felt stupid. I immediately regretted telling a complete stranger my business, but at the same time, it felt therapeutic to get it off my chest. I closed my eyes and exhaled, reopening them to a look of sympathy. Becky smiled, reached over the table, and closed her hand over mine.

"She didn't appreciate you. Let's not talk about our sad stories. From now on, we'll just talk about things that make us happy, deal?"

"Deal."

Neither Dennis nor Gabby's names were mentioned the rest of the night. Our chatter was fun. The conversation between us flowed naturally and freely. We laughed and talked as if we'd known each other for years. We were so deep in conversation that we barely noticed when the waitress brought our food.

"What do you dream about?" Becky asked.

"You and these questions." I laughed. "I don't know. I dream of graduating at the top of my class and landing a job at a prestigious law firm one day. I dream about becoming a name partner in the firm and starting a family."

Becky nodded.

"What do you dream about?" I asked.

"My dream is to have my own column in a national magazine and become a bestselling novelist."

"What's the book going to be about?"

"I'm not sure yet, but I want to write something that's a game changer, something that will make people think."

We continued to talk about everything. When our waitress returned, I reached for the check to pay.

"It's OK. I got this one," Becky said.

"No way."

"I asked you out, remember?"

"That doesn't matter. I got the bill," I said, winking at her.

We stepped out of the Applebee's.

"Well, it's getting late. I guess we better call it a night," I said.

"Where do you live?"

"I live near campus on Morningside Avenue. You?"

"I'm in Harlem on 126th Street. Walk me to the train station?"

"Sure."

Becky slid her hand in mine. I smiled, and we strode hand in hand, enjoying each other's company on our way to the train station on Forty-Second Street.

We said our goodbyes outside the station.

"I needed a friend tonight, and you were exactly that. Thank you," Becky said.

"It's no problem."

"Can I see your cell one sec?" she asked.

"Sure."

I handed her my cell phone. She typed something in and handed it back to me.

"I put my number in your phone so that we can stay in touch. Don't be a stranger. Call me," she said and kissed me on the cheek. I smiled as she walked away. She turned around and winked at me.

She was nice, but I was naïve and still held on to the small glimmer of hope that Gabby would come around.

The next day, I went back to the library. I couldn't get Becky off my mind. I could've easily called her, but I didn't want to admit to myself that I was feeling her. I figured if it were meant to be, fate would bring us to meet again.

I sat at the same table I did the day before. An hour passed, and then Becky walked into the library wearing a shimmery, curve-hugging black dress. The black heels she wore accentuated her ass. She looked like she was dressed more for partying than studying.

Her eyes lit up at the sight of me.

"Hey, you," Becky said, flashing a warm smile. "Do you mind if I sit with you again?"

"Nah, I don't mind," I said, smiling back.

I couldn't stop staring at her. She smiled again, letting me know she noticed. "I hope I'm not interrupting your studying."

"No, it's cool. It's good seeing you again."

"I figured it'd be a long shot, but I came at the same time I did last night, and I hoped you'd be here."

"Why?"

"I was just wondering if maybe we could help each other study. If we're together, we won't be alone to drown in our sorrows about our heartaches."

"We have different majors," I said.

"That's OK. It'll be fun."

I still hadn't heard from Gabby, and this girl that I'd just met wanted to spend more time with me than my best friend.

"Sure. Studying together sounds good."

She lightly clapped her hands. "Yea, but let's start tomorrow. Tonight, let's get dinner and talk again."

"You're making me break my rules," I laughed.

"That's a good thing. It's always good to shake things up now and then."

We went to Mel's Burger Bar on Broadway and continued from the previous night, laughing and getting to know each other.

I looked up from my menu and saw two sistas sitting across from us, cutting their eyes at Becky and me. One woman whispered something to the other. They shook *their heads and stared us down. Becky was oblivious to the drama. She looked up and saw my irritated expression. She followed my line of sight, and the women continued to give her the stank eye. Becky looked back at me.*

"What's their problem?" she asked.

I sighed. "They're talking shit because they know we're dating."

Becky's eyes sparkled, and her face lit up. "So, this is a date?" she asked.

I smiled. "Yeah, I guess it is."

"Good. I'm enjoying our date," she said, patting my hand.

She didn't flinch at the looks we got from the two women. She acted as if only she and I existed.

Soon, Becky stood up, excused herself, and went to the bathroom. My phone vibrated, alerting me to a text. I checked to see if it was from Gabby, but it was Terrence.

Terrence: Just checking to see if you're still alive, man.

I laughed.

Ben: Yeah, I'm good.

Terrence: I hope you're not still caught in your feelings because of Gabby.

Ben: Nah, I'm getting over it. I'm actually on a date now.

Terrence: What! Well, play on, playa. Text me later.

Ben: No doubt.

Becky came back to the table. She looked irritated.

"Are you OK? You look mad," I said.

"I'm good. Those women that were staring at us decided they'd give me a piece of their minds in the ladies' room about our date."

The women came back to their table and gave us the finger.

"What did they say?" I asked.

"It's not important. I won't let them have the satisfaction of ruining my night with you."

I smiled at that.

We fought over which one of us was paying the bill, and when she finally let me take care of it, she made me promise I'd let her pick out our next activity, and I wouldn't complain no matter what.

Becky surprised me with a cab ride to the 40/40 Club on West Twenty-Fifth Street. She grabbed my hand and pulled me toward the club.

"Oooh, let's go dancing," Becky said.

"You look good, but I'm not dressed for that."

I had on khakis, with black shoes and a black Polo shirt. I was dressed decent enough, but not nice enough for clubbing.

"There's no way we'll get in there," I said.

"Ye of little faith. Come on."

I laughed. "OK, but answer this one question: did you have this planned?"

"Not entirely. If I didn't see you in the library, I was going to go dancing regardless, but I wasn't sure which club I'd go to."

Becky dug inside her purse and pulled out a wad of money. She walked to the front of the line, dragging me with her up to the bouncer.

"My friend Ben and I are on the VIP list."

She flashed him what had to be over $500 and handed it to him. He quickly snatched the money from her hand, pointed at his clipboard, and said, "Oh yeah, I see his name right here. Go right on in."

He moved the rope and let us inside. Becky smiled and winked at him. There was a lot of cursing and angry faces from the people who were waiting in line to get in.

Becky took me by the hand, and we immediately went to the dance floor.

"Don't worry, I won't embarrass you. Contrary to popular belief, this white girl can dance. I took dance classes almost all my life."

She wasn't kidding. She was twerking and gyrating better than most of the sistas in the club.

After we'd danced for a while, Becky held my hand as we maneuvered through the crowd to the bar.

My ears were buzzing from the music bumping loudly all night. We did all types of shots. I was tipsy but sober enough to function. Becky, on the other hand, was really knocking them back. Our date was cut short when it was obvious she was shitfaced. Her cheeks were bright red, and her words were slurred. She hopped off her barstool and could barely stand.

"I think it's time to call it quits tonight," I said.

"Why? We're having a good time," she said, wobbling as she struggled to pull her dress down.

"Yeah, but you might've had a little too much to drink tonight."

Becky laughed. "Maybe just a little," she said, stumbling to the ground.

I helped her up.

"Can I stay at your place? I don't want to go home to my lonely apartment," she said.

I didn't know where she lived exactly in Harlem, and I wasn't going to let her take the train or even a cab alone while she was drunk.

"Sure," I said.

We took a cab to my condo. I looped her arm over my shoulder, half dragging, half carrying her inside to my room, and placed her in the center of my huge bed. Becky's summer dress rose up around her thighs. She sat up, kissed the side of my face, slipped her hands inside my pants, and massaged my dick. I closed my eyes as she stroked me, but came to my senses and stopped her. *Becky stood up unsteadily. She swiftly fidgeted with the shoulder straps on her dress and slid her dress off her curvy frame, and it dropped to the floor. Then she quickly stepped out of her black lace panties and unhooked her bra. She stood in front of me completely naked, her eyes showing me her desire.*

"Come on. I want you so bad right now," she moaned.

Becky kissed me and slid her tongue deep into my mouth. She tilted her head, leaned back, and lay naked on my bed, rubbing her clit. I was tempted, but I wasn't going to take advantage of her when she was drunk. I smiled.

"I want you too, but not tonight. I'm going to sleep on the couch. Get some sleep and I'll see you in the morning, OK?"

Becky pouted. "I really like you. Why don't you want me?"

I kissed her and slowly eased away. "I want you too, just not like this. Rest up, and I'll talk to you in the morning."

"OK," she said, sounding disappointed.

I pulled out some clothes from my dresser, and when I faced Becky again, she was sound asleep.

I took a cold shower and went to bed wondering what tomorrow morning would bring.

The next morning, I went to the Hamilton deli near my place and bought Becky and me coffee and breakfast sandwiches. I thought about waking her up before I left, but she looked so peaceful sleeping that I decided just to leave her be and bring the food back home.

When I opened my bedroom door, I saw Becky lying on her back with her forearm across her eyes. I set her breakfast and coffee on the nightstand next to my bed and said, "Good morning."

"Ugh, you're a morning person," she groaned.

"Yup. I bought you breakfast and coffee."

"Thank you."

I handed her the food, and the comforter moved and exposed her bare breasts. I couldn't help but stare. She noticed and gradually raised her arms to cover up.

"I'm sorry, Ben. I'm so embarrassed."

"Don't be. It's fine. There's nothing wrong with partying hard now and then."

"I really like you, Ben, and now you probably think I'm some wild white girl that gets wasted all the time."

"I don't think that. It's OK."

"You promise you'll still hang out with me?"

I laughed. "Yes."

The next three days, Becky and I met at the library to study.

"I'm never going to get this shit," she pouted.

"Yeah, you will, but you gotta focus," I said.

"I'm stupid."

"Stop saying that. Look, why did you major in journalism and English literature?"

"I like to write. My dream is to work at a major magazine and have a bestselling novel."

"So, what's stopping you? You have the talent, Becky, but you need the heart and the will to make these things happen. Now, let's build that together. Come on, focus."

At first, I saw our hanging out as just a distraction. Nothing serious, just a meaningless way to not think about Gabby, but I couldn't lie to myself—I liked Becky. We were both healing from our past, and I felt so comfortable with her. Becky was a lively free spirit, while I was more laid-back. She shared bits and pieces of her past with me and got me to be open with mine too.

Our friendship changed forever after the first time we were intimate.

We had finished our study session when I asked her, "Do you want to hang out at my place tonight?"

"Sure."

We stepped inside my condo, and I tried to tidy up quickly, moving the magazines off my sofa and repositioning the pillows on my couch.

Becky giggled.

"What are you doing? Your place is ridiculously clean," she said.

"I'm sort of a neat freak."

"I'm the total opposite."

I laughed to myself. We were opposites in a lot of ways, I thought. I leaned forward and picked up the TV remote from my coffee table.

Becky eased down next to me on the sofa.

"I thought we could order Chinese and watch something on Netflix."

"So, you wanted me to come over to 'Netflix and chill,' eh?"

"You're making a dark man blush," I laughed. "As much as I'm attracted to you, I'll promise to be a gentleman."

"You're attracted to me?"

"You know I am."

"I'm feeling you too."

Becky casually edged closer to me. She leaned toward me, her face inches from mine. I stared into her eyes. Our lips grazed against each other's, and I pulled her close and kissed her.

I felt my hardness straining in my jeans. Becky noticed and traced the outline of my cock through my pants. We continued to kiss, our hands exploring and roaming over each other's bodies. I raised her dress and rubbed my hands over her firm ass. Becky broke the embrace of our kiss and asked, "You want to go to your bedroom?"

"Yup."

She held my hand, and we walked to my bedroom. I lightly kissed her neck as I worked my way down to her collarbone. Then I slowly slipped her dress straps off her shoulders and tugged it down until she was only standing in her bra and panties. I unhooked her bra and fondled her soft breasts. Within seconds, she had me undressed. Our hands explored and roamed over each other's bodies. I rubbed my hands all over her firm ass, giving it a smack.

Becky pushed me down on the bed. She dropped to her knees, rubbed her hands over my chest, and kissed her way down my stomach. Then she grasped my cock and quickly sucked on the head of my manhood, stroking it with both hands.

I positioned the head of my dick at her entrance and gently slid inside her moist treasure. Becky's lips parted. She drew in a slow breath. Her eyes opened wide as my cock filled her. Her legs squeezed me tightly, teeth clenched, her fingers digging into my back. Her moans gradually became louder as I drove into her and spread her thighs apart.

"Right there . . . Right there!"

Becky bucked and shuddered around me as her fingers raked my back. She gripped my ass and pulled me deeper into her as she came. I tried to convince myself to not catch feelings, to just enjoy what this was, but the moment we changed the dynamics of our friendship and became intimate, I knew I had feelings for her.

She rested her head on my shoulder. The warmth of her body felt good on me as we cuddled.

Becky looked at our intertwined bodies. Her soft hand held mine. Dark skin resting on top of peach-colored skin.

"I love the way your skin contrasts with mine. It's . . . beautiful."

I smiled.

"Can I spend the night?" she asked.

"You can spend the weekend."

We laughed and spent the rest of our night sexing each other up and holding each other.

The next day, Becky and I were going to spend the whole day cuddled up together on the couch, but my doorbell buzzed.

I stood up and answered the door—then sucked my teeth when I saw Gabby standing in my doorway, smiling.

"This is a surprise. I've been calling and texting you for the last two weeks," I said.

"Yeah, I've been busy."

"What's up?"

"Aren't you going to invite me in? It's early, and I want to get a quick run in. It's nice outside, and I want you to keep me company."

Gabby attempted to walk into my place, but I blocked her with my arm.

"I can't. This isn't a good time right now. I have company."

"So? It's not like I haven't hung out with you and your boys before. Who's here? Terrence?"

She tried to step past me, but I blocked her again.

"No, it's not Terrence."

"Why are you acting all weird and secretive?"

"Because I'm not hanging out with a guy. I'm sort of continuing a date."

"What?" Gabby said. "Since when?"

"Since now. I'll call you later," I said, slowly closing the door.

"She must be ugly if you're not trying to be seen with her outside." She laughed, trying to look past me.

I sighed. "Later, Gabby."

Her eyes narrowed. "Is that her fucking bra in the hallway?" Gabby asked, pushing the door open and rushing past me.

Becky was only wearing my Carmelo Anthony jersey and panties but stood up as soon as Gabby stormed into the living room.

"Hi, I'm Becky," she said, smiling and extending her hand.

Gabby stared daggers at her, looking her up and down, mentally dissecting her, and left her standing there with her hand hanging. She glowered at her, then shot her eyes at me.

"Who's this, Ben?" Gabby asked.

"This is my . . . friend Becky." I turned and faced Becky. "This is Gabby, my friend I was telling you about."

Becky smiled and extended her hand again. "Hi. Ben has told me so much about you. It's nice to meet you."

Gabby rolled her eyes and turned back to me. "No wonder you're keeping her inside. You don't want people to see you're a sellout. What? I shoot you down after our one-time fuck, and you swear off of black women?"

Becky's smile waned, and she put her hand down.

I tried my hardest to speak calmly, but Gabby kept interrupting me.

"Stop!" I yelled.

Gabby stood there, stunned at my loud outburst.

"I haven't seen you in two weeks. You made it very clear that our night together meant nothing, so don't come to my place talking to me like I'm a piece of shit."

I thought back to how I felt when she wouldn't return my calls, texts, or emails. She'd shut me out, and I was tired of chasing after a woman I knew I'd never get. I was tired of knowingly being toyed with, catering to her, and the constant games of her playing hard to get. It was at that moment that I made up my mind and decided I was moving on from her.

"It did mean something. I was going through shit, and I'll admit I handled the situation wrong, but you didn't have to run into the arms of a white girl—"

"And you didn't have to ignore me. Gabby, I'll talk to you later. Like I told you before, I have company."

"You're kicking me out?"

I didn't answer her. I just stared at her.

"Fine, but whatever this shit is you have with her, it won't last."

She walked out, and I slammed the door behind her.

"What a bitch," Becky said.

"Yeah, but she's one of my best friends."

"I know. I'm sorry. If it helps, I hope our friendship lasts and blossoms into more."

"Me too."

Becky and I started doing more activities together. I took her to hip-hop concerts with me, and she took me to rock concerts with her. She gradually got me into listening to Linkin Park, and I got her into listening to Drake.

I introduced her to Terrence, and after getting the approval from him, I knew she was someone special. I invited him over to watch the Knicks game with us. Becky didn't know anything about sports, but another thing I liked about her was that she wanted to learn so we could bond over it.

Becky was in the living room. She bent down to pick up the remote that dropped on the floor. Terrence pulled me into the kitchen.

"Damn, Ben, I didn't know your snowflake had it like that."

"Yeah, she's nice in all the right places."

"She's thicker than a bowl of oatmeal, bro. Does she have family, friends—anyone that looks like her that she could hook me up with?"

"I'll ask."

"Seriously, though, I'm glad you stopped chasing Gabby." Terrence took another look at Becky. "You did good, brother. She's not a sista, but at least she's hot."

We laughed and shared a brotherly hug.

It was the little things Becky did regularly that made me fall in love with her. She never made me feel like I was less of a man or put me down. She was supportive and uplifting, qualities I never felt with Gabby. We balanced each other out. Becky was spontaneous and adventurous, while I was always calculated and cautious. She helped me to live in the moment, and I kept her grounded and responsible.

Our relationship was blossoming, but we still hadn't made things official. It was as if we were avoiding talking about it out of a fear of ruining our good times. The true test came the day I went to her parents' house for the first time.

"Why do you look so nervous? I'm the one meeting your parents for the first time," I said.

"Yeah, but my parents can be snobbish assholes, and I don't want them tainting your thoughts about me."

I squeezed her hand affectionately, winked, and said, "Never."

Becky's parents lived in a huge, ritzy, gated community, and had the biggest house in it. She fumbled in her purse. "I can't find my damn keys. Ugh, I'll just ring the doorbell."

A white man who looked like he was in his sixties opened the door.

"Is this your dad? It's good to meet you, Mr.—"

"That's our butler, Bernard," Becky said.

I leaned in close and whispered in her ear, "Your parents have white servants? Now, I know they're loaded."

She playfully nudged me.

Mrs. Preston appeared and walked toward us. "Thank you, Bernard. I'll take it from here," she said.

Becky's mother was stunningly gorgeous. She didn't look a day older than forty. I saw where Becky got her looks, breasts, and hips from, because her mom was sexy for an older woman. She wore very subtle makeup, and she didn't even need that, because she was naturally beautiful.

"There's my favorite daughter," Mrs. Preston said.

"Mom, I'm your only daughter."

"I see you're still as cynical as ever."

"Hello, Mom," Becky said, rolling her eyes.

"Hello, Rebecca. Who is this young man with you?"

She stuttered a little then said, "This is my boyfriend, Ben."

I was taken aback by Becky giving me that title, especially since we hadn't discussed our relationship yet, but I smiled and shook Mrs. Preston's hand. She wasn't smiling. Her expression looked more like one of disappointment.

"It's very nice to meet you, Mrs. Preston," I said.

"I'm sure. Call me Susan." She stared at Becky. "Come, Rebecca. Your father is already in the dining room."

We walked across spotless marble floors to the dining room.

"Becky Bear."

Rebecca's eyes lit up. "Hi, Daddy," she said, running to hug her father.

Mr. Preston was a tall man, about six-three. He had thick, graying brown hair with a bushy but well-groomed mustache.

"And who is this gentleman?" Mr. Preston asked.

"This is Rebecca's friend, Ben," Susan said before Becky had a chance to answer.

"It's nice to meet you, Ben," he said, shaking my hand with a firm grip.

We sat at the dinner table, and Becky tried to talk me up to her parents, telling them how I was the top of my law school class.

"What's your stance on politics, Ben?" Mr. Preston asked.

I laughed off his question. "My parents told me there's two things you should never discuss: religion and politics."

"That's true, but we're all friends here, right? I'll tell you this: I can't believe we have that disgrace of a president Barack Obama in office. Did you support McCain?"

I didn't know which would piss him off more, declining to comment, or telling him I voted for Obama.

"I wasn't a fan of McCain," I said, deliberately being vague.

"Don't tell me you supported that monkey Obama. Well, what should I expect? You probably loved that loser."

I clenched my teeth and took a deep breath, trying my hardest to remain calm and civil.

"Daddy," Becky yelled.

"Steven," Susan said.

Mr. Preston raised his hand to cut both of them off. "Obama is going to be the worst president this country *has ever had, and your people looked at him like he's some type of fucking hero. He's nothing. He's less than nothing."*

It took every ounce of self-restraint to stop myself from reaching across the table and knocking him out. Unfortunately, men like him would only take my outburst as typical "black behavior." The negative image of black people in society was built off stereotypes that we were still trying to overcome. Reinforcing them only proved ignorant pricks like him right, so I kept my composure and asked, "How many white role models would you say you've had in your lifetime?"

"A few, but what does that matter? Obama isn't a role model. He's a Muslim socialist," Mr. Preston replied.

"I'm sure you had your father, and numerous presidents, and so forth. I'm not the spokesman for black people, but for me, Obama gives me hope. He being elected transcends beyond politics. He shows a generation of black children and even adults that we're not limited to being just athletes and musicians. While society, TV, and music give the message to black people that ignorance is cool, Obama shows black people that being smart, family-oriented, and selfless is most important."

Mr. Preston began a slow, obnoxious clap. "Oh, bravo. A black guy who's the exception to the rule and influences some other blacks to do things they should be smart enough to be doing already. It's all bullshit."

"Daddy, do you hear yourself right now? You're being extremely rude and acting like an asshole," Rebecca said.

My leg was bouncing. I was regretting coming here and was ready to leave. Becky calmly placed a hand on my leg.

"Don't worry. I'll defend you. You're worth fighting for," she whispered.

Seeing that she was upset and embarrassed calmed me down immediately. I looked up at Mr. Preston. His eyes bored into me. He looked inquisitively at both of us. My defenses were up.

"So, dear, do you have anyone special in your life?" he asked.

"Well, yes, isn't it obvious?" Becky said. "He's sitting at the table with us."

Mr. Preston's eyes narrowed. "I'm not sure I'm following what you're saying, Rebecca. All I see is your 'friend' here."

"Dad, Ben isn't my friend. He's my boyfriend."

His eyes widened. "The hell he is. No daughter of mine is going to be dating a black boy," he yelled.

He shook his head vigorously. His nostrils flared, and his face was beet red as he continued. "First, we have a darky in the White House, and now my daughter, my only child, is fucking one. Unbelievable. Haven't you embarrassed yourself and our family enough ho'ing around when you were growing up? You have to do this now too?"

"Daddy, stop it!" Rebecca yelled.

Susan covered her mouth like she didn't know what to say. Mr. Preston continued.

"Rebecca, I raised you better than this. We've taught you to stick with your own kind. You don't see lions mating with panthers. There's a reason for that. God wanted us to stick with our own race. He wouldn't have made other races if he wanted us to all be the same."

"Your logic is false and outdated, Dad," Becky said. "Ben is smart and funny, and he treats me better than any white man I've ever dated. I don't see life in black and white like you do. Life is in color, and you need to open your narrow-minded way of thinking to understand that."

"Steven, dear, calm down," Susan said, patting Mr. Preston's hand.

A scowl was all over his angry, red face. "Ben, let's talk in my study like civilized men," he said.

Becky held my arm. "You don't have to if you don't want to. We can leave right now if you want to go home."

After everything her father said, there was no way in hell I was going to back down from him. I also appreciated Becky sticking up for me. The fact that she defended me made me want to be strong for her.

"It's OK. I'll hear him out," I said.

I followed him to his study, where he closed the door and let out a loud, irritated sigh. His study was impressive. It was a huge room filled with mahogany furniture, plaques, trophies, and pictures of all of his accomplishments. There were mounted animal heads on the walls and a bearskin rug near the fireplace. Apparently, he liked to hunt. I felt like I was being hunted now.

"Have a seat, Ben," he said, standing by his liquor cabinet.

I sat in one of the black leather armchairs in front of his desk.

"Drink?" he offered, pouring a large amount of scotch into his glass.

"I'm fine," I answered.

He shrugged, tossed back the scotch, and said, "Suit yourself. More for me." He refilled his glass and sat behind his huge desk in a chair that looked like a throne. I waited to see where this conversation would lead.

"Ben, in this room, we leave all the politically correct bullshit at the door. We're unfiltered and open in here. Bottom line, I don't want you dating my daughter. I don't believe in anyone dating outside their race," he said bitterly before tossing back his second scotch.

I didn't respond. I kept quiet and let him continue.

"Rebecca has always been challenging. As a kid, she never colored in the lines of her coloring books. She was always rebellious, always wanted to be different. If I try to stop her from being with you, it'll only drive her to want you more. She went through a very . . . promiscuous phase as a teenager. I'm sure she's just curious to see if the stereotype is true and wants to fuck you for sexual gratification."

Mr. Preston snickered to himself and went on. "For now, I'll play the game. I'll tolerate this . . . whatever it is you have with my daughter. I know it won't last."

"But what if it does? What if we're soul mates?"

"I'd never let my daughter marry a nigger or have nigger children. Let's pray she gets over whatever phase she's going through right now, and it never comes down to that. If it does go that far, I guarantee I'll put an end to it."

I stood up. "Are we done here?"

Mr. Preston smirked. "Yeah, we're done here. Oh, and, Ben, whatever we say in this room stays in this room. I hope you're man enough to keep our conversation private."

"Don't worry. I won't tell your little girl how much of a racist you are."

"I'm not racist. There are plenty of exceptions to the rule. Blacks like you that work for me . . . I value them, but I just wouldn't want them ruining my family's gene pool."

I stomped out of the office and sat back down next to Becky.

She analyzed my pissed-off expression.

"Are you okay?"

"I'm fine. It's nothing I can't handle."

***

We went to my apartment after dinner.

"Can I talk to you about something?" Becky asked.

"What's on your mind, beautiful?"

"What are we doing, Ben? We spend time together like we're in a relationship, but we've never discussed it. Where are we going with this? I really want more than just a friendship."

"Becky, I like you a lot, but we come from two completely different worlds. Tonight, meeting your parents confirmed that. I'm not sure either of us is ready to handle the stress and drama that would come from us being in a relationship."

"I'm not scared. We never know unless we try, right?"

She held my hand and looked me in the eyes. I couldn't deny the fact that I really liked her or the fact that she made me extremely happy and proud when she had no fear in claiming our relationship and defending me to her parents. Those actions gave me confidence that we should at least try to make our relationship official and see how things work out.

"All right, let's do it."

"You mean yes?" Becky said excitedly.

I sighed. "I want to be with you, but are you sure you really want to do this? It's not too late to just stay friends."

"My feelings for you go deeper than a mere friendship. I'm with you because I want to be. I can handle whatever happens. I know we'll face shit, and I don't care. I love you, and I'll fight for us because you're worth fighting for, but this'll only work if you feel the same way."

Hearing her say "I love you" further proved to me that we weren't just fuck buddies. Her words helped solidify that our feelings were mutual and real, and we were now in a committed relationship.

"I love you too. I feel the same way . . . I needed that."
"Needed what?"
"I needed to hear that you love me and you'd fight for us. I'll protect and love you too . . . always."
We kissed.
"What about Gabby?" Becky asked.
"I've known Gabby a long time. She's one of my best friends, but that's where it ends. I don't want anyone else. I don't love her like that. I just want to be with you."
I stared into her eyes.
After that day, it was us against the world.

My trip down memory lane was interrupted by Gabby snapping her fingers in front of my face. I was instantly pulled back to the present.

"You looked like your mind was somewhere else for a minute. You all right?"

I shook those memories away. "Yeah, I'm cool. I'm just thinking about my case."

"Yo, yo, what's up, Ben?" Terrence said.

Terrence was about six-two. He had a brown complexion and always had on the latest fashions. Today, he was wearing a charcoal-gray suit with matching purple bow tie and socks. I gave him a brotherly hug.

"Gabby, I see you're still suffering from resting bitch-face syndrome," he teased.

"Shut up, punk," she said jokingly.

I told Terrence everything that had gone down so far with the case and about the partnership if I won.

"I don't want to sound negative, but your firm is playing you. They know damn well you can't win that case," he said.

"Rarely do I agree with Terrence, but he's kind of right," Gabby added.

"You need to drop that firm anyway and start one with me," he said.

Terrence had his own solo law practice, and he tried to convince me to start a firm with him nearly every time I saw him.

"Why would Ben want to work with your broke ass?" Gabby asked him.

"I guess you didn't see the brand-new Porsche I'm driving, huh? My life is like a sandwich. No matter which way I flip it, my bread comes first. I'm always about getting my money, and with Ben and me working together, we'd be unstoppable."

I laughed. I looked at my watch and said, "I got to head home. If y'all want, we can keep this conversation going and hang out at my place for a while until I get ready to go to dinner with Becky."

They nodded.

"Hey, babe," I called, entering my apartment.

We stepped inside.

"We're in the living room," Becky shouted.

"We?"

"Yeah, Simone is here."

"I got Terrence and Gabby with me."

"Oh . . . OK."

I knew she wasn't thrilled to hear Gabby was with me. I placed my briefcase on the hardwood floor. Gabby and Terrence were still arguing. They walked in, sat on the love seat, and continued their comical bickering. Simone was sitting on the sofa with Becky, flipping channels, while Becky had her legs crossed on top of our ottoman, typing away on her laptop.

"Hey, cuz," Simone said.

"What's up? What are you doing here?"

"Can't I visit my favorite cousin and my best friend?"

"What's the *real* reason you're here?"

Simone laughed. "I have a date picking me up here at seven. I don't want Uncle Curtis or Aunt Mabel to question me about my new guy, so I told them I was hanging out with Becky tonight."

I shook my head, tugged off my tie, and kissed Becky.

"So, I got that case with that rapper who killed the cops and the gay couple. He claims he didn't do it, and as crazy as it sounds, I kind of believe him. If I can clear him and win this case, I'll be made partner."

"That's great, baby. You're like Atticus Finch in *To Kill a Mockingbird*."

I looked over at Gabby, who was pretending to vomit.

"What are typing?" I asked Becky.

"I'm just finishing this article about the importance of women wearing lingerie for their partners."

I kissed her and said, "You would know. It drives me wild seeing you dressed up all sexy, then working to get you out of it. It's like unwrapping a gift on Christmas."

Becky playfully slapped me on the ass.

"Aw, I want what you guys have," Simone said.

"Ugh, get a room," Gabby said, breaking away from her conversation with Terrence.

Becky cut her eyes at Gabby.

"You see that?" Terrence said. "That's why brothers are going to these white girls. Sistas got too much attitude."

"Don't say shit like that. Race has nothing to do with it," I said.

"No, don't correct him, Ben," Gabby said. She adjusted herself in the love seat, faced him, and scowled. "When I see sorry brothas like you choose white women, I take it as a personal rejection of the women who birthed them. It's bad enough we're devalued in society. To see it happen from our own is just hurtful."

She was upset, but I took offense to that too, since I mirrored the men she was talking about.

Gabby continued, "We're immersed in a culture where society subtly tells us black women like me aren't viewed as beautiful. Do you know how much it tears me apart inside and hurts when I hear the white boys at work say how hideous Michelle Obama is and drool over how hot they think Melania is now that she's the first lady? I think Michelle is beautiful, but to them, everything about her is ugly. When I see Michelle Obama, I see myself, so what do you think of me? Why does Melania set the bar for beauty standards?"

"I agree with you, Gabby, but don't blame all white people for the few that made those silly comments," Becky said.

"Of course, you would say that. If I had blond hair and blue eyes, I'd see the world with rose-colored glasses too. It wouldn't make sense to try to make you understand the constant rejection from society that blacks suffer on a daily basis. No matter how much you see it or Ben explains it to you, you'll never know what it feels like. You can at least have compassion and stop insulting blacks further by pretending that racism doesn't exist."

"I think Michelle and Melania are both pretty," Simone inserted.

That made Terrence and Gabby laugh.

"You're no better than Terrence. You're a black woman so ashamed of your race that you won't even date a black man because society has programmed you to believe they're inferior," Gabby snidely replied.

"I'm not even going to argue with you today. You're always talking about other people's problems when yours is simple: you need some dick."

Terrence and I laughed. Simone and Becky high-fived. Gabby folded her arms and pouted.

"Laugh it up, Simone, but playing ostrich by sticking your head in the sand and pretending problems don't exist doesn't make your problems go away. You're a sorry excuse for a black woman."

Simone's cell phone chimed. She waved off Gabby's comment, glanced at her phone, and smiled. "It's Trevor. I've been waiting for this text all day. He's here. Later, guys."

"Don't sleep with him," I yelled as she rushed out the door.

"Don't judge me," Simone fired back.

"All right, I don't mean to kick you guys out, but Ben and I have plans to see my parents in a few," Becky said.

"That's tonight?" I joked.

"Yes, babe. I've been telling you this for the past week."

I laughed. "I'm kidding."

"Well, I guess that's our cue to leave. Get up, punk," Gabby said, nudging Terrence.

We said our goodbyes, and then I walked back to the couch with Becky.

"Whatcha doin?" I asked.

"Working on my book."

I tried to sneak a peek, and Becky playfully covered the monitor.

"I don't want you to read it until after it's published. This book is special to me, and I wrote it for us."

"All right. How's the book coming along?"

"Ugh, good, I guess. I did some revisions and sent it out to two more publishers. There's a letter from a publisher now on the counter."

"Open it."

"I'm afraid it's another rejection letter."

"If it is, you'll just have to keep trying." I handed her the letter. She opened it and read it.

"What does it say?" I asked.

She sighed and handed it to me. I winced as I scanned through the rejection letter. The letter was professional and tactfully written, but it was crystal clear they weren't interested.

"Hurry up and get ready," she said. "I told my parents that I didn't know if you'd be able to come to dinner tonight because of your case, but I'm glad you're going to be with me."

That made one of us.

Chapter 7

Bill

Ill Bill

"Yo, who's that white guy? Is that a cop?" a teenage boy asked Shakir, a kid that lived in my mom's apartment building.

"Nah, that's no cop. That's my man, Ill Bill."

Shakir waved. "Yo, B, what up? You playing ball with us today?"

"Nah, not today," I said. "I know you don't want me to come on the court and embarrass y'all. You already know why they call me 'Ill Bill.'"

"Yeah, yeah, 'cause your skills are sick on the court," Shakir said. "I know, but come on, B. What, you scared you gonna mess up your pretty suit?"

"Don't think I can't cross you over in wingtips," I joked.

"Prove it. You got next."

"All right, I'll play one quick one."

After the arraignment, I was on my way to visit my mom. She still lived in this housing project. My case was heavily on my mind, but this was a welcome distraction from the petty games played at the firm. When I was at work, I listened and smiled at the bullshit comments and racist jokes the partners made when there weren't minorities around. I nodded and pretended to agree with their opinions, but their bigoted way of thinking wasn't me. I didn't belong in their narrow-minded world. Here—this neighborhood—these were *my* people. Being here was where I felt comfortable. I grew up here, found love here, but most importantly, I could be myself here. I was at home in Queensbridge.

I hung up my suit jacket on the black metal fence, rolled my shirt sleeves up to the elbow, cuffed my pant legs, and tied the laces as tightly as they could be on my brown wingtip shoes, preparing myself for the next game.

Being on this basketball court brought back so many memories. Memories of my mom, Ebony, and why I became a lawyer. At first glance, a lot of people believed that because I was white, I never had to struggle and had a perfect life growing up, but that couldn't be further from the truth.

"Now, class, I want you all to welcome our newest student, William O'Neil," Mrs. Foy said.

I was a skinny, dorky, twelve-year-old standing awkwardly in front of the classroom, noticeably sticking out because I was the only white student in the class.

"Can you call me Billy or Bill? I hate my full name," I said to Mrs. Foy.

She nodded.

"Can you call me Billy or Bill?" one of the kids sporting a high-top fade nasally mimicked me.

"Knock it off, Jalen. Keep it up and I'll make another call home to your mother."

The class laughed at his scolding.

Back then, my mom was sick regularly and couldn't understand why she constantly felt tired and had pain in her back. She saw numerous doctors and eventually had an MRI done, which showed she had lesions covering her brain and spine. She was diagnosed with multiple scle-

rosis, and the doctors said it was incurable and would only worsen over time. Multiple sclerosis is an unpredictable, sometimes crippling disease of the central nervous system that disrupts the flow of information inside the brain. Those disruptions cause pain and physical malfunction in the body. There are treatments like pills, shots, and physical therapy, but there's nothing that can permanently make the disease go away. The treatments only help to slow it down, and all of them are expensive.

Feeling sick and in pain all the time, Mom missed a lot of work, which led to her eventually losing her housekeeping job. With my mom working sparsely as a waitress and hardly having money to support us, we got kicked out of our apartment in Kew Gardens and had to move to the only place she could afford: The Queensbridge Housing Projects. We lived in a small, run-down, two-bedroom apartment and were the only white family in there, so we stuck out. This neighborhood was different. Hiding under our beds whenever we heard the sounds of gunshots outside our bedroom windows was something we weren't used to.

"Is he your son or something? There ain't no white kids around this neighborhood," an extremely dark-skinned boy with beady eyes said. His complexion was as black as his shirt.

I felt my face turning as red as Mrs. Foy's hair.

"No, Draper, Billy and I are not related."

Mrs. Foy turned to me. "You can take the empty desk next to Ebony in the third row, OK?"

I nodded and walked to the only empty desk available in the class.

The first time I saw Ebony, I thought she was the most beautiful girl I had ever seen. She had a deep mocha complexion that matched her eyes, and a long, silky ponytail that ended down the middle of her back. She had *the prettiest smile. I couldn't stop myself from staring at her. Ebony giggled, but the boy sitting next to her was giving me a death stare. I'd seen him and the kid Jalen in passing before. They lived on the floors above me in my apartment building.*

"Hi," I said, sitting down next to her.

"Hey," she said, smiling back at me.

"Stay away from my twin, white boy," the kid next to her said.

I realized he had the same complexion and eyes that she had. "Huh?" I stammered.

"I saw you gawking at my sister. Don't try frontin' like you weren't."

"Chill out, Akeem. He's just being nice," Ebony fired back.

Akeem ignored her and kept his gaze on me. "You heard what I said. Keep looking at her, and I'ma fuck you up."

"Akeem, I'm not going to have you using that language and threatening kids in my classroom. Go to the principal's office now," Mrs. Foy yelled.

Akeem stood up and pushed my forehead. "This isn't over, chump."

He left the room, staring me down. All I wanted to do was fit in on my first day, but instead, I'd already made an enemy.

"Stop running like a bitch, white boy," Akeem yelled.

I ran at full speed. Some of the neighborhood kids chased me from school all the way to my apartment building. Fighting my way home after school had become an everyday occurrence. They picked on me daily for no reason other than me being white and living in their neighborhood.

One of the boys tackled me from behind and held my arms down. Eight kids my age circled me.

"Fuck him up," Akeem ordered.

Jalen sucker-punched me, while Draper yanked me to the ground. All of them stomped and kicked while I tried my best to protect my face and head. Then I heard a police siren. A cruiser with flashing lights screeched to a halt.

"Shit, that's O'Sullivan. Fall back. Let's bounce," Akeem said.

The group quickly dispersed.

"Run. Scatter like fucking roaches, you bunch of savages," O'Sullivan said, sprinting out of his cruiser and swinging his nightstick.

I was left bloodied and beaten, curled up in a fetal position on the concrete. My hands shook. Tears streamed down my face. A muscular cop with a receding hairline and a black, bushy mustache held out his hand and helped me up. He stood up straight, and his eyes widened when he said, "You'll be all right, kid. Stop crying. Be tough. What's your name?"

I quickly wiped my face. "Billy O'Neil."

"Ah, an Irish boy, huh? What are you doing around here?"

"I live here," I said, pointing to my building.

"You live in this neighborhood with the niggers?"

Mom told me never to use that word, so I just repeated, "I live here."

"What does your dad do?"

"I never met him, sir."

"What about your mom?"

"She's sick . . . She has multiple sclerosis."

"Jesus, why were these punks fighting with you?"

"Because I'm white. They said blacks have been getting beaten up by whites and even worse for no reason for

years. They figured they could take some of that revenge out on me."

"What? You see, this is why you shouldn't be around these savages. I'm taking you to your apartment. Come on."

We walked inside the building.

"What floor do you live on?" he asked.

"The third floor."

He pulled on the elevator door.

"It's broken," I said.

"Of course, it is. I don't know how you and your mother live here with these animals."

We walked to my floor, and I opened the door to my apartment. My mom was grimacing in pain, bent over in the kitchen. I ran over and helped her up.

"Mom, are you OK?"

She looked up at my bruised face. "My God, are those boys still beating on you?"

I watched Mom run to the bathroom and dampen a towel at the faucet sink. She came back and cleaned up my face.

"Mom, don't worry about that. How are you feeling?"

"I'm all right. Did you get in trouble? Why is there a cop with you?"

"How are you, ma'am? I'm Officer O'Sullivan from the 114th Precinct. I stopped those niggers from attacking your son, and I figured I'd introduce myself."

Mom glared at him after his statement.

"Don't worry, Ms. O'Neil. Billy told me his father wasn't around, so I'll make sure to keep an eye on him and keep him out of trouble. Have a good day, ma'am."

He left. I helped my mom to the couch in the living room.

"Sit down, Billy."

I did as she instructed and sat beside her.

"Billy, there are bad people in every race. I never want to hear you refer to black people as the N-word. Don't ever use it. That term can be applied to any race, but its history is ugly. I know it's hard not to be angry. It'd be easy to just hate all black people for what they're doing to you, but don't become a bigot like Officer O'Sullivan."

"Mom, they're beating me up every day because I'm white."

"I know, and it's terrible. I'm going to talk to their parents, but in the meantime, I need you to endure until they get to know you. Things will be better. They'll see that you're not their enemy, and vice versa."

I rolled my eyes.

"There was a time when I hated minorities and thought I was better than them, but life has a way of humbling us all," Mom said.

"What happened?" I asked, grimacing as I clutched my side.

"Back then, I used to bad-mouth any race that wasn't white. I wouldn't acknowledge or talk to them at work. When I married your father, that first year, he lost his job. He couldn't find a new one, which forced me to work double shifts at my housekeeping job at the Hilton. I struggled to take care of both of us. There were times when I could barely keep a roof over our heads and had to choose between paying the rent or buying food. We went to bed hungry often. Our church, our neighborhood, our people . . . knew we were struggling, and they did nothing to help us. When I couldn't pay tithes every month, our church excommunicated us. Our so-called friends and community stuck up their noses and called us white trash. To them, we were no better than 'N-words.' Your father and I didn't have much family, and the little family we did have lived in different states and were broke too. You wanna know who picked us up when we were at rock bottom?"

"Who helped?" I asked.

"The black women that I worked side by side with every day, the same people I used to bad-mouth and wouldn't talk to put together a collection and gave us money to help with our rent, food, and clothes to survive."

I slowly nodded.

"I realized I was wrong and needed to change. In time, those boys will see they need to change too," Mom said.

"I hope they figure it out before they kill me."

"I'm sure they will. Clean yourself up and start your homework while I work on dinner."

I did as my mom asked.

Later that night, I heard what sounded like crying coming from my mom's bedroom. I crept to her door and slowly pushed it open. I peeked my head in and saw my mom sitting on the edge of the bed, crying.

"Are you OK, Mom?"

Mom wiped her eyes and kissed my forehead. She put her nose against mine and said, "I'm sorry. I'm sorry I can't give you a better place to live or picked a better father for you." Her lips trembled. She turned away from me so I wouldn't see her crying. "I'm sorry I couldn't give you a better life. I hate that you have to suffer because of me."

My mom was going through a lot with my dad being gone and her being sick. I hated that I was powerless to help her. I hated that my drama with Akeem was adding more stress to her already stressful life. I didn't want her to get any sicker because of it. We were all we had. I knew I had to be strong for her.

"I'm fine, Mom. We'll be OK."

As promised, Mom talked to Akeem's mother about my daily ass whoopings, but they didn't stop. She was determined to befriend Jalen's and Akeem's mothers and stop the bullying once she had a better relationship with them. The first month, every day whenever Mom saw them talking outside and smoking their cigarettes in front of our building, she went up to them and said hello, and every day, they ignored her. Despite them snubbing her, she still smiled and spoke to them. Eventually, she got the women to engage in a conversation, and slowly but surely, they bonded when they realized her life was similar to their own.

"Billy, I need you to go to the grocery store for me," Mom shouted from her bedroom.

"OK." I sighed and got ready.

As soon as I stepped out of my apartment door, I saw Akeem sprinting up the stairs at full speed, panic and fear in his eyes.

"O'Sullivan's gonna kill me," he said.

He tugged on the janitor's closet door, and it flung open. Akeem put his finger to his lips, indicating for me to keep quiet, and slowly closed the door behind him.

I heard heavy footsteps coming up the stairwell. O'Sullivan's face was red, his nostrils flared. He grabbed me by the collar and said, "Where is he? Where'd that fucking pickaninny go?"

I shook nervously. I thought about telling O'Sullivan the truth, but I remembered what Akeem said and the look of terror in his eyes.

"He ran up the stairs," I said, my voice shaky.

"You better not be lying to me and trying to help that nigger. He's not your friend. He and his homeboys beat your ass every day. I hope you're not stupid enough to protect him."

I shook my head nervously. "I'm not lying."

O'Sullivan scanned the area; then his eyes narrowed on me. He shoved me, then released my collar.

"I don't believe you. Is he hiding in the fucking elevator?" He quickly tugged on the door.

"The elevator is still broken."

He walked toward the janitor's closet. As soon as he was about to pull on the door, my mom swung open our apartment door.

"I've been listening to you this entire time. My son answered your questions. Why are you chasing after a child, anyway?"

O'Sullivan stammered. "I'm sorry, ma'am. Those little hoodlums threw eggs at my car, and I wanted to teach them a lesson. I didn't mean to take my frustration out on Billy."

"The way you were yelling at my son, I'm scared to see what that 'lesson' would've been. They're just children."

"Don't mind me. My bark is bigger than my bite. I wouldn't give him more than a firm yelling."

Mom folded her arms. "Well, my son answered you. If you don't mind ending this interrogation, he's going to the store to pick up a few things for me."

"No, no, I don't mind. I'm sure I lost Akeem by now anyway, so I'm heading out. You have a good day, Ms. O'Neil."

"Yeah, you too," she said and slammed the door shut.

O'Sullivan leaned in close, his lips almost grazing my ear, and whispered through clenched teeth, "You tell that little black bastard when I catch him I'm going to beat his ass. You hear me?"

I nodded.

O'Sullivan walked down the steps. After a good minute had passed, Akeem stepped out of the closet.

"Yo, thanks for not diming me out to O'Sullivan. I owe you one."

"No problem."

"I'll see you around."

I hoped that incident would prove that I wasn't a bad guy.

"Can I get next? Can I play?"

"Hell no!" Jalen, Draper, and some of the other boys on the basketball court yelled.

"White boys can't play no ball," Jalen said.

They all continued to curse me out and rejected my request, but Akeem shut them down.

"Yo, he's got next," Akeem said.

"C'mon, man, you know he's gonna suck," Jalen argued.

"Chill, J, it's better this way. Now we can play three on three."

Since I didn't snitch when O'Sullivan was hunting for him, my daily ass-kickings ended, and Akeem didn't look at me like he wanted to kill me anymore.

I stepped on the court. I figured they thought I would suck because I was "the white boy," but I used to practice all the time in my old neighborhood. I knew my best chance of earning their respect was playing defense and passing them the ball, so that was exactly what I did. I threw fancy passes, made defense stops, and knocked down open shots. We blew the other team out. Akeem was impressed.

"I didn't know you had game like that. You busted my boys' asses."

Jalen sulked. I smiled and said, "Thanks."

"Good looking out for not giving me up to O'Sullivan."

"It's cool."

"Nah, that's a big deal to me. I already gave the word for everyone around here to stop beating on you."

"Thanks."

"You should play ball with us from now on. We play almost every day after school. We're getting ready to try out for the school team. You should too."

"I can't. I take care of my mom after school. She's sick . . . She has multiple sclerosis."

"Where's your pops at? Can't he take care of her?" Akeem asked.

"I've seen pictures of my dad, but I never met him. He left when I was younger. It's just my mom and me."

"I didn't know your dad wasn't around. I thought all white people had both parents in their lives."

"Not in my family."

Akeem laughed. "Between you being good at ball and your pops not being around, I swear, Bill, I'm starting to think you're secretly black."

I smiled. Akeem's face got serious.

"My pops took off when me and my sister were babies. The coward left us to fend for ourselves. It's all right, though. I didn't need him then, and I damn sure don't need him now. One day, I'm gonna be paid, and my mom and Ebony will never have to worry about money again."

"I'm right there with you, man," I said. "I want to do the same thing for my mom and me."

"Cool."

Akeem faced Jalen. "Bring it in, J."

Jalen was already within earshot of us but reluctantly came closer. Draper glared at us since Akeem didn't bother to call him over.

"J's my right hand. Now that you're down with us, we'll get this money together."

The three of us fist-bumped, and after that day, Akeem, Jalen, and I became best friends. Akeem's and my anger toward our fathers being deadbeats, our dreams of being rich, and our love of basketball strengthened our bond. Being around Akeem and Jalen got me respect and street credibility. Akeem let everyone know that I didn't rat him out to O'Sullivan and I could be trusted. My mom being cool with Akeem's and Jalen's mothers was a plus too. She was known as "the cool-ass white lady on Tenth Street." A lot of people around the neighborhood still weren't fond of white people, but we were the exceptions. I wasn't "the white boy" that lived in the hood anymore. Since my skills were "sick" on the basketball court, Akeem had everyone in the neighborhood calling me "Ill Bill."

Luckily for me, Mom's multiple sclerosis went into remission. She was doing better healthwise, or at least she pretended to be, and pushed for me to hang out with Akeem and Jalen and try out for the basketball team.

Since I was hanging out at Akeem's house all the time, that meant I also got to see Ebony. We flirted when no one was around, but I tried to keep my feelings hidden. I didn't want to piss Akeem off and get on his bad side again now that we were friends. Once Akeem and Jalen realized I had a crush on her, they teased me relentlessly about it.

Things were good for a while until one summer day that changed Akeem's and Jalen's lives forever.

We were sitting on the wooden benches in front of our building when an Escalade with huge rims and a sound system we heard from blocks away pulled up to the curb and stopped at the hydrant. A black guy in the chromed-out Cadillac Escalade pointed and shouted, "Yo, Akeem, lemme holla at'cha real quick."

Akeem smiled and ran over to the truck.

The guy was dark-skinned, with a long, thin scar that ran down the side of his face.

"Who's that?" I asked Jalen.

"That's Drastic and his right-hand man Boogie Brown," Draper answered for Jalen. "He's got crazy *loot. He always has the latest Air Jordans and the best clothes. Sometimes, he pays us good money if we drop off packages in certain buildings for him."*

"I want those new Jordans, so I hope he asks me to do a drop-off. I already know my mom can't afford to get them for me," Jalen said.

Jalen's little brother, Jerami, had cancer back then. Jalen's dad was killed in the crossfire of a shootout several years before. With his dad gone, Jalen's mom, Juanita Wilson, was always working to pay for his brother's treatments and household bills. Often, when my mom was feeling decent, she'd watch Jerami for Mrs. Wilson to help her out since his aunt Carina, who lived with them, was a flake and wasn't dependable. Jalen hated the life of being a poor latchkey kid. He never wanted to go home, because being home for him was depressing. It reminded him that his family was broke and his brother's sickness might take another person he loved out of his life.

I stepped closer to Akeem and strained to listen in on his conversation with Drastic.

"Yo, you and your boy Jalen wanna work for me again?" Drastic asked.

"I don't know," Akeem said. "My mom would kill me if she found out. Me and J can't get picked up by the cops again, or we're going to Spofford for sure this time."

The Spofford Juvenile Detention Center was located in Hunts Point in the Bronx and served as a youth jail for kids that got caught up with the law.

"Don't worry about that. It won't be like last time. I don't want y'all stealing shit for me anymore. Don't worry about your mom, either. Mine's was the same way when I was coming up. All you gotta do is hit her off with some cash every now and then, and she'll chill out."

Akeem stood there, thinking.

"Look, I'm a busy man. I need an answer now. You're my first choice, but if you can't handle it, I'm moving on."

"Nah, I can handle it," Akeem said. "All right, bet. I'm in."

"Call your boy over here. Let's see if he wants to make some consistent money too."

"Yo, J, Draper, Ill Bill, y'all come here."

"Chill kid—Draper and the white boy can't be down with us. They're bad for business," Drastic said.

Akeem waved us off. Jalen stood by with Draper and me.

"Draper's cool and my boy B is good people. Bill wouldn't snitch or nothing. I can vouch for that," Akeem said.

"Draper got a big fucking mouth," Drastic said. "The last time he did a drop for me, the block was hot with cops for weeks. Putting Draper and the white boy on would draw too much attention. If you wanna make money with this, bringing notice to yourself can fuck you up. You wanna stay under the radar."

Akeem nodded. "Yo, J, come here."

"Y'all ready to make some real money? I'm tryin' to have y'all sell for me on the block. No more of the little kiddie shit I had y'all doing before. Both of y'all can make some serious money," Drastic said.

Drastic turned to Jalen and said, "Your boy Akeem said he was down. What about you? You in?"

"Fuck yeah, I'm down," Jalen said.

"That's what I like to hear. Drop these two and I'll show y'all what I want y'all to start with. Hop in."

Draper looked furious, watching Drastic talking with Akeem and Jalen.

"Yo, Bill, Draper, me and J gotta do something with Drastic. We'll catch up with y'all later," Akeem said.

Things weren't the same with Draper and them after that day.

Akeem did well selling crack for Drastic. His reputation on the streets was growing, but the bigger he got, the more Draper hated him. Akeem was a natural-born leader, and in a different environment, he could've been anything, but he was consumed by the street life. Draper eventually stopped hanging out with us altogether. Seeing Akeem's reputation growing and watching him make good money made him jealous. He picked arguments with Akeem often and eventually became his competition in the street when it came to selling drugs.

High school came around. With all the money Akeem and Jalen were making, they felt the streets taught them way more than school ever could, so they dropped out. They stopped playing basketball for our neighborhood leagues, too, focusing all their time and energy on the streets. Even though they stopped playing, they always went to my games and supported me. Seeing their success and observing my mom struggling over the years, I often begged Akeem to let me sell drugs too, but he always refused.

"You're meant to do more in life than this, B. You're smart. Keep your head in the books. The streets aren't for you."

"You're making good money, though," I said. "I'm broke. My mom barely has money to buy groceries after paying all the bills, and she won't let me quit playing ball to work because she says she wants me to enjoy life right now."

"If you need money here and there, I got you."

"Nah, I'm not cool with that. I'm no charity case."

"It's not charity. You're like family to me. You always got my back, and I got yours."

We gave each other a brotherly hug. After that conversation, every other week, Akeem slipped money under the door for my mom for groceries.

The cops had been cracking down hard. Eventually, Drastic got caught by the cops in a traffic stop gone wrong. The cops found drugs and a gun linked to a few homicides in his truck. With that stuff and his priors, Drastic was sentenced to life in prison. With him gone, Akeem was number one in the streets. This made him a target for Officer O'Sullivan and Draper, who despised him. With his new power came those who tried to test him. To "keep my hands clean," as Akeem would say, he didn't have me around when he had to "take care of business," but he was notorious for being vicious and ruthless. I knew he hurt people. He was known for being stone cold in the street, but he never showed that side to me whenever we hung out.

Scholastically, Ebony and I were doing well and were in a lot of the same honors classes. We were officially dating but kept things on the low out of fear of how Akeem would take it. Surprisingly, he was happy about it.

"B, come here for a sec," Akeem called from the living room.

Ebony and I were laughing and working on a group project together, sitting at their kitchen table. I walked up to him.

"What's up?" I asked.

"Sit down. I want to talk to you about something."

"Is everything good?" I asked, concerned.

"I know you and my sister got something going on."

My heart raced. I was stuttering and stammering, trying to find the right words to explain myself.

"It's not-I wasn't trying to-I won't—"

"It's fine, B, relax. You're a good dude, and you're going somewhere in life. I don't want her to be with a guy like me. She deserves the best, and I know you would give her that type of life. Just don't hurt her."

"I won't."

"I know."

Before I knew it, it was my senior year in high school. While things were going great with Ebony and me, the tension between Akeem and Draper was at an all-time high. Whenever they saw each other, it was a fight. Things were getting violent, and it was drawing a lot of attention from the cops.

"What the hell is your bum ass looking at?" Akeem shouted at Draper.

Akeem, Jalen, and I were hanging out on the benches near the basketball courts when Draper walked past us with his boys, pointing in Akeem's direction.

"Keep talking shit. I got something for your big-ass mouth," Draper fired back.

"That sounds real gay. I knew you were a homo."

"What'd you say, motherfucker?" Draper said, rushing over and pushing Akeem.

"All right, jiggaboos, break it up," Officer O'Sullivan said, seemingly coming out of nowhere.

Everyone was so focused on the argument with Akeem and Draper that the cops caught us slipping and crept on us. Every one of us sucked our teeth. Lately, O'Sullivan and his new partner, McIvor, had been stopping and frisking us nonstop. Akeem never kept any hard drugs on him, but O'Sullivan was determined to bust him and send him to prison like he did with Drastic.

"You all know the drill. Spread your legs and place your hands on the fucking table," O'Sullivan said.

Five more officers surrounded us, so there was no use in trying to run. O'Sullivan walked next to me and whispered in my ear, "How many times do I have to tell you? Stop hanging around these niggers. Go home, Billy." Then O'Sullivan shoved me and shouted, "Get outta here."

In his twisted mind, his racist view was his way of looking out for me.

"They were just arguing. Nothing happened," I said.

O'Sullivan swiftly punched me in the stomach. My knees buckled, and I dropped down to the ground gasping for air. He manhandled me, yanking me off the ground and pushing me out of hearing range of my friends.

"Don't you ever backtalk me in front of other cops again. I'm trying to protect your stupid ass, and you insist on trying my patience and ending up like these lowlifes."

I looked over at my friends. Akeem took his hand off the table and motioned for me to calm down.

"Keep your fucking hands on the table where I can see them," Officer McIvor yelled.

O'Sullivan turned my face back to him and continued. "Look at me, kid. They don't have futures. They're gonna be stuck in this hellhole for generations to come. I'm trying to keep your record clean so you can amount to something in life and get out of here. I'm nice, but don't take my fucking kindness for weakness."

"I'm not asking you for your help, and I don't want it," I shot back.

He punched me in the stomach again.

"I'm not going to say it a third time . . . Get the fuck out of here. Your mother is under enough stress with her sickness. She doesn't need this bullshit from you. Go home."

Akeem looked at me and said, "It's OK, man, just do what he says. We know you got our back."

McIvor put him in an arm bar and slammed him on the ground. The gravel scraped Akeem's face, and his lip was cut and bleeding.

"Nobody was talking to you, boy," McIvor said. "Let's get something straight—we run shit here."

I didn't want to be the cause of anything else negative. I walked home, praying nothing bad happened while I was away from my friends.

Two weeks passed. Word on the street was Draper was going around the neighborhood telling everyone he had enough of Akeem punking him and was going to shoot Akeem if he got in his face again. Not trying to ruin his reputation, Akeem went looking for him. I tried to convince him to let me go with him and Jalen, but he wasn't having it.

"B, things might get real out here tonight. I don't want you getting caught in the middle," Akeem said.

Two hours passed. I was sitting in my living room when I heard three loud shots, boom, boom, boom, and ran to my window. I carefully stood off to the side and saw marked and unmarked cop cars speeding down the blocks blaring their sirens. In the distance, I saw Akeem sprinting past buildings headed toward ours with his gun in hand while Draper continued to fire at him. O'Sullivan's patrol car stopped in front of them. Draper hauled ass in the opposite direction while Akeem ran around the car. O'Sullivan and McIvor chased Akeem with their guns drawn.

"Drop your weapon!" O'Sullivan yelled.

Instinctively, Akeem turned around quickly with his gun still in his hand. O'Sullivan and McIvor riddled him with bullets.

"Nooooooo!" I screamed.

"Billy, get away from that window," Mom yelled.

I rushed past her, frantically putting on my shoes.

"What are you doing? Where are you going? You can't go out there right now," Mom said.

"They shot Akeem," I said, rushing out the door.

I ran past Jalen in the stairwell.

"You gotta tell Ms. Williams and Ebony. Hurry up," I yelled to him, not stopping to talk further.

I rushed outside. My heart was pounding so hard, it felt like it was going to beat out of my chest. Akeem was slumped on the side of the fence leading to our building. His blood was gushing out at a rapid rate and seeping on the concrete. I held him as he gasped for air.

"Help . . . Help. Call an ambulance. He's dying," I yelled to O'Sullivan.

O'Sullivan rolled his eyes, grabbed his radio, keyed the microphone, and said, "Central, shots fired. The perp was hit, and we're going to need a bus at this location."

"He's not a perp, and he doesn't need a bus. He needs a damn ambulance," I said.

"Relax, kid. A bus is cop jargon for an ambulance," McIvor said. "They're on their way."

"Let me get a rush on that bus, Central," O'Sullivan said nonchalantly on his radio.

"What's the condition of the perp?" I heard the woman on the radio say.

"The perp is likely, Central," O'Sullivan answered.

"What's 'likely' mean?" I asked.

"Kid, it means I don't think he's gonna make it."

"You knew him. He was terrified of you. He wouldn't have shot you, and you know it."

"Look, when someone turns around with a gun pointed, you don't have time to assume they're not going to *shoot at you. You said it yourself: he was terrified of me. Wouldn't you want to kill the boogeyman that you're afraid of? Wake up. They're all the same. They're all killers, and I took him out before he killed me."*

Our neighbors and other people from the surrounding buildings ran outside to see what happened. Jalen pushed his way through the crowd. He dropped down to the ground next to me. He was trembling and crying, too shocked to say anything. Akeem shook as he struggled to raise his head and look up at me. He let out one last pant, and I wept as I rocked his lifeless body in my arms.

I heard the wail of approaching sirens, but I knew it was too late. When the ambulance finally arrived, the paramedics slowly pried Akeem's body from my grasp. Jalen and I watched them work quickly in the ambulance while we sat on the ground in shock, drenched in our best friend's blood. Time moved in a blur. There were about twenty patrol cars out, and cops were everywhere trying to calm the community down.

Mrs. Wilson, Ebony, and Mrs. Williams ran out of our building.

"Billy, where is Akeem? Where's my brother?" Ebony yelled. I couldn't stop crying. Ebony shook me by the shoulders and asked again, with her eyes welling up with tears, "Billy, where is he?"

I point to the paramedics, who were using a defibrillator on him. Ebony and Mrs. Williams sprinted over to them.

"Ma'am, you can't come in here," a paramedic said to Mrs. Williams, extending his arms to block her.

She batted his hands away. "That's my son," she shouted as she and Ebony tried to jump into the ambulance.

The paramedics were moving frantically in the ambulance, working to stop the bleeding and attached an

AED to Akeem's chest. Akeem's eyes were shut, and his arms dangled off the sides of the stretcher.

While the paramedics were struggling with Ebony, Mrs. Williams pushed past everyone and rushed into the ambulance. She caught sight of Akeem, reached for the gurney, and tried to pick up his lifeless body, but the cops took her off so the paramedics could continue to work on him without any distractions.

Mrs. Williams dropped to her knees and wept. Ebony crouched and held her. Then Mrs. Williams jumped to her feet, rushed over to a random cop that was closest to the ambulance, and pounded on his chest. Some of the other cops tried to restrain her. Even Ebony tried to hold her back. Mrs. Williams finally stopped, her eyes pained as she stared at her son's blood on the concrete and his dead body in the ambulance. The cops and EMS workers tried to console her and Ebony.

"Get off me. Get the fuck off me. You murdered my son." she wept.

Jalen's mom, Mrs. Wilson, consoled her, but the hard reality was that Akeem had died that night.

Ebony and I were in her bedroom after Akeem's funeral. She was sitting on her bed, staring out the window, deep in thought. She was hurting, and I had no idea what I could say or do to take her pain away.

Then she sighed and asked, "What do you want to be after high school?"

I shrugged. "I don't know. I was thinking maybe a lawyer. I like arguing with people, and I want to fight for good people that the world is fucking with. I'm still thinking about it. What do you want to be?"

Ebony didn't take her eyes off whatever she was looking at outside her window. "I want to be a cop."

"A cop? Why?" I asked.

"I should hate them after two of them killed my brother, but I learned something from all of this. My brother was far from being a saint, but he didn't deserve to die. The cops in this neighbor prey on minorities and think we're all savages. For things to change, communities and the way they are policed need to change. I want to become a cop so I can show other minority children that there are other ways to make it besides selling drugs. I know it sounds crazy, but I want to become one to help change things for people of color. If I'm a cop, at least I know there'd be one good one in the world. A lot of these white cops come in our neighborhoods and don't know how to handle situations with people of color. Instead of running from the cops, I want to make changes from the inside."

"Why?" I asked.

"How do you think scientists create vaccines? They have to get the virus first before they can create what's needed to cure it. I'm going to become a cop and rise so high in the ranks that I'll have the power to make changes to police procedures and the way cops interact with minority communities. I know, it sounds crazy."

"That's not crazy," I said. "Hearing you talk about it like that, it makes a lot of sense. I already know you can do anything you put your mind to. You always have my support. I got your back."

After high school, Ebony and I went to John Jay College. She majored in criminal justice, and I studied law. Both of us used Akeem's death as motivation and graduated at the top of our classes.

Once we were finished with college, Ebony went straight to the police academy with one goal in mind: rising through the ranks and making real changes within the NYPD.

I was a financially struggling public defender with a good case record. Seeing that I was struggling, Jalen's mom asked me for my résumé and begged the partners at the firm she worked at to hire me. I worked my ass off so I wouldn't embarrass her, and every day, I made sure to hug and kiss her to show my appreciation.

Ebony and I moved on from Queensbridge to a nicer neighborhood in a condo in Jamaica Estates. Queensbridge made me who I was, and I could never forget it. It taught me how to adapt to whatever surroundings I was in, and it showed me that there were good people that lived in these neighborhoods. It made me street smart and book smart, but most importantly, the lessons I learned from this community gave me the motivation to become a lawyer.

The basketball bounced against my leg, interrupting my train of thought and instantly pulling me back to the present.

"You ready to get this game in, or are you just gonna sit there and daydream all day?" Shakir asked.

I smiled and said, "Let's do it."

Chapter 8

Ebony

Temptation

After talking to what felt like a million people about the murders, I flopped down on the beat-up brown leather sofa in the lounge at my precinct. I'd been so busy handling things at the hospital and crime scene that I forgot to clean off the dried blood all over my trembling hands and uniform. It was so fucking hard doing this job every day. I woke up, put on this uniform, and went to work with the intention of making the world a better place, but sometimes, I felt the world was so damaged that it was beyond repair.

I took out my notes for the lieutenants' test I was studying for and started reading. The TV played in the background, and I heard the channel go from a commercial to a press conference with the police commissioner. The reporter's voice pulled my thoughts off my notes and brought my attention to the news conference.

The commissioner was standing in front of a podium loaded with microphones at the murder scene. Reporters listened closely as the commissioner gave the details of the case so far. The commissioner said, "At approximately two fifteen this morning, officers responded to the corner of Gansevoort and Washington Streets and found the perpetrator standing over the bodies of two of the victims, brandishing a weapon while allegedly having the blood of the couple on his body and clothing. Two officers were also killed during the incident when they were attempting to exit their vehicle. The perpetrator opened fire on the patrol car, and the officers passed away when they were en route to being rushed to Bellevue Hospital. When the second group of officers approached the suspect, Mr. Brown fled and resisted arrest when he was apprehended. As of now, Mr. Brown is being held without bail at Rikers Island, and the suspect has denied killing any of the victims."

I took a deep breath as I tried to rein in my thoughts and focus back on my study material. Rashida, my partner, walked into the lounge. "You all right, boss?" she asked.

"I'm hanging in there."

"I'm gonna head home . . . Maybe you should too."

"I am. I just needed to sit down for a sec. I'm trying to keep my mind occupied by studying."

"I know how you feel. I'm drained all around too."

Rashida Harrell had been my partner since day one. She was what I called a triple minority: black, a woman, and a lesbian—all the things society hated. Rashida was light-skinned, with a slender, sexy figure, dreads, and a no-nonsense attitude that matched mine. She was one of my best friends.

"Some of us are going to the Delancey around six tonight for drinks," she said. "After everything we've been through last night, we all need to unwind. You think you can put off studying for one night and come with us?"

"Who is going to be there?"

"So far, me, Rayna, and Morgan."

"The rookie, Rayna Osborne?"

"Yup. I hung out with her last week. She kissed a girl, and she liked it," Rashida joked. "I found out she's gay too. Now I'm trying to see if I can get her to do more than just kiss me."

I laughed and said, "TMI. So, Morgan is going to be there too?"

"I told him I was going to ask you to come out tonight, and he said he'd be there. Can you at least make an appearance? It'll make my courting Rayna so much easier if she's relaxed and having a good time with us."

"I'll try. Let's see how I feel after I get some sleep."

"Well, hurry up and go home so you can rest and come out with us tonight," Rashida said, pulling me up off the couch and helping me to my feet.

"All right."

As soon as I got home, I jumped in the shower, grateful that the nightmare of an evening I had last night was over. I turned on the faucet, and the hot water spewed from the showerhead. I leaned against the wall and let the water cascade down my weary body. Billy was on my mind. He hadn't called me yet, but there was also another man on my mind: Morgan. Morgan St. Clair was another sergeant at my precinct, and I couldn't lie. I was attracted to him. Morgan was the definition of tall, dark, and handsome. He was around six foot six, with a rich espresso complexion. He was built like a fitness model and had dimples that could light up a room. We often joked that we were each other's work spouses, but neither of us could deny there was an attraction between us. Despite our flirty exchanges, he knew I'd never cheat on Billy. At least, I thought he did.

At times, when the stress of my job was too much, he helped me cope and handle things. He was just as into giving back to minority communities as I was. He was smart, driven, and had the same goal of rising in the ranks as I had. We were steady study partners for the lieutenants' test that was coming up in two months. Often, we'd meet up at the library at the police academy and drill each other with questions. I saw in his eyes that even though he knew I'd never cheat on Billy, he wanted to drill me in other ways. Morgan was single and very popular with women, and while he was a bit of a player, he was always honest and open with me, and vice versa.

We had in-depth conversations regularly whenever we were alone in the lounge at the precinct. One of those conversations that made me question everything about myself and my relationship happened last week.

"So, I gotta ask, how are you so Afrocentric and dating a white boy? That's like an oxymoron."

I laughed. "I love Billy. He's my soul mate. Besides, I plan to marry a man that is smart, loyal, loving, attentive, and supportive. Billy is all of those things, and the last time I checked, those characteristics weren't attached to a specific race."

"I hear that," Morgan said.

"Honestly, though, when I see Billy, I don't see his race. He grew up with me in Queensbridge, so he isn't your typical white guy."

"He might be conscious of black plights, but he's still white," Morgan said. "Plus, I know he's not holding it down like a brotha."

I blushed and chuckled. "I'm very satisfied. Billy holds it down in the bedroom. I have no complaints in that department."

"So, you're telling me he pleases you better than all the brothas you dated in the past?"

"I wouldn't know. I never dated a brotha."

"You gotta be kidding me."

"Don't look at me like that," I said, playfully punching him in the arm.

"Look at you like what?"

"Like that. Like 'oh, you're one of those.' You know, the type that talks pro-black but doesn't live that lifestyle. I see that expression on people's faces every time I take Billy with me to my community events."

"I'm not judging you," he said.

"Uh-huh. I see that look on your face."

He smiled. "Well, my dear, of course, you don't know any better. Ignorance is bliss. You can't miss something you never had."

That conversation made me question a lot of things. Did people view me as a hypocrite when I did community events? Was it possible to be pro-black and date outside my race? But another question that I didn't want to admit that I was curious about was: by settling down and dating Billy so young, did I do myself a disservice by not seeing what else was out there?

I knew I shouldn't let questions like those influence me or my feelings toward my relationship with Billy, but I felt them seeping into my subconscious, and it fucked with me.

I felt stupid for even thinking about those things, but all I knew was my relationship with Billy. I didn't have experiences with other men or boyfriends to compare him to. Billy had been my one and only since I lost my virginity to him our senior year in high school.

The war inside my mind was fucking with me. I put all my energy into studying until I fell asleep.

Several hours later, Billy called me. He told me he was letting Mrs. Wilson have the night off from taking care of his mom. He explained that he got assigned a *big case, and if he did well, he'd make partner. I figured that was the reason he gave Mrs. Wilson the night off. He probably felt he could win the case, and wanted to tell his mom the news. Since he wasn't going to be home anytime soon, I figured that gave me the green light to relax and go out with Rashida. It was time to get ready.*

Chapter 9

Ben

Blessings

We arrived at Becky's parents' house. Their butler, Bernard, greeted us at the door and escorted us to the dining room.

"Hey, Dad. Hey, Mom."

Susan hugged Becky and gave me a light peck on the cheek.

Mr. Preston greeted us with a faux grin, hugged Becky, and grudgingly gave me a weak handshake.

"Glad to see you could make it, Ben," he said nonchalantly.

"I'm glad I could make it. Mr. Preston, can I talk to you about something later?"

He looked at me skeptically. "Sure thing."

Becky leaned over and asked me, "What do you have to talk to him about?"

"Nothing. Just man stuff."

She smiled. "You're up to something."

I gave her a quick kiss.

We sat down at the table, and as usual, Becky tried to impress her parents by telling them about my recent accomplishments and successes, but they were unmoved. She told them about my new case and how important it would be for my career.

"Ben has been working so hard at his firm that he was given that case that's all over the news."

"What case is that, dear?" Susan asked.

"You know, the one with the rapper that killed the two cops and gay couple. He's being considered for partnership."

For once, Mrs. Preston looked impressed by the news. "That's wonderful!"

Mr. Preston grunted and faced me. "Who else is up for consideration?"

"Bill, another lawyer who has also been winning a lot of cases for the firm," I said.

"Let me guess: Bill is white."

"Not that it matters, but yes."

Mr. Preston sighed. "Of course, you wouldn't think it matters. Are there any black partners in your firm?"

"No, but—"

"I'm sure it doesn't matter how hard Bill works. You'll end up getting the position over him. That's how things work nowadays."

Becky squeezed my hand, attempting to keep me calm while he continued.

"You'll get it automatically because you're black, and the white guy will probably never move up in your firm." Mr. Preston snickered. "The media is always talking about white privilege, but the only privilege I see is with you people."

I curled my bottom lip to hold my tongue from cursing him out. He was part of the reason why I worked so hard. He fueled my endless motivation. Every day I busted my ass to show people like him that black people weren't just thugs, criminals, and drug addicts. I wanted to prove to him and other small-minded individuals that my people were sophisticated, intelligent, and just as good as his were. Even though I knew he believed his race was superior, I wanted him to see there was no difference or gap between us. I was equally as capable and as smart as anyone in his race.

"You know what *you* minorities will never understand?" Mr. Preston asked me.

"What would that be, sir?"

"Steven—" Mrs. Preston said.

"No, society coddles minorities too much. He needs to hear this, Susan." He faced me. "You people always want more and think things should be equal. When does it end? I'm not blind. I know that right now, white people hold the majority of power in this country, but why should we give it up? We built this country—"

"Off the backs of those minorities you're talking about," I said.

"Regardless of that, it was white men who built this country, and if minorities had it their way, they'd push white people out of power and make *us* the minority. While that's good for you and your people, what about *my* race? Why would I want to see a shitty world like that?"

"It wouldn't be a bad world. It would be how races should be treated in this world: equal."

"Again, you're still not grasping, how does that benefit me as a white person?"

"You wouldn't feel good doing what's right?"

"Please, don't talk to me about morals," he said. "You're getting paid well to represent a murderer, and I'm sure as an attorney, you've manipulated the law plenty of times to benefit your firm when you knew it wasn't morally right. The same rules apply to me. I'm not worried about your race or any other minority. I'm concerned about my own benefit."

He laughed and said, "Frankly, as a white man, I don't give a shit about minorities killing each other. It's one less mouth on welfare mooching off of my tax dollars."

Becky rested her hand on my thigh to calm me.

Before things got out of hand, I said, "Let's just agree to disagree."

"Ben, that's the smartest thing you've said all night," he said.

After listening to Mr. Preston talk for a good two hours about how he was so happy to see Obama out of office and proud to have a strong, wealthy white man back in the White House again, he finally shut up and asked me to speak with him privately.

"Ben, while the women gossip, let's go into my study so we can talk, man to man."

I nodded and followed him.

As soon as the door shut, Mr. Preston stopped smiling.

"Have a seat, Ben. We can drop the bullshit now. You know my daughter can't hear us in here."

I sat down. Mr. Preston leaned back in his black leather executive chair, lit a cigar, and blew the smoke in my direction.

"Now, what do you want?" he asked and took another long puff on his cigar.

"I won't beat around the bush. I love Rebecca, and I wanted to ask you for your blessing when I ask her to marry me."

He laughed at me. "Absolutely not. I've entertained this phase she's going through and put up with your sham of a relationship for years because I love my daughter, but there's no way in hell I'd allow you to ever marry her. No matter what you do, you'll never be good enough for my daughter."

"Why is that? I'm no slouch. I've worked hard all my life, and I've always done well—"

"You people are all the same. You might be wrapped in a nicer package, but when it comes down to it, you're no different from the other blacks I've met."

"What's that supposed to mean?"

He sighed. "I thought you were smarter than that. Do you need me to spell it out for you? OK, here goes. You've gone to prestigious schools, so you're not a complete dummy. You have a decent job, and you drive around in a nice car, but nothing will change the fact that you're black. It doesn't matter how many fancy degrees you have or how much money you make. You can't change that fact. I don't want my daughter to just do 'well.' If she married you, it would be a downgrade."

"Downgrade? I work just as hard, if not harder, than you."

"But you're still black."

"So?" I asked.

"I don't want people in power to look at my daughter in pity when they know she's married to you. If you were married, any children you had would be black, and I don't want your race ruining my gene pool. I'd rather my daughter be a lesbian than marry a nigger. That might sound harsh to you, but I'm being honest."

With his last comment, I stood up and headed for the door. My hand on the doorknob, I turned to him and said, "With your blessing—or without it—I love Becky, and nothing you say or do will stop me from asking her to marry me."

"I'll never let it happen."

"We'll just have to see, won't we?"

The tragedy of it all was that I'd been law-abiding all my life, received an excellent education, a great career, and now I was rising to gain the American dream by being a black partner in a white-dominated firm, but in the eyes of many ignorant people like Mr. Preston, I would never be more than a nigger.

Chapter 10

Bill

Borrowed Time

After schooling Shakir and his friends on the basketball court, I called Ebony as I walked to my mom's building.

"Hey, honey," she said, sounding groggy.

"Did I wake you up?"

"Yeah, but it's OK. Where are you?"

"I'm at my mom's place. I'm giving Mrs. Wilson the night off. I feel bad that instead of going home and relaxing after working at the firm all day, she goes to take care of my mom."

"She volunteers to do it. She said she doesn't mind, and she enjoys spending time with your mom."

"I know, but I think she does it because she feels she owes it to her for helping to take care of Jerami when he was sick as a kid."

"That might be one reason, but she's one of your mom's best friends. She loves her," Ebony said. "She knows how hard it is for you to try to juggle things with your own life . . . Well, since you're going to be with your mom, Rashida and some of my other coworkers asked me to go to the Delancey for some drinks with them. I'm going to get ready and head over there. If you want, after you finish with your mom, you can meet me there."

"Nah, I'll just see you when you get home," I said. "I'd tell you about the case now, but it's too much to explain over the phone. Long story short, if I win, they're going to make me a partner. Life will be a lot easier for us if I get this partnership."

"Wow! That's great, baby."

"Go ahead, get ready, and go unwind with your friends. I'll tell you all the details later."

"All right, babe. Well, take care of your mom, and I'll see you when I get home."

We said our goodbyes and ended the call once I stepped inside the building.

I made my way up the musty, narrow, urine-scented staircase to Mom's apartment.

I opened her apartment door, and Mrs. Williams, Ebony's mom, was sitting in the living room, watching TV.

"Hey, Mrs. Williams. How's Mom doing?"

"She's holding up. She's in her room taking a nap, but you should go on in there and see her."

I nodded.

Luckily for me, Mrs. Williams and Jalen's mom, Mrs. Wilson, helped me out a lot with caring for my mom. I tried to do as much as I could when I came to visit her during the week—grocery shopping, cleaning, and cooking—but Mom had been depressed lately because she felt like she was a burden to all of us. She cried and went on about how she felt useless because we only wanted her to rest. I'd seen my mom fighting hard for a long time, but I'd never understood the full scope of her sickness. Once her leg was amputated, it scared me and motivated me to work harder to move her into a place that could take better care of her.

"Why are you so sweaty?" Mrs. Williams asked.

"I had to show these kids who's still the king on these courts."

She laughed. "You taking care of my baby girl?"

"Always."

"Tell her I know she's out there trying to save the world, but she needs to visit her mother from time to time."

I winked and said, "I will."

I slowly opened the door, and my mom was sitting against her headboard, grimacing in pain.

"Hey, Mom, how are you feeling?"

"I'm all right," she said.

She was getting worse. All I could picture was her slowly deteriorating and one day dying alone. My mom had been through too much already. I couldn't sit back and let that happen.

Mom was completely bedridden and couldn't do anything for herself. A year ago, her neurologist told her to stay on bed rest because she was having severe relapses. She had a stroke, kidney stones—which mostly formed from all the medications she took—chest and kidney infections, and recently, her left leg had been amputated. She pushed herself past her limits and said the moment she allowed her illness to define her was the moment she'd begin her death sentence.

Her MS had made it hard for her to talk to me like she used to. Most times, she lost track or interest in conversations and found it difficult to string together long sentences.

"I talked to the powers that be at my firm today, and if I win this big case, they're going to make me a partner," I said.

"That's great, Billy."

"If I get the partnership, I can afford to move you out of here to someplace more comfortable . . . where they can take care of you."

"Don't worry about me," she said. "Use that money to pay for a nice wedding for you and Ebony. I'm not going anywhere. All of my positive memories are here. This is my home. I've been blessed with friends that take care of me. I don't have much time left anyway. Don't waste your money on me."

"Don't talk like that, Mom. You're the only family I have."

"That's why you should stop worrying about me and focus on marrying Ebony so I can at least try to be alive to see my grandkids' births. We can't stop the inevitable with me."

"Can we drop the negative talk?"

I told my mom some things about the case and took care of her until she went to bed for the night. I prayed that she would live to see the birth of my future children.

Finally, I went home, showered, and looked at today's case files. I got into bed and tried to stay awake and wait up for Ebony to come home but ended up dozing off before she got there.

Chapter 11

Ebony

Ashamed

Usually, when I go through heavy shit at work, I tend to either stay to myself or just spend time alone with Billy until I get my mind right. When I got to the Delancey, I thought about turning back and going home to do one or the other . . . until Rashida spotted me and waved me over. My coworkers were all drinking, talking, and laughing. I didn't feel I was in the mood for any of that.

"Hey! We're all sitting over here."

Mendez, Mahoney, Osborne, and St. Clair all raised their beers to salute me. Rashida had her arm around Osborne, and the two of them looked very comfortable together. Osborne was a cute girl. She had hazel eyes and long, wavy, jet-black hair. She was sporting a red blouse that showcased her cleavage, with matching pumps and leggings that showed off her thick legs and ass.

I expected the atmosphere of the lounge to be overly loud and crowded, but there were just enough people in there, and the volume of the crowd was calm.

Morgan flashed his beautiful smile at me and patted the spot next to him. "I saved you a seat."

I smiled and sat down.

We laughed, drank, and made a toast to Roberts and Gomez. After the toast, we didn't discuss anything work-related for the rest of the night. Some of the televisions in the lounge had the news on them. The media replayed the reports of the murders over and over again. Talking about it would only pain us more, and seeing how all of us got quiet, avoided looking at the screens, and had uncomfortable looks on our faces, I knew Mendez, Mahoney, and Rashida felt like I did and wanted to push that night as far into the back of our minds as possible— at least for tonight.

Dancing, drinking, and having fun with Morgan, I looked at my watch and realized I had lost track of time. It was eleven p.m. I was off for the next two days, but I wanted to talk to Billy before he had to head back to work in the morning. Always considerate, he knew I needed time to relax and clear my head, so he didn't stress me by calling and texting me.

"All right, guys, I'm outta here," I said.

"Yeah, I'm right behind you," Mahoney said.

"Me too, as soon as I finish my Corona," Mendez added.

Rashida was too busy tonguing down Rayna to acknowledge me. I was sure Rayna was going home with her.

"You leaving so soon?" Morgan asked.

"Yeah, I haven't seen my man all day. I want to spend some time with him before he goes back to work."

"Are we still studying for the lieutenants' test together this week?"

"Yup."

"All right, beautiful, I'll see you later."

Morgan gave me a soft kiss on the cheek. His plush lips felt good against my skin. Feeling his impressive bulge as he ground on me when we were dancing and feeling his lips on my skin just now made me question what other things would feel like. I shook those thoughts out of my head and went home to my man.

It was around midnight when I finally got home. The only light in the house came from our bedroom off the muted TV that Billy left on. He was probably waiting up to tell me about his case or wanted to sneak in a quickie before I went to bed. As exhausted as I was, I missed him. I wanted to talk to him, even if only a few minutes. I took a quick shower, dried myself off, and nuzzled next to my man. Then I gently shook him.

"Hey, baby," he said, yawning and stretching out. His hand grazed my bare thigh, and once he realized I was naked, it was on.

Billy kissed my breasts, wrapped his tongue over my hardened brown nipples, and worked his way down my body.

"Lie down," he said softly.

I did as he asked. Billy stuck two fingers inside me and massaged my G-spot. He worked me until I writhed and moaned. Then he slid down and gently licked the sides of my folds.

My head lifted off the pillow, and my thighs were pressed tightly around his ears as he flicked his tongue across my clit and nibbled on my pussy lips. Then he drove his tongue inside me.

"Oooh! Don't stop, baby!" I said, wrapping my hands around the back of his head, holding him in position.

I moaned out his name. I couldn't prolong it anymore. The way he worked his tongue and hearing the slurping sounds he made when he lapped up my pussy juices gave me an atomic orgasm that rippled through me.

I lay there twitching as Billy went to the bathroom to grab a condom. He returned, slipped the condom over his hard cock, and spread my legs wide. I felt his cock push through the opening of my pussy and fill me with his thickness. Billy propped himself up on his forearms as his cock pounded into me. I watched his broad shoulders, chiseled back, and firm ass in our bedroom mirror. I gripped his bare ass and pulled him deeper inside me as he pumped away at my treasure.

His powerful, fast thrusts made my orgasm sneak up on me quickly this time. I bucked and cursed as I came for the second time, digging my fingernails deep into his back.

Billy's face was red and flushed, and his body stiffened as he came inside me.

We were both limp, sweaty, and gasping for air. We lay together in bed. He held me in his arms and traced the contours of my curves. As he spooned me in the dark, I felt guilty. Even though I loved this man so much, and I knew he loved me unconditionally, a part of me felt like maybe Morgan was right. Maybe I was missing out on more in life because I didn't know anything but life with Billy. I was ashamed of my thoughts. I shook them away and kissed Billy's arm. After all the stress I'd been dealing with, I desperately needed the sexual relief that Billy gave me.

Chapter 12

Becky

Reflections

"So . . . Is it true?" Brooke asked, her crystal-blue eyes inquisitively wide.

"Is what true?"

"You know, about their cocks?"

I sighed. There were a million questions people could ask me about my interracial relationship, yet all they seemed to want to know about was my man's dick.

Brooke and I were sitting in my cubicle at *Cosmopolitan* magazine in Midtown Manhattan. She was like me, a wealthy trust fund girl that used her parents' connections to land a job here at *Cosmo*. I didn't have a lot of female friends or friends in general, so we bonded over that. Next to Simone, Brooke was one of my closest friends.

I mostly worked from home on my articles, since I worked part time. I wrote a weekly column on sex, love, and relationships, so it didn't require me to show my face in the office all the time. I mainly came in when I had staff meetings or an appointment with a publisher. Today, I blessed the office with my presence because I was meeting with another publishing company to pitch my novel, *Black and White,* that I'd been working on for the past three years, but I didn't let anyone read it.

I didn't realize Brooke was reading it over my shoulder when I was tinkering with it after I finished my article for the magazine.

I answered her question. "From my experience, it's true, but Ben's the only black guy I've been with."

"Nice. So how big we talkin'? So big you're sore-for-a-couple-of-days big, or, oh my God, you're in agonizing pain, and you feel like you're-being-ripped-in-half big?"

I had to laugh at that. "Brooke, I'm not discussing my man's dick with you. It's funny. All these years we've been friends, and you've never asked me that question."

"I never read a sex scene so descriptive before. Is your book going to have lots of interracial sex scenes?" she asked.

"Yes, but it's not all about sex. This book is about the trials and tribulations of being in an interracial relationship. I want people to fall in love with my characters and root for them. Wait, why do *you* care? You'd never sleep with a black guy anyway."

"True, I could never be as adventurous as you, but I *am* curious about them. Wait a minute. This book is fiction, right? You're not going to kill yourself and have the book published as a sort of suicide note, are you?"

"Of course not."

"Let me read some more of it," she said. "What are you doing, anyway?"

I handed over the manuscript I planned on showing to the publisher this afternoon. "I finished the manuscript that I'm shopping around, but I've been making improvements here and there. I want it to be perfect. I need this book to get published." I leaned back in my chair.

I knew my book was good, but something was missing. I kept getting rejected by publishers. Every time it got rejected, I retooled my story to find that missing link, but I kept falling short.

I wanted to write a book that showed how, with patience and perseverance, interracial love could conquer all obstacles, but that wasn't the kind of book that I felt ended up on my pages.

"Doesn't your rich and powerful daddy have all sorts of connections? Just ask him to help you get it published," Brooke said.

"Nah, I'm not asking my dad for any favors. I need to do this on my own. My parents, Ben's parents, Ben's annoying best friend Gabby, and the rest of the world think I'm a helpless, incompetent bimbo. I'm determined to prove all of them wrong."

"I get it, but everyone needs somebody sometimes. You'll prove them wrong when the book is published, and you're a bestseller. Anyhoo, I'm going to sit right here next to you and read more of this juicy story."

I was determined to make it with my writing. My parents expected me to fail. They expected me to come running to them with my tail between my legs, begging for help, but I wouldn't give them that satisfaction.

I knew my parents loved me, but growing up, I never felt good enough for them. I was never pretty, smart, or thin enough for them, so I spent most of my life rebelling. When they wanted me to be a ballerina, I became a gymnast. When they wanted me to stay home and study, I went out and partied. They wanted me to be their perfect little angel, but since they were constant destroyers of my confidence, I was the neighborhood slut that slept with any guy that told her she was pretty. My mom, always the prim and proper woman, was too busy doing events with other well-kept women at the country club. She was fine with having my nannies handle the responsibilities of raising me and hiring the finest therapists in New York to talk to me rather than listen to any of my problems.

Every action I did growing up was my big "fuck you" to them for always making me feel like I was a disappointment, and even though I knew they believed my relationship with Ben was a continuation of that behavior, it wasn't. I was sure they felt my relationship with him was due to some liberal guilt, or he was with me as a trophy for his success, but they were wrong. What Ben and I had was real and beautiful.

At the beginning of our relationship, my parents' hatred toward Ben didn't surprise me. They never accepted me for who I was, so I didn't expect them to approve of any guy I brought home—let alone a black one.

Recently, my parents had lectured me on everything they felt I was doing wrong in life.

"When are you going to choose a serious career and stop with this writing foolishness?" Mom always critiqued my life decisions and weight.

I sighed.

"Maybe I should just marry wealthy like you did so I don't have to worry about it," I fired back.

Dad laughed. Mom's face was red. She was clearly embarrassed, but now she got a taste of how I felt around her.

"That's a shitty thing to say, Rebecca," Mom said. She huffed. "Anyway, it won't happen for you. You insist on dating your black guy, and even if you smartened up and broke up with him, you're not thin enough to marry well."

"There's the mother I know and love."

"You're so cynical. No wonder you couldn't find a nice white man to date you."

I tuned my mother out and played with my cell phone. Dad chimed in, "Seriously, Rebecca, when is this bullshit relationship going to end? You both know it isn't going anywhere."

"Dad, we live together. We've been in a relationship for eight years. Why is it hard to see our love is real?"

Mom stood up. "I'm going to the gym. Steven, there's no point trying to reason with her. She's too stubborn."

I rolled my eyes as she left the room. "Daddy, honestly, what's so bad about my relationship with Ben?"

"Besides him being black? Nothing."

"So, you just don't like him because he's black? Don't you think that's a silly reason?"

"That's the only reason I need, Rebecca. Blacks are mostly uneducated, poor, filthy, and diseased."

"And you're basing this off of . . .?"

"Facts. They live in crime-riddled neighborhoods, and they're thieves."

"Daddy!"

"If you don't watch them, they'll steal everything you own from right under your nose," he said. "Every race needs to stick with their own."

"You know Ben is none of those things you just mentioned."

"Rebecca, remember this and remember it well: You can polish a turd, but it's still a piece of shit. Just because Ben has a little bit of an education and has a decent career doesn't change the fact that he's black."

"You're downplaying everything that Ben is," I said. "He graduated from an Ivy League school, and he's on his way to becoming a partner at one of the most prestigious law firms in the country. That's way beyond merely having a 'little education and a decent career.' Ben is a great guy who treats me like a queen. What does it matter what race he is? Don't you want your only child to be happy?"

"You can be happy with someone white. Eventually, Rebecca, you're going to have to make the decision to drop him. No man is worth your family. Remember that."

Dad stood up and kissed me on the forehead. "I'm going to the country club. After this discussion with you, I need to unwind."

What my parents never seemed to understand was I didn't love Ben because of his race. I loved him for who he was.

After the streak of losers I dated, I knew Ben was different.

Some guys dated me because they knew I was well off financially. Some men dated me because they just wanted to fuck me. Then there were guys that dated me for both, to use me for my wealth and get some ass. Most times, I could clearly see through those types. I was used to being treated as merely rich eye candy, but Ben was different. Ben knew I was wealthy and never asked me for anything. I loved that the fact that I had money didn't matter to him.

While most of the men I dated in the past wanted me to dumb myself down for their enjoyment, I never had to for Ben.

Beyond my physical attraction, I loved Ben's drive, his intellect, and his surreal ability to bring the best out of me and make me feel good about myself when so many people brought me down. He made me feel beautiful, smart, and, most importantly, special.

The Virgo in him paid attention to detail, and he noticed little things about me. He knew when I was sad or hurt and what to do to make me happy. Unlike the guys I dated before him, Ben read all of my articles. He didn't give them a bullshit skim job, either. He took the time to read and understand everything.

Ben opened my eyes to a lot of things. He introduced me to new music and foods and gave me a new perspective on life in general. Dating a black man was not the same as dating a white one. The adversities we faced pushed me out of my comfort zone, and I learned more about the sad truth about race than I ever would have if I dated someone white.

I knew our love wouldn't be easy. I remembered being approached by two women in the ladies' room on one of our first dates.

I was standing in front of the bathroom mirror, washing my hands and checking my makeup when two black women approached me.

"Don't you hate seeing these white girls stealing our men?" a brown-skinned woman with short hair and a shapely figure asked.

"Uh-huh, it's tragic," the other woman said. She was a dark-skinned woman with flawless skin and al-mond-shaped eyes.

Thinking back on that day, I should've ignored them and walked away, but I confronted them.

"Excuse me, are you talking about me?" I asked.

The brown-skinned woman stepped up to me and answered, "Yup."

They both crowded around me.

Her friend chimed in, "You're nothing special, yet we always have to compete with white bitches like you."

I wasn't moved. I wasn't intimidated by loudmouthed women. I'd been bullied by girls all my life growing up. I didn't back down then, and I wouldn't back down now. I looked them both in their faces.

"Look, you don't know me, so you can't say I'm nothing special. I'm sorry if you feel like you're losing your men to white women like me, but maybe you need to step your game up."

Before they could say anything else, I shoved past them.

"Pardon my back," I said, walking out the door.

Ben and I were getting ready to leave when the women saw us and gave us the finger.

I held Ben's hand and smiled at the women. I wasn't ashamed or intimidated by them. I was proud to be with him, and I didn't care who thought otherwise.

Back then, when we were in college, I often found myself staring at Ben in admiration when I watched him studying and working his ass off. He inspired me to have a strong work ethic, and he always encouraged me to stick with my dream of being a novelist. The truth was that Ben made me a better person.

I loved the life I'd built with Ben, but there was one obstacle in my way of complete happiness: his best friend, Gabby. That bitch had broken his heart before we dated, and he was *still* best friends with her. She'd love to have me out of the way so she could have him for herself, and that scared me. Ben constantly tried to convince me that it was all in my head and assure me that Gabby didn't want him, but I knew women. I saw the way she eyed him possessively, like she was ready to take him from me. Whenever Ben and she were around each other, I saw their chemistry, and it made me insecure. They were both movie fanatics, so they often amused each other by having full conversations in just movie quotes.

They had a history together and bonded in a way that made me question if he could ever truly be happy with me, a white woman. His relationship with Gabby made me question if I were good enough for him on all levels.

At one point, I was so intimidated by Gabby that I tried to overcompensate for growing up sheltered and wealthy by acting how I felt Ben would be more comfortable.

I remembered putting on my tightest, ass-hugging jeans, my Jimmy Choo stilettos, and, to complete my ensemble, my big gold hoop earrings.

"Baby, what are you doing?" Ben asked.

"Nuttin', just representin'!"

"Baby, stop. Don't do that."

"Don't do what?"

"Don't act like something you're not. I fell in love with who you are. I don't want you to pretend to be something else. Just be yourself."

"Was I acting stereotypically?"

He laughed and nodded. "Very."

"Would other black people be offended if I acted like that in public?"

"Definitely," he said with a smirk.

I sighed. "Fine. I'm sorry. I'll knock it off . . . but I'm keeping these hoop earrings. I'm really feeling them."

We laughed together, and I appreciated knowing that Ben accepted and loved me for who I was, flaws and all.

The first time I met Gabby at Ben's apartment in college was a disaster, and over the years, it'd only gotten worse. She always seemed to be in my way. I remembered the first time I met Ben's parents.

"Mom, Dad, I want you to meet my girlfriend, Rebecca," Ben said, smiling.

Mr. Turner smiled and said, "It's very nice to meet you, Rebecca. Call me Curtis."

"Hello, Rebecca," Mrs. Turner said.

The apparent dislike in her tone made it obvious she wasn't feeling me.

"Please call me Becky," I smiled.

"Where's Simone?" Ben asked.

"Your silly cousin is out on another date with one of her white boys. This one will break her heart too, just like they all do. She never learns," Mrs. Turner said, looking at me.

His mom didn't seem too thrilled about his cousin dating someone white, so I felt like I needed to impress his parents.

I spent a good twenty minutes telling them about myself. I told them about the private schools I went to and my father being the head of a major brokerage firm on Wall Street. I told them about all of the volunteer hours I did at homeless shelters and the work I did with minority children at the Boys and Girls Clubs. I thought that would give me some Brownie points and show them that I was far from prejudiced. I hoped everything I said was enough, but the blasé looks on their faces made me feel like everything I said put me even further out of their favor.

I finished my babbling by sharing my plans to gradu- ate from Columbia with a bachelor's degree in journal- ism and English literature, and standing side by side proudly with Ben on that day. I added that I already had a job lined up for after college, but his parents still seemed unmoved.

Then the doorbell rang.

"I'll get it," Mrs. Turner said.

Ben whispered in my ear, "You're doing great. They're judges, so they're big on listening and observing more than being vocal about what they're thinking, but I know they like you."

I smiled, but that quickly went away when Mrs. Turner came back to the table, joking and laughing with Gabby.

"Hey, Big Head," Gabby said to Ben. She turned to face me. "Hi, Becky."

I nodded, but I couldn't hide the pissed-off expression on my face.

"What are you doing here?" Ben asked.

"I always hang out with your momma on Sundays. We usually have our mani/pedi date Sunday mornings, but I had to work this morning. Your mom texted me and invited me to dinner, so here I am."

Gabby turned to Mrs. Turner and said, "I never turn down a free meal." They laughed and high-fived.

I knew for sure Ben had specifically told his parents he was bringing me so they could get to know me. If his mother openly invited Gabby to this dinner, it meant she already knew she wasn't going to like me.

Mrs. Turner's disapproving gaze only got worse as she and Gabby drank more wine.

The next time I hung out with his family wasn't any better. His parents were throwing a barbecue.

"Is Gabby going to be here?" I asked.

"Probably. Our families have been close most of our lives. Our parents are best friends, so there's a good chance she'll be there."

"Oh, great," I said sarcastically.

"Don't worry. I'm going to introduce you to everybody. You'll have plenty of people to talk to," Ben said.

We walked to a beautiful deck overlooking the backyard down the steps past the patio where Ben's dad was grilling on the barbecue, and his mom was entertaining guests. There were lots of people drinking, laughing, playing cards, and having a good time.

"Hey, everybody, this is my girlfriend, Rebecca," Ben said to his family and friends.

I mostly got questioning stares with a couple of half-hearted waves here and there. I was the only white person at the party. I nodded, smiled, and chimed in during conversations, but hardly anyone acknowledged me.

"Don't mind them. They act all rude and militant, but they aren't that bad. They do the same thing when I bring white guys home. Hi, I'm Simone, Ben's cousin."

She was a beautiful girl. She had gorgeous green eyes, a firm, shapely figure, and her thick, wavy mixture of brown and black hair fell past her shoulders.

I shook her hand.

"Ben has told me so much about you. It's nice to meet you finally," I said.

"He's told me a lot about you too. He thinks you're the one."

"Did he say that?"

"Yup."

I couldn't stop myself from blushing.

Ben smiled when he saw Simone and me laughing and having girl talk.

"The party can start now, y'all. I'm here," Gabby said.

Everyone stood up and was excited to see her. They perked up and didn't hesitate to kiss, hug, and talk to her, which made me jealous, because they were so dull with me.

"Hey, Mama Turner," Gabby greeted.

Mrs. Turner hugged and kissed her like she hadn't seen her in years.

"Papa, don't lose too much weight now. I like seeing you fill out your suits," Gabby said to Ben's dad.

He grinned and gave her a kiss on the cheek.

"Uncle George, now you know that plate has too much on it," Gabby said. "You have to watch your sugar."

He smiled and said, "I know, I know. I need you around to keep me in check."

"That's right," she smiled.

Gabby turned to face his wife, Aunt Valerie. "Aunt Val, save my spot at the spades table. Nobody here is taking us down tonight."

"I know that's right, chile," Aunt Val said, high-fiving her.

Gabby walked up to Ben and me. She gave me the stank eye and kissed Ben on the cheek.

"What's up, Big Head? Hello, Becky."

I gave her a weak wave.

"Hello to you too," Simone said.

"Oh, hey, Simone, I should've known you would be sitting next to the only white person at this party," Gabby said.

"I should've known you'd be the only bitchy one to make a negative comment like that."

"I see you made a grand entrance," Ben said.

"I make an entrance wherever I go," Gabby replied. "You know this."

Once Gabby got settled in with the guests, it was like I didn't exist. Ben and Simone knew I was uncomfortable, so they stayed by my side the entire time. After that day, Simone and I became best friends. Simone saw I was a good person, while Mrs. Turner and Gabby didn't.

Women like Ben's mom and Gabby saw me as some silly white girl that only wanted to sleep with a black man so I could run back to my girlfriends, giggle, and brag about the experience, but that wasn't true. I loved him for everything he was. Since dating Ben, I wasn't the rebellious, lost little girl I was in college anymore, but even though I'd grown a lot when it came to Gabby, I never felt like I measured up.

***

"Becky, your book is amazing," Brooke said. "I don't know how a publisher hasn't picked this up yet."

I was lost in thought, forgetting that I wasn't alone. I smiled.

"Not to toot my own horn, but me neither. I just hope the publisher I'm meeting today feels the same way."

I was at home, sitting up in my bed, typing away on my laptop, pissed off that another publisher had rejected me after my meeting with them today. Brooke came over to cheer me up and keep me company. Simone had stopped by too before she went on another date with her new guy.

Brooke toyed with Simone's hair, staring at it with her nose scrunched up.

"It's so thick . . . How can anyone manage this?" Brooke asked.

I looked up from my laptop. "Stop playing with her hair," I told her.

"It's all right," Simone said.

I wasn't sure if she was oblivious to the fact that Brooke was insulting her hair or just didn't mind it.

Simone stood up and twisted from side to side, admiring her shape in the bedroom mirror.

"Your butt is huge," Brooke said.

"Trevor can't keep his hands off it," Simone said. "He *loves* my ass."

Brooke didn't say anything. She just sat next to me, eyeing Simone and sulking.

Brooke, Simone, and I hung out a lot together, but Brooke often seemed jealous of Simone and acted like a total bitch.

"So, Uncle Curtis keeps stressing me to find my sister," Simone said. "He thinks once I find that piece of my life that's missing, everything will turn around. I don't see anything wrong with my life the way it is."

"You don't?" Brooke said. "Maybe instead of telling you to find your sister, he should tell you to find a job."

"Brooke!" I yelled.

"I haven't found a career yet that moves me," Simone said. "I'm still trying to find myself. Besides, if I'm right about Trevor, he's going to be my Prince Charming. I'll marry him, have his kids, and be a stay-at-home mom."

Simone's cell phone rang. "Hey, handsome. Are you outside? OK, I'm coming out now." She turned to me and hugged me. "I'll call you later."

I worked on my book and watched TV with Brooke as I waited for my own Prince Charming to come home.

Chapter 13

Simone

Vicious Cycle

I felt hurt, abandoned, alone, and emotionally drained by yet another man who just wanted to fuck me because of my race. This time, the inconsiderate dickhead kicked me out of his place early in the morning. A part of it was my fault for using my pretty face, tits, hips, and ass to entice these shallow guys, but sex was all I ever felt I was good at. I'd been so desperate to find true love that I'd mistaken cheap pickup lines from jerks for actual interest in me.

I'd always longed to be loved, but I was constantly getting my ass kicked by it. I was aware that I had serious, deep-rooted abandonment issues that dated back to my childhood, but I wanted to feel that unconditional "you are my world, I can't live without you" type of love that Ben and Becky had. Instead, I was on a corner on Broome Street in Manhattan at four a.m. I was in high heels and a short dress, being catcalled and offered "the dick" by every drunk asshole awake. My hair and clothes were disheveled, mascara running, and I looked like a hot mess hailing a cab as I did the walk of shame to my cousin's place.

"Hey, baby! You wanna have a date with me?" a home-less, toothless white man asked.

I cringed, ignored him, and continued waving my hand to get a cab. The homeless man laughed at me and said, "Stupid bitch."

Unfortunately . . . I felt like I was.

I rang the doorbell to Ben and Becky's townhouse. Becky checked to see who was at the door and saw me in tears, my eyes puffy and bloodshot. She opened the door.

"Are you OK? You look like shit." She stepped aside so I could come in.

"No, I'm *not* OK. As always, I got fucked over again."

We walked to the living room, and I plopped down on the couch. Ben was getting ready to go to work. There had been so many times when I waited for him to leave for work before coming over here to do the walk of shame and cry on Becky's shoulder, but I couldn't wait this time.

Ben saw me sitting on the couch, shook his head, and hugged me. I guess the look on my hurt face told him now was not the time to lecture me.

"If you need me, even if it's just to talk, call me. I'm here for you."

I patted his hand. "Thanks, Ben."

Becky mouthed, "Thank you," to him. He gave us both a kiss and headed out.

I was grateful he'd spared me the embarrassment of a lecture on how slutty I was.

"What happened?" Becky asked.

"I always find the fucking losers that use me to cross 'fucking a black chick' off their bucket list."

Becky gently stroked my back as I held my face in my hands and wept. "Why do you think that?"

I sat back on the couch and took a deep breath as I prepared to relive the whole ordeal from start to finish.

For the past month, my latest guy, Trevor, had been wining and dining me. I told him early on that I wanted something "real" and wasn't looking for a purely sexual relationship. I didn't fuck him right away, but we did talk about all the dirty things we wanted to do to each other when the time came. Trevor told me he'd never been with a "black girl" before, but I thought I was more than that to him. I legit thought he liked me.

Last night, I was tipsy after partying with Trevor. We went to his place, and things got heavy.

"Take off your clothes," he ordered in a sexy, demanding tone.

I smiled and did as he asked.

"Now, turn around and bend over. I want to see that big, juicy black ass of yours."

I smiled. I heard the condom wrapper rip and the rubber slap against his penis as he put it on, then felt his manicured hands grab hold of my hips and pull me to the edge of the mattress. I watched Trevor in the mirror hold the base of his cock and ram it inside me. He wound his fingers through my hair, closed them into a fist, and yanked my hair so hard my head flew back. He was rough with me, putting me in every position imaginable as he fucked me like a whore, but I was fine with it as long as I was exclusively his. But his dirty talk made me really uncomfortable because it was race-driven. He shoved his dick in my mouth and asked me if I loved sucking his big white cock. He wasn't huge, about average in length and girth, but he had stamina. He then fucked me anally and asked if I liked feeling his white dick in my big black ass.

Despite being turned off by his dirty talk, I did every freaky thing he asked of me. I wanted him to see that if we were in a relationship, I could please him.

"Yes, baby! That's it. Don't stop!"

His faced turned red. I felt him become rigid, shudder, then relax as he pumped his load inside me. The bastard couldn't hold on just another minute for me to come, and I was so damn close. We collapsed side by side on the bed.

"Can you go down on me so I can come?" I asked.

He laughed. "I don't think so."

I held him and gave him a false smile to hide my disappointment in the sex. Trevor pulled away.

"Can you get off me?" he asked.

I released him and said, "Huh?"

After the douche bag had got his rocks off, he did a complete one-eighty on me. His whole demeanor had changed. He stood up, belched, rolled off the condom, and flushed it down the toilet. He reemerged from the bathroom and lay down with a look of satisfaction.

"So, I hope you see what you're getting in a relationship with me," I said, tracing my fingers along his chest.

"If we're talking about a fuck-buddy type of relationship, then I'm all for it."

"I told you from the beginning that's not what I wanted."

"Well, that's the only type you'll get from me."

That hurt. I sat up, folded my arms tightly against my breasts, and shook my head.

"You used me. You fucked me, and now that you got what you wanted, you don't give a shit about me or what I want and feel."

"Don't act like a victim. You owed me."

"What did I owe you?"

"After all the dinners, drinks, gifts, and money I spent on you, I paid for this fuck in full."

I curled my lip in, holding back tears. "Was that all I was to you?"

"Look, don't make me out to be the villain. I really enjoyed fucking you."

"But you don't see yourself dating me?"

He laughed. "I don't believe in dating outside my race."

"Didn't we just have sex?"

"We're not in a relationship. I don't have to like you to fuck you."

"So, I'm good enough to fuck, but I'm not good enough to date?" I said, even though it was more of a statement than an actual question.

"Hey, it is what it is . . . Anyway, I think it's time for you to leave," he said, flinging my clothes at me.

"You're kicking me out?"

"You're trying to make me out to be a villain, but you're a pretty smart girl," he said. "You can't tell me you didn't know what this was."

"I guess I'm not that smart, because I didn't."

"I guess not. Well, it was nice meeting you, Shaniqua."

"It's Simone."

"Sorry, nice meeting you . . . Simone."

His racist, inconsiderate ass had kicked me out and left me standing there looking stupid in front of his closed door.

I turned and faced Becky.

"Why does this keep happening to me? Every time I get my heart broken, it always makes me question if there's something wrong with me. Men always see me as a good enough fuck, so why wouldn't they want to be in a committed relationship with me?"

"I know how you feel," she said. "Trust me. Before I met Ben, I was in the same boat."

"This *always* happens to me, though. Awhile back, I was dating another white guy, Matthew. He gave me the sob story that his friend Mike was getting deployed to Iraq and could die over there. He convinced me to have a threesome with him and Mike because it was something they always wanted to try. I was stupid and gave in. I let them film it—only to find out that his friend Mike wasn't even in the military. When I called them out on it, they laughed at me and told me I was a stupid black bitch that deserved to get played."

Becky looked at me with sympathetic eyes and rubbed my shoulders as I continued.

"I remember them saying, 'You acted like a ho, so we treated you like one.' Hearing them refer to me as a 'ho' made me feel like my mother. I was ashamed of myself, but instead of stopping dating, keeping my legs closed, and healing from the experience, I went out that night, got drunk, and had another meaningless, one-night stand. I probably helped another white guy cross fucking a black girl off his bucket list."

I held my face in my hands and wept. All of my shitty past experiences were rising to the surface, and it was becoming overwhelming.

"Please don't take this the wrong way, but maybe you should take a break from white guys or maybe even dating in general until you're mentally ready," Becky said.

"I know what you mean. I don't know what's wrong with me. I know black men aren't evil. I have my uncle and my cousin that are great examples of that, but when I get approached by black men, it makes me think about my parents."

"I know things were bad with your parents, but you were a little girl back then. You're grown now. Don't let your past control your future."

"You want to know the truth?" I asked. "I don't date black guys because I try to shield myself from anybody and anyone that reminds me of my parents or my old life in their old neighborhood."

I took a deep breath.

"Underneath my designer clothes and fancy shoes, I still feel like that poor little black girl. Do you know how it felt growing up knowing my mother was a junkie that sold pussy for money, and my father was a pimp? I remember my first day of school when Uncle Curtis first gained custody of me. All the kids were talking about what their parents did for a living, and I was embarrassed and ashamed of mine. No matter what I did in life or what clothes I wore, I could never shake that feeling that I'd never amount to anything—just like my parents. My mom never called or came to see me. As a kid, it felt as if she were just as embarrassed by me as I was of her. I never met my father, and according to Uncle Curtis, it was never going to happen anyway. He keeps trying to get me to meet my sister."

"You told me."

"I don't know if I should, but all this talk from Uncle Curtis has me thinking about her every day. I wonder if she's as fucked up and wounded as I am."

Chapter 14

Ben

The Same

"Shit," I mumbled as I rewound the clip of Reggie arguing with the victims.

I was sitting in my office watching all the surveillance videos from the club and local businesses around the area on the night of the murders. The video showed Reggie shove one of the guys and throw his drink in the other's face. Reggie's two linebacker-sized bodyguards pulled him away from the men, but he shook out of their grasps, sprinted over to the couple, and swung wildly at their faces.

Suddenly, there was a knock on my door. Mark Cruz, another associate for the firm, poked his head in and said, "What's up, Ben? You got a minute?"

I gave him a halfhearted wave. "Yup."

He walked up to my desk. "Richard wants you to focus your time and energy on your murder case. He assigned all your other cases to me. I need your case files."

I nodded.

Mark was Puerto Rican but very fair-skinned and could pass for white. He wore a thin mustache and kept his black hair slicked back. When around other Hispanics, he spoke fluent Spanish, but in front of the partners and white people, he pretended to struggle with the language. He was a decent lawyer but was favored by the partners because his father was heavily involved in politics.

Mark tossed a manila envelope on my desk. "It's the forensic tests for your murder case."

"Thanks."

"No offense, but I'm glad I got all your other cases and not this clusterfuck."

"Gee, thanks."

"I'm sorry, but it just seems like a lost cause," Mark said. "Well, on the bright side, you did all the legwork for these cases I'm taking over, so they should all be easy wins for me and improve my case record."

I gave him a faux grin, shuffled through the files in my desk drawers, and handed him two boxes full of files and paperwork for my reassigned cases. "Glad I could help."

He winked and nodded as he left my office with the boxes.

I didn't like him.

I opened the envelope, and, as expected, the forensic tests came back showing that the gun that was in Reggie's hand was the murder weapon used to kill the two cops and gay couple. The test also confirmed Reggie's DNA was found on the trigger. The other tests came back positive, showing that the blood on Reggie's clothes was also from the murdered couple. There was another set of fingerprints found on the magazine of the gun. They belonged to Kuwuan Mitchell, a known criminal arrested several times for selling illegal guns. Even though the cops had no idea where he was right now, they didn't suspect him because he was never arrested for violent crimes, and Reggie was found at the scene holding the weapon. Things weren't looking promising for Reggie's defense. The only things I had going for me were Kuwuan's fingerprint on the magazine and the grainy footage that showed the killer wearing a red and black hat and matching sneakers. Reggie was found wearing black boots and no hat. It was all I had so far to save him. I needed to talk to him and see if he could help me get more.

Reggie strutted into the lawyer room at Rikers Island wearing his orange prisoner attire. "What's up, Oreo?"

"Reginald."

He gave me a death stare but got my point.

"How are things going in here?" I asked.

"Shitty, but I'm mentally preparing myself to spend the rest of my life in here, so I'm adjusting."

"Don't say things like that. It's bad for your psyche. I'm trying my best to make sure that doesn't happen, but I need you to help me understand this case, Reggie. All signs are pointing to you. Give me something. What am I missing or not seeing? I need you to help me."

"Are your folks still together?"

I rubbed my hand down my face and curled my lip. "Reggie, I'm not here to talk to you about my parents. We're fighting for your life here. My parents' marriage is irrelevant in this case, but, yes, they're still together."

"My dad wasn't around growing up," he said. "He was out running the streets. My mom tried the best she could to raise my three brothers and me on her own."

I could hear in his voice that this situation made him reflect on his life and the actions that got him to this point. I put my pen down on my notepad and heard him out.

"Your mom must be a very strong woman. That's a hard task to ask of anyone, to raise four kids alone."

He smiled. "Yeah, she was strong. That's a lot of mouths to feed, you know? She died of a stroke when I was fourteen."

He nodded and continued, "Since I was the oldest and the man of the house, I did what I had to, to help us survive. I didn't have the luxury of living a *Cosby Show* life like you did. I was slinging dope at twelve."

"Now that you finished giving me your family history, do you think we can get back to discussing your case?" I asked.

"In a few. I like you, Ben. You're not as big of an asshole that I thought you were, but I still have a feeling you don't see that you and I are the same."

"We're the same, huh?"

"Yup—the only differences between you and me are our environments and circumstances. If the roles were reversed and we traded pasts, you'd be where I'm at, and I'd be sitting in your seat."

I nodded and questioned if he were right. If I grew up in his surroundings, would I have turned out like him?

"Reggie, I don't doubt that we have similarities, but what overrules your environment and circumstances argument is choice. You had a rough environment and a dysfunctional family life, but you could've chosen not to sell drugs. That 'choice' led to you going to prison. You could've not fought with people after prison, which would've not given you a history of violent assaults. Your choices were what led to why we're here now."

"You're right. Some of my choices could've been avoided, but that doesn't change the fact that you and I are the same," he said.

"Can we get back to discussing your case? Your record label is spending a lot of money on your defense. You're important to them, so let's not waste any more time."

Reggie sucked his teeth. "I'm important to them now because I fill their pockets. I watch the news in here. I know my drama is making all of my albums fly off the shelves, and they're making money hand over fist right now, but if I'm found guilty and convicted, best believe they'll drop my black ass like a bad habit. I'm no different than you. Your bosses use you as their golden boy and make tons of money off the cases you win, but don't get it twisted—they don't think you're anything special. Trust me: lose a couple of cases in a row, and I'm sure they'll look at you as just another nigga the same way how the record executives will look at me once they can't make money off me anymore."

I nodded. There was some truth to what he was saying.

Reggie laughed. "You got a lady at home?" he asked.

"What?"

"Do you got a lady? A girlfriend? A woman at home?"

"Yeah."

Reggie smiled. "I bet money your girl is whiter than Wonder Bread."

I didn't confirm or deny his claim. "Why do you think that?"

"Because I can tell you're the type that likes things easy. You guys probably never argue. She's probably really submissive, and she doesn't challenge you with anything."

"My girl is white, but as far as things being easy, that couldn't be further from the truth," I said. "Nothing about our relationship is easy. Between people like you calling me a 'sellout' and her a 'nigger lover,' people openly insulting us to our faces, my family and friends picking on her, her family and friends believing I'll never be good enough for her, and society in general thinking interracial relationships are bullshit, *nothing's* easy about it. My girl and I challenge each other to be better every day. We argue and have problems just like any other couples, but I love her enough to endure all that shit."

"See. I love when you get like this," Reggie said. "You're a fighter. I told you we weren't different. Deep down in you, I know you see it too. I bust your balls a lot, but I'm trying to pull that fighter out of you, so you'll stay motivated to help me beat this case."

The scary thing was that he was right. He was much smarter than I thought he was. His way of thinking was different than mine, but he also made good points and a lot of sense. Reggie had me questioning how I viewed myself and what the world thought of me.

Chapter 15

Ebony

Irritation

"No justice, no peace for the racist police," the crowd shouted.

It was pouring over Washington Square Park. Rashida and I were soaked. I was tired and cranky from spending hours being cursed out by angry protestors. Their outrage came about because a cop in North Carolina shot and killed an unarmed fifteen-year-old black boy. People all over the country were protesting, but these protesters weren't mad at just the cops involved in the incident—they were mad at the system and law enforcement in general. The crowd seemed to heckle me more because I was black. Protesters stood inches from my face and yelled, "You should be ashamed of yourself, sista!"

"Look at you, taking orders from your new-age slave master. Don't you know they're just using you?"

"You're lost. You need to stop disrespecting yourself."

One woman shook her head and folded her arms. "Does it feel good oppressing your own people to suck the white man's dick? How do you sleep at night?"

I looked at all these angry faces, and they didn't see me, a woman that fought and worked her ass off for the community—they just saw the uniform. My skin was as black as most of theirs, but they only saw me as blue. It was hard to stop yourself from developing that "us versus them" mentality when you felt like the world hated you because of your profession.

"What's wrong with you, sista?" a young protestor asked.

She was brown-skinned, in her early twenties. I stared at her and curled my lips to hold my tongue.

I knew I shouldn't respond. Nothing I said would make this situation better. It would be best if I just stayed quiet, but I replied, "How do you know that I'm not as pained by this as you are? Why do you assume that I don't care about this young man's life?"

"Because we know you don't. You're under the blue wall of silence. Once you took that job, you stopped giving a shit about your people because you think you're safe and one of them. You ain't shit either, and as soon as you take off that uniform, they'll treat your ass just like the rest of us."

She didn't know about the community service I'd done and still did on a regular basis. I fought day in and day out when I was a kid against racist cops like O'Sullivan and manipulative drug dealers that corrupted young boys the way Drastic corrupted my brother growing up. She didn't know that the purpose of me being a cop was to help make a change for the better in our communities. To her, I was just a sellout with a badge.

"You don't know me or what I'm about. You're judging me the same way you say the cops judge the community," I fired back.

"Oh, please," she said. "Once you put on that uniform, you're just as fucked-up and corrupt as the rest of them. You're no exception. All of you cops need to apologize for the shit y'all put communities through."

I ground my teeth. I was angry about her comments and was cold, hungry, and wet from the rain. Then, on top of being yelled at for hours for an incident I had no involvement in, it was all starting to bubble my anger to the top.

"Would you apologize for all black people if a black person you didn't know committed a violent crime toward a white victim?" I asked her.

"Nope. Shit ain't have nothing to do with me."

"So why should I, a black female cop who isn't guilty of anything, be treated like a villain because some other cop that I don't know, in a state I've never been to, shot someone? You wouldn't expect or want everyone to hate, distrust, or mentally condemn all black people because of the actions of a few. So why do you feel I should apologize on behalf of all cops because of a situation I wasn't involved in?"

The woman waved me off, dismissing my comments.

"Using the guilty-by-association argument is hypocritical when you protest day in and day out and cry foul when it's done against minorities," I said. "You're doing the same thing to me, and I'm as black as you."

"You're black, but you'll *never* be black like me. I'm not a sellout who preys on her own people," she fired back.

I felt myself getting ready to scream at this woman when I suddenly felt a hand on my shoulder.

"Take a minute to cool off. Sit in the car for a while and study your flashcards for the lieutenants' test. I'll take it from here," Morgan said.

He was right. I didn't argue. I got in my patrol car, closed the door, and leaned my head back on the headrest. I took a deep breath and studied my test material. While being around protestors was discouraging, I couldn't lose focus. I needed to keep my mind on my goal of rising in the ranks. Once I calmed down and did a good amount of studying, I went back out to my post with Rashida.

Morgan wrapped his arm around me. "You good now, Williams?" he asked.

"Yeah, I'm cool."

"As sexy as you look when you're mad, I didn't want you to lose your temper on one of these protestors."

"I appreciate it."

"I got to look out for my girl. I'll be around. Text me if you need another break."

I smiled. "Thanks."

I watched his firm, muscular ass as he walked away.

"Boss, you need to be careful," Rashida said.

"Why do you say that?"

"It's obvious he's feeling you, and it looks like you're feeling him too. Playas recognize playas, and, boss, I'm tellin' you, he wants to fuck you."

"I won't become a statistic. Trust me."

I didn't know who I was trying to convince, her or me. I felt guilty. In my heart, I could never cheat on Billy, but I feared what would happen if I were ever in a situation where I was alone with Morgan.

Was it that obvious that I was attracted to him? If she could see it, could other cops I worked with see it too? Was this just an innocent crush, or was there something deeper? I put those thoughts aside and focused on the protestors.

Chapter 16

Bill

The Truth

"Nope, not like that. Let's try it again," I said.

I was in my office trying my best to hide my frustration as I prepared Johnny for what the prosecution could ask him on trial. I needed this prep to be perfect so he'd be ready for the questions the prosecution would throw at him if we had to put him on the witness stand.

His answers were decent, but after years of experience dealing with shady clients, my gut was telling me there was more to his story.

"So, this is your lady, huh?" Johnny said, holding a picture of Ebony and me he picked up from my credenza.

"Uh, yeah, that's my girlfriend."

"Yo, I knew you and I were cut from the same cloth."

I didn't respond. I just let him talk.

"I love fucking black bitches."

I tried to keep my face expressionless. Everything about him pissed me off. He wasn't from the street, but he pretended to be. I also didn't appreciate him referring to my woman as a "black bitch" or thinking he and I were anything alike. I thought about what winning this case would do for my mom and Ebony and calmed myself down.

"C'mon, stop frontin' like you don't got a black-girl fetish too," he said.

"Let's focus on our trial prep. You gotta answer the questions exactly how we rehearsed, and you seriously need to stop smiling when you answer them too. You don't want the jury to think you're some pompous asshole. Now, did you rape Sophia?"

He chuckled. "Nope."

"Johnny, be serious."

"How you want me to answer it . . . like this?" He put on a nasal voice and said, "No, sir, I did not forcefully have sexual relations with that woman."

"If you say it like that, they'll know you're being condescending."

"Well, I wouldn't call it rape. At least, I paid the bitch."

I held up a hand to stop him. "That won't fly with the jury in the courtroom. What do you mean by that, anyway?"

"Well, I did rough her up a bit to convince her to let me fuck, but it's not like she didn't get paid."

"You can't say that on the witness stand."

"I'm tired of prepping for this shit, yo," he said. "I'm ready to go."

"No, you're not. Now stop avoiding the question. Did you rape Sophia?"

"Nah."

"You're smiling again."

"Look, between me and you, blacks are beneath us anyway, so fucking them only feels right. I know you feel the same way when you fuck your girl." He laughed.

I rubbed the bridge of my nose, trying to keep my composure. I was insulted. This asshole really believed our views were the same, and he wouldn't stop talking.

"Black bitches will do any nasty thing you want when you got money. They'll let you fuck them any kind of way, and even if they don't want it—fuck it. No one will believe them anyway."

"Wait, what did you just say?" I asked.

"No one in their right mind would take some black stripper bitch's word over a successful white dude. We can do whatever we want to them."

"You're making it sound like you actually raped that girl."

"Well, I paid her, but I knew she definitely didn't want it." He laughed. "I took what I wanted, and I'm sure she spent the good money I gave her on drugs or some other bullshit."

I stood up from my chair, charged Johnny, and shoved him hard in the chest. He stumbled back. I grabbed him by his collar and slammed him against my office door.

"You son of a bitch. You swore to me that you didn't rape that girl. Now, you're telling me you did."

"Get your fucking hands off me. Are you crazy?"

I let him go, realizing what I had just done.

"You wanna hear me say it, fine. I fucking raped her, and I'm not sorry about it, either."

There it was—the truth—and I wasn't ready for it. When I was in law school, I knew there'd be times that, as a criminal defense lawyer, I'd have to represent guilty clients, but I figured I'd deal with it when the time came. The time was here, and I didn't want to handle it. Under attorney-client privilege, I still had to defend him despite now knowing he was guilty.

Johnny continued, "That bitch has been fucking for money for years. I wasn't gonna let her turn me down. I'm not payin' you to judge me. After I got some ass, I paid her just like I'm payin' you. I'm paying you to get me off. I thought we saw the world the same, but you're actin' all boujie. I'm just gonna have to treat you like I treated that bitch. She got me off sexually, and you'll get me off legally. I'm out."

Johnny walked out of my office. I sat back in my chair for a few minutes and thought about how I should handle this situation. I decided to talk to Francis to hear his opinion, so I walked to his office and knocked lightly on his closed door.

"Come in," he yelled.

He was on the phone. He held his index finger up to stop me from interrupting and listened as the person on the phone spoke to him.

"It's not a problem. I'll talk to him. This won't happen again. I promise you that. Goodbye, sir."

Francis slammed the phone down.

"What happened in your office with Alfieri?" he asked.

I told him what went down, and he didn't give a shit.

"So what? A good criminal defense lawyer doesn't ask, 'What did my client do?' He asks, 'What can the prosecutors prove he did?' You shouldn't care about what your client did. He's not legally guilty until the prosecutor has enough evidence to convince the jury to convict him. Come on, Billy, this is basic stuff. You're better than that. Tactically, for trial, your arguments should be focused on the prosecution's failure to prove Johnny raped the stripper. You need to get your shit together if you're going to win this case."

The hardest question I was having trouble answering was: If I did something morally wrong to accomplish something good, did that make *me* a bad person? Morally, representing Johnny was wrong, but winning this case would make me a partner, and I could take care of my mom and comfortably marry Ebony. Did that make me selfish, wanting those things for myself, even though it meant getting Johnny off?

I couldn't dwell on that. I needed to win this case. I'd feel bad about it after my mom was taken care of and I was married to Ebony.

Chapter 17

Ben

Answers

I needed answers. The trial was quickly approaching, and I needed more ammo to defend Reggie. I went back to Rikers to talk to him and see what he could tell me.

"Who is Kuwuan Mitchell to you?" I asked.

"Hello to you, too," Reggie said.

"I don't . . . We don't have time to be polite right now. The clock is ticking, and Kuwuan Mitchell's fingerprints were found on the magazine of the gun you were holding that night."

"I don't know him."

"What did the guy look like?"

"I dunno. Dark-skinned guy, around my height. He had a red and black Chicago Bulls hat on and matching Air Jordans."

"And you don't know him?" I asked. "You never saw him before?"

"Did I stutter?"

"You're sure you weren't wearing a hat that night?"

"Yeah, I'm sure."

I rubbed my hand down my face.

"You look worried. You all right?" he asked.

"I'm fine. I'm not going to lose this case."

"So, you believe I'm innocent?"

"Yes."

"Why?"

That caught me off guard. "Your story is always consistent. It never changed."

"Because I didn't do it. You're different from all the other lawyers I've had. You got this corny Wayne Brady demeanor going for you."

"What does that mean?"

"White people love sellout brothas like you. I think it'll help convince the jury that I didn't do it."

Reggie was good at touching that sore spot with me. Every day I'd been questioning myself, wondering if I were considered black enough, or if people viewed me as authentic since I'd started defending him.

I took some more notes and headed back to the office.

On the drive back to the office, I saw a cop car in my rearview mirror. The car had been following me for a while. I tried to play it cool, but I accidentally made eye contact with the cop in the mirror. I knew I was going to get pulled over. Like clockwork, his lights and siren went on, and I pulled over.

I rolled down my windows and turned my radio down. Tensions were high with cops, since two were just killed in my case. I was nervous when I saw those lights come on. I quickly fished in my glove compartment and had my license, registration, and insurance in my hands with both of them placed on top of my steering wheel by the time the officer came to my window.

"License and registration," the officer said.

His hand was on his weapon. His eyes darted around my car, searching for anything out of the ordinary.

I handed him everything in my hand and placed them back on the steering wheel. "Is there a problem, Officer?"

"A lot of these BMWs have been getting stolen lately in this area. Is this your car?"

"Yes, sir, it is. I have all the proper documents and paperwork if you would like to see them."

He laughed. "You don't speak like you're black. What do you do for work?"

You don't speak like you're black. This dumbass statement was meant to be a compliment to say I was articulate, but it was demeaning to me and my race.

I gave him a fake grin to mask my irritation. It wasn't any of his business to know what I did for work, but I wanted to get out of this car stop without any problems, so I answered.

"I'm a lawyer."

"Well, that explains it. Have a good day, sir."

I got out of the car stop without a problem, but Reggie's comment was still in the back of my mind after hearing the cop tell me that I didn't speak like I was black. I hated feeling like I was a sellout.

Chapter 18

Becky

Rejection

"Mr. Simonetti will see you now, Ms. Preston," the receptionist at Gotham Publishing said.

She walked me to his office, and he greeted me at the door.

"I'm glad you could make it. We have a lot to discuss," he said, smiling.

That sounded like a good sign.

"I'll cut right to the chase. Your story is witty, sexy, and well written, but it's also a bit dark, and I don't know if I can sell an interracial story. I'm sure with your fan base from your articles with *Cosmo,* my company would break even, but I don't know if we'd see much of a profit the way the story is now."

I frowned. "What do you feel is missing to make it marketable?" I asked.

"Do yourself a favor. Take the interracial element out. Keep it a love story between two white people, and that would definitely increase the book's profitability. I've seen you at events, and I know your boyfriend is black. I know you probably wanted to use this story to profess your love to the world, but interracial books between a black man and white woman just don't sell."

"The book is called *Black and White*," I said. "The basis is to show the trials and tribulations of being in a relationship that society shuns. Without the interracial part, the book wouldn't even make sense."

"White people don't have trials and tribulations in their relationships? Don't some Italians and Irish people believe they should stick with their own? We can spin this in a million ways that would be more marketable. Realize this: *Fifty Shades of Grey* started out as *Twilight* fan fiction. E. L. James wasn't making money with her story until she took out the vampire element. If you change the black-and-white relationship, we have a deal. If you can't do that, I'm sorry. I can't help you."

I couldn't control the disappointment on my face. I stood up but couldn't look Mr. Simonetti in the eyes. "I appreciate that you took the time to talk to me in person, but I put my heart and soul into this book. While it might be a simple fix to you to change the interracial part, I couldn't live with myself, no matter how popular the book would be, if I didn't publish it the way I want it."

Mr. Simonetti shook his head. "I'm sorry to hear that. Look, I know your father. I've been to a couple of investment seminars he's done. He has a lot of connections. I'm sure he could pull some strings with another publisher that could put your book out there the way you intend it to be, but book sales have been on the decline lately, and I can't make that type of risky business move. I'm sorry."

I nodded. "I understand. Thanks for taking the time to meet with me."

"It's no problem. Look, here's my card." Mr. Simonetti handed me a thick business card. "If you decide to change that little part of your book, I'll publish it with no problem. Take some time and consider it."

I smiled and said, "Thank you."

I walked out of the building, depressed. I texted Ben.
I knew he wasn't too far from here, and I needed him to
make me feel better.

"Two venti caramel lattes and one Frappuccino for
Ben," the barista called.

I nodded. Ben and I walked to the counter and grabbed
the drinks. I'd told Ben a little fib that I was in the neighborhood because of an interview with the *Village Voice*
to write a column for them on a regular basis. I didn't feel
like telling him the truth—that I'd met with another publishing company for my book and got rejected because of
the concept.

After being turned down again, I decided to crash his
usual Starbucks coffee date with Gabby.

"Do you always buy drinks for Gabby?" I asked.

"No, most of the time he's the late one, and I usually
buy for him," Gabby said from behind me, scaring the
shit out of me.

Ben chuckled. "Hey, Gabby."

"Hey, Big Head."

She walked past me like I wasn't there.

Ben handed Gabby her coffee.

"Is it black, the way I like it?"

"Black with no sugar, the way you always get it." He
cleared his throat.

"What?" she asked.

"Did you forget something?"

"Nope."

"You're being rude."

Gabby rolled her eyes. "Hi, Rebecca."

"Gabby," I said.

"I know Ben likes milk in his coffee, but I didn't know
he was bringing you here. What's up? Writing in your

little column isn't cutting it, so you're going to apply for a job here?"

I wasn't taking her shit today. I was already furious about my book being rejected by another publisher, and while I knew I should let it go, her snide comment put me over the edge.

"What's your problem with me?" I asked. "Are you that insecure and intimidated that you have to put me down to boost yourself up every chance you get?"

"Baby, let it go. Both of you, please, let's try to have a nice, peaceful lunch today," Ben said.

"I'm not letting it go," I said. "Not today. She has a problem with us being together, and I want to know what's so wrong with interracial dating?"

Gabby sipped her coffee and stared at me with a smirk. "Insecure? Hardly. Intimidated by you? Never. Listen to him, *Becky*. You don't have the wits to have a debate like that with me."

"Oh yeah? Let's see about that," I shot back.

Gabby chuckled as if I were pathetic. The way she'd condescendingly called me "Becky" pissed me off.

"Baby, please. Don't do this. Let's all calm down and drop it," Ben said.

I knew he loved me, but I also knew he didn't have confidence in me being able to hold my own against Gabby.

"No, I can handle myself. I'm not afraid of her, and I'm tired of backing down every time she acts like a bitch. I got this."

Ben sighed, closed his eyes, and rubbed the bridge of his nose.

Gabby faced him. "May I start with my opening argument?" she asked.

"Neither of you listen to me anyway, so proceed," he said.

"Gladly." Gabby turned herself to face me better. "Becky, I am absolutely against interracial dating. I'm pro-black love. Honestly, interracial dating disgusts me, especially when most white women only date black men as a novelty—not because they love them and truly understand what black men face in this country on a daily basis. Before I school you, answer this: how many African American friends do you have? *Real* friends—not Ben's cousin, Simone, coworkers you're friendly with, or people on your Facebook friends list. How many *real* black friends do you have?"

I stuttered and stammered a bit, but caught myself.

"I don't keep a tally of the number of friends of different races I have. For me, people are people. I'm sorry you believe that I see Ben as a novelty, but I never looked at him like that. I genuinely love him, and you'd see that if you weren't so busy being racist toward me, but since we're on the topic, how many white friends do *you* have?"

"To answer your question, *Becky,* I don't have any white friends," Gabby said. "I have a few associates, but none that I would consider a close friend. There are some Caucasians that I'm cordial with, but that's where it ends. Second, black people can't be racist. Racism is a problem and concept that operates on both an individual and institutional level, where a dominant race benefits from the oppression of another. To be racist, I would have to have the power and influence to take my prejudices and exercise them with immunity under the law. African Americans in this country have never had that type of authority or influence. Therefore, we could never be racist."

"Racism, by definition, means to view another race as being inferior, and isn't that how you view me?" I asked. "You look at me as if I'm less than nothing. You don't like or respect me. You think I'm some stupid, spoiled little white bitch that is beneath you."

I felt my anger bubbling. Gabby clasped her hands together and placed them on the table. "I can't help that I see you for who you are."

"Gabby—" Ben snapped.

"Sorry. It slipped," she said, smiling at him, then looking back at me before she continued.

"You're interchanging racism and prejudice. They *aren't* the same thing. How I treat you is just a taste of what Ben and I go through on a daily basis. We live in a challenging time for black people. Women like you won't help him through these struggles. When he gets pulled over for driving while being black, followed, and harassed in stores because of the color of his skin, or passed up on getting this partnership, when everyone knows he busts his ass and is probably more qualified and deserving than the white guy he's in competition with, who is going to console him—you?"

"All right, before this gets further out of hand, let's stop this now," Ben said.

"No, I'm a big girl, Ben, I got this. I can take anything she dishes out," I said, cutting my eyes at her.

"Baby, I have all the confidence in the world that you're strong, but you don't have to prove anything to Gabby or me," he said. "Let this go."

"No, Ben, she needs to hear this," Gabby said. "Too many times I've seen white women like her date black men just to piss off their fathers, or because they want to have exotic-looking babies, or just to escape the label of being racist."

She pointed at me. "Do you know how many white girls I know will date, marry, or have babies with black men but don't associate with any other black people or African American culture whatsoever?"

I knew the expression on my face showed I hated her. I couldn't be weak in front of her. I couldn't let her see she was getting to me. I needed to hide my emotions better.

"I care about African American culture, and I have black friends."

Gabby continued to push and goad me. "Hanging out with Simone and watching *Save the Last Dance* and *Roots* doesn't mean you have black friends or care about African American culture."

She made me so angry. I was holding back tears, and I curled my bottom lip and bounced my foot under the table.

"Look at you with your fake tan, wearing your big hoop earrings, stealing our cultural styles," she said. "It's funny how y'all hate us but want to be us so much. Is that all supposed to make you appear more 'down for the cause'?"

"Now you're attacking my appearance and fashion choices?" I said. "I don't see you wearing a dashiki. All the designers you have on are European. Doesn't that makeup you're wearing make your skin appear lighter than it is? Who is *really* stealing whose style?"

"So, you think all African Americans should wear dashikis, huh?" Gabby said. "Maybe we should live in mud huts too and be primitive like your people believe is in our nature, right? I wear clothing and makeup because they're tools to help me succeed in this country that is controlled by your kind. What's *your* excuse?"

I rapidly tapped my fingers on the table.

"Am I striking a nerve?" she said. "Help me understand. Why do you want to be with a black man? Since you're not a twig and have some hips and ass, were you rejected by your precious white men and gravitated to brothers as a default because they showed you attention? Oh, I get it. It's a sex thing. You just love you some black dick, huh? Knowing that sistas have been enjoying something so good that you didn't have must've driven your cracker ass to want it full-time, huh?"

"Fuck you, you stupid black bitch."

I covered my mouth as soon as the words left it.

"You see that, Ben? All it took was a little prying and irritation, but her true colors showed. She doesn't give a shit about you or black people. She's just another spoiled boujie white bitch that doesn't know the struggle and is trying to convince herself she isn't racist."

My lips trembled, and I felt myself on the verge of tears. The last thing I wanted to do was cry in front of her. I rose to my feet, grabbed my purse, and quickly ran toward the door.

"Shit." I tripped on the edge of a chair and dropped my purse. Nearly everything spilled on the floor. People chuckled at my clumsiness, but no one helped me. I quickly began to pick up the contents. I was still within earshot when Ben said, "Gabby, you're my best friend. I care about you, but you have to stop this shit. Stop picking on her."

"I'm not picking on her—"

"Whether you or my family approves, I love her, and I'm going to protect her, even if it's from all of you."

"She's an adult, Ben," she said. "The bitch doesn't need her big black man to save her all the time."

Ben shook his head. "I love you, Gabby, but if you call Becky out of her name or treat her like shit again, we're done!"

Gabby gave him a look of confusion. Even I momentarily stopped picking up my things in shock.

"We've been best friends since we were kids. You would throw away a lifetime of friendship for *her?*" she asked.

He didn't answer. They stood in silence and stared at each other long and hard.

Hearing Ben defend me warmed my heart and calmed me down somewhat, but I was still embarrassed and hurt.

I finished gathering the things from my purse and stormed out of the restaurant. Ben caught up to me.

"Baby, wait," he said.

I stopped and faced him. "She's a vapid bitch, and I fucking hate her."

"I know you do. Look, I'm going to talk to her *and* my parents. This can't keep going on."

"Will anyone ever think I'm good enough for you?"

"I could ask you the same thing. You think I have it easy with *your* family?"

I knew he wasn't wrong, but I was still fuming.

"Look, it's hard for both of us, but we knew this when we started dating," he said. "The only opinion that matters is our own. As long as we love each other, we can handle it."

I knew he'd just said back there that if Gabby didn't stop, their friendship was over, but I didn't believe him.

"What if I can't handle it anymore?" I asked. "What if I told you that you had to choose between her and me? Who would you choose, huh?" I looked at him intently and waited for an answer. "You know what? Don't say it. I know the answer."

I didn't want Ben to answer because, deep down, I was scared he might answer truthfully. I hated Gabby because, overall, I felt she was better than me. She was graceful and sexy, with serious curves that made men and even women turn their heads. She was strong, confident, articulate, and I was intimidated by her. I knew if I saw all these things, it was obvious Ben saw them too. I knew he loved me. When I looked him in his warm, almond-shaped, brown eyes, I knew what we had was real, but deep down, I was afraid he'd come to his senses one day and choose to be with her over me.

Ben cradled my face in his hands before he kissed me. "I love you, Becky. You're worth fighting for."

I hugged him. Ben always knew what to say to make me happy.

***

We came home, and I was still fuming from our lunch with Gabby. I plopped down on the couch with my arms folded.

"Baby, don't be mad, OK?" Ben said.

"I'm not."

"You sure?"

"Yup."

"All right, you did this to yourself . . ."

Ben tickled me into submission, and I couldn't help but laugh my ass off. I playfully slapped his arm.

"I love you," he said.

Seeing the sincerity in his eyes somewhat soothed me, but I kept thinking of her. "I love you too. Let me show you how much," I said, pulling down his zipper and dropping to my knees. A smile grew on Ben's face.

I unbuckled his pants and slid his boxers down to his ankles. His huge cock bobbed in his lap and dangled in front of my face. I took him all in, deep-throating as I worked him in my mouth, toying with him as he writhed in ecstasy. His legs trembled, and the veins inside his thick cock pulsated. I stopped, taking my mouth off him.

"Shit, babe, I'm almost there, don't stop."

"I don't want you to come yet. I want you inside me. Let's take this to the bedroom."

I took him by the hand, pulled him to his feet, and led him to the bedroom, where I quickly undressed while he lay down on the bed. I lay next to him and stroked his meaty shaft. Then I braced myself as I swung my legs over him, reached back, grabbed his cock, and, in one smooth motion, inserted it inside me.

I placed my soft hands on his chest and slowly found my rhythm. Ben held his hands on my hips, thrusting into me until we were in perfect sync.

I pictured Gabby fucking him like this. I envisioned Ben in total ecstasy while she rode him. Her holding her nose up high as if she were fucking him out of some sort of charity. Ben reached up and caressed my breasts. I closed my eyes. I worked my ass up and down on his dick, quickening my pace when I heard his breathing quickening and his moans getting louder. I needed reassurance that I could please my man. I wanted to fuck him so good that he'd forget about ever being intimate with her and any other women that came before me.

Ben slapped my ass. "Damn, baby," he moaned.

I needed to see him lose control, to know that I made him reach nirvana like this. I was desperate to see that look of satisfaction in his eyes, but most importantly, I needed to feel powerful. The lack of finding a publisher and my constant battles with Gabby had me feeling powerless and inferior. I needed to feel and believe that Ben wanted me—and only me.

"Oh, shit, Becky."

I felt my own orgasm rising inside me. My body became lost in the moment. "Ahhhh!" I moaned.

My orgasm snuck up on me. I bucked and shuddered. Ben continued to thrust upward, and I savored the feeling of his dick filling me. I gathered my composure, and he pounded into me, faster and harder. Then he moaned and pinched my nipples.

We held each other as we came. Ben moved behind me and spooned his body against mine, nuzzling his face into my neck and running his fingertips along the contours of my body.

"I love you, Becky."

"I love you too."

I needed that reassurance. My thoughts went to my spat with Gabby, and inspiration hit me. Suddenly, I knew what was missing from my book. I reached for my laptop on top of my dresser.

"What are you doing?" Ben asked.

"Today inspired me. I know what will make my story better."

I start typing, infusing every new paragraph with the frustration and pain and hatred our relationship dealt with on a daily basis. I wrote about the things we did to combat those factors that tried to pull us apart, and I loved the outcome. I felt like my story was finally complete.

Chapter 19

Ben

Acceptance

I walked into my parents' house. Dad was watching that show, *The First 48*.

"Hey, Dad."

"What's up, son? What brings you around here today?"

I told him about the incident with Becky and Gabby at Starbucks and how I wanted to talk to Mom about her relationship with Becky.

"Is Mom home?" I asked.

"Yeah, she's outside in the backyard reading one of her favorite novels."

"Dad, I gotta ask—how come you aren't as mad about me being with Becky as Mom is?"

He took a long breath and exhaled. "Son, I've dealt with my fair share of racism, but not like your mother. I lived in New York all my life, where racism wasn't as prevalent as it was in the South. Your mom grew up in Tennessee during the segregation era. If you know your history, Pulaski, Tennessee, was where the Ku Klux Klan originated. As a kid, your mom witnessed family members and friends get beaten and killed by white people. I was blessed to not have the same negative experiences with white folks as your mom, so my views are somewhat different about it than hers, but no matter how much time has changed and race relations have slightly improved, those memories will always be ingrained in the back of her mind."

"I get it, Dad, but how does that help me with showing her that Rebecca is different?"

"It doesn't," he said. "It's not up to you to show that to your mother. Your mom has to change on her own. She knows you love Becky, and even though she isn't fond of it, and it may take awhile, she'll come around. Rebecca has to do her part by continuing to show her love and support to you, and trust me, it will soften your mom's heart."

"How is that fair to Becky or me?"

"Fair? There's nothing written in stone that anything in this life has to be fair. Black people in this country have endured troubling times for generations. All our lives, your mother and I had to prove to the world that not all black people are the same, that we aren't all uneducated, lazy losers. Through hard work and our actions, we show people every day that we're different. We've changed some people's perspective on us. Some people we haven't. It feels like a never-ending battle, but that's life. Rebecca is going to have to endure that same fight with you. If it's too hard for her, she can take the easy way out and leave you, but if she loves you like you say she does, she'll be able to handle it."

I nodded. "I'm going to talk to Mom and see if I can help speed things up and spark that change in her heart."

Dad laughed. "That's the spirit."

I walked into the backyard and saw my mom sitting in the shade on a lounge chair drinking iced tea and reading Ralph Ellison's *Invisible Man*. I kissed her on the cheek and sat next to her.

"Hey, Ben. How's everything going with the case?"

"I'm struggling, but I'll fight with whatever I have."

"That's what I like to hear."

"While I'm in the fighting spirit, Mom, I need to talk to you about Becky."

Mom sighed. "What do you need to say to me about that weak girl?"

"Why don't you like her?"

"She's not the right woman for you."

It never mattered how good I made Becky sound. Mom always compared her to Gabby, and she paled in comparison in her eyes.

"Baby, help me understand something. I just don't get it," Mom said.

I sighed. I knew where this was going. "Mama—"

"I raised you and Simone to value black families."

"Mama—"

"Don't 'Mama' me. Let me speak. When parents are raising their children, they envision their kids will find prospective mates that will resemble them. As a parent, you picture who your son brings home as a reflection of yourself, but that isn't the case with you and Simone. Both of you are sleeping with white people, people who don't resemble your father or me, and it just . . . feels like rejection. It makes me feel that, as black parents, we weren't good enough, strong enough, or smart enough for either of you, so it caused the two of you to look outside of your race."

"Mama, that's not true," I said. "You're the strongest woman I know. I love you and admire you more than anyone."

"Then why are you with Rebecca? You have a strong black woman in Gabby. She's beautiful. She's smart, she's successful—she's everything that your white woman isn't. How could you pass up on having a strong partner for a weak one?"

"Mama, you and Dad taught me to see the person and not the skin," I said. "You raised me to know that people shouldn't be judged by their skin color, but for their hearts and actions. Gabby is more successful than Becky, but Becky has a lot of similarities with you."

Mom sulked. "Yeah, right. I highly doubt I have anything in common with that . . . that woman."

"You're both determined to try to prove everyone wrong, even when the world is against you."

Mama tried to hide a slight grin.

"You're both confident that when you apply yourself, you can achieve anything."

"What else?"

"Behind all of your strengths, you're both sensitive, loving, and nurturing. I watch how you take care of Dad—even when he doesn't ask you for anything, you like to take care of him."

"Your father gives me the world," Mom said. "It's only natural I'd enjoy taking care of my king."

"Becky has that same mind-set, Mom. I know she can be a little naïve and seem spoiled, but she's a great person who gives me the same love you show Dad."

Mom nodded.

"You'd see that if you would just give her a chance. I know you love Gabby. She'll always be my friend, but that's where my relationship with her ends. I love Becky, and I need you to give her the same love and respect that you give Gabby."

"I'll try, Ben, but it does bother me that she's white."

Chapter 20

Becky

Damaged

"What's got you acting all pissy?" Simone asked.

Simone and I were hanging out in my living room. She was flipping through channels while I groaned at what I just read after checking the mail.

"I got *another* rejection letter from a publisher. I'm getting these daily at this point."

"What do those pretentious dickheads know anyway? People love your column in *Cosmo*. Just ask your dad to pull some strings with his contacts and get published already. Once your book is out, I'm sure it'll be a bestseller."

I crumpled up the letter and threw it in the garbage can. It had been a month since I submitted my latest rewritten manuscript to this particular publisher. In my eyes, it was perfect, and there was nothing I could add that would improve the story any more than it was, but I guessed wrong. Each rejection crushed me, but no matter how much I wanted to just give up and say, "fuck it," I couldn't. This book meant too much to me. I wanted this book to show the world how special and beautiful my relationship with Ben was. I wanted to prove to everyone that I could do this on my own and become a successful bestselling author without anyone's help. Most importantly, I needed to prove it to myself. I opened my laptop that was sitting on the coffee table and tinkered with my manuscript.

"Look, I don't want to see you stressed out all night," Simone said. "Ben's gonna come home and be lost in his annoying case all night. Why don't you call Brooke, and the three of us go clubbing? We can dance and get shitfaced drunk. Besides, we're way overdue for a girls' night out."

I laughed. "I hate going clubbing with you two. You guys always end up abandoning me to go home with guys you met at the end of the night."

"Thanks for making us sound like hoes. Come on. It'll be fun."

I closed my laptop and texted Ben to let him know I was heading out with Simone. I needed a night to clear my head.

"Cool, let's go," I said.

We went to the B66 Club in Brooklyn. For the most part, Simone wasn't as flirty as she usually was, but she was still getting a lot of attention from white men. She was sitting at the bar talking with a cute guy in a light gray suit. Brooke was jealous.

"I just don't get why every guy here is all over her," she pouted.

"Guys have been hitting on you all night too. Relax."

"Yeah, the ugly ones. It's not fair."

"What's not fair?" I asked.

"How easy she has it because she's black."

I didn't like her answer. She sounded like my dad.

"Trust me, her life is far from easy," I said.

"She's an unemployed college dropout that's babied by her rich aunt and uncle. Sounds pretty easy to me. Sure, you and I have trust funds, and our parents do a lot for us, but we also work and make our own money. You're even working on publishing a book—what is *she* doing with her life? It's just not fair that the pretty black girl gets all the attention while pretty white girls like me, who deserve to be with these rich white men, get shafted."

"I think your drinks are speaking for you tonight."

Brooke took a long sip of her mojito. "Maybe. Or maybe I'm just tired of her only getting fucked by these guys when they could be my potential husband."

"Every time we hang out, you leave with a guy too."

"I get the consolation prizes while the quality guys look at her as some easy ho they can fuck . . . just like her mother."

"What's wrong with you tonight?"

Brooke kept glaring at Simone. "It doesn't make you mad that we work hard, yet this unemployed bum has a better wardrobe than us?"

"She's our friend," I said. "We shop together at the same stores. You could buy the same clothes she has. Our dads paid for ours. Her uncle paid for hers. What does it matter?"

"Why do you always defend her?"

"Because she's our friend, and you sound really fucking racist right now."

"And what if I am?" Brooke said. "Just because you're fucking one, don't act all high and mighty."

"Wow, Brooke. The truth finally comes out."

Simone looked at Brooke and me, cutting her conversation short. Then she walked over to us.

"What are you guys arguing about over here?" she asked.

"Nothing of importance," I said.

Simone kept tugging down on the back of her grey skirt because her thick thighs and ass kept making the back rise.

"Hey, beautiful, come back over here and keep me company," the guy she'd been talking to said after observing her wardrobe troubles.

Brooke was still sulking.

"Nah, I'm going to keep my friend here company, but my girl Brooke would love to talk to you."

Brooke's eyes narrowed. "I don't want your fucking sloppy seconds. I can find a man on my own."

The guy tossed up his hands and walked away.

"Ouch. What's *wrong* with you?" Simone asked.

"*You're* what's wrong with me. Why can't you just stick with your own kind?" Brooke yelled.

"I didn't know who I dated bothered you—"

"I'm just tired of you acting like you're white."

Simone looked taken aback and hurt by Brooke's comment. "I know I'm not white. How would you like me to act, Brooke? Should I talk loudly and only speak in slang? Should I drink grape soda and eat fried chicken every day? I know you hate me. I figured in time after being around me and getting to know me, you would accept me, but you only see my skin color."

That said, Simone walked away toward the exit.

"Wait for me," I said.

We stood in front of the club. Simone wrapped her arms around herself. "People have been telling me I talk and act 'white' since I was a little girl. I fucking hate hearing that. What am I supposed to sound like?"

"People are ignorant. Don't let it bother you," I said.

"It shouldn't, but it does. I didn't want to get involved with that guy tonight because I'm trying to change things about myself. I don't want to be standoffish to black guys anymore, and I sure as hell don't want to be a statistic to another white guy with a black-girl fetish." She shook her head.

"I used to close my eyes and pretend others didn't see my skin color. I used to act like racial problems didn't exist, but Brooke's outburst proved that people only see me as a black girl trying to be white."

I'd seen Ben frustrated about these same problems, and I felt her pain. I didn't know what I could say or do to console her.

"I'm sorry," I said.

"It's not your fault."

Brooke walked out of the club and met up with us.

"Seriously, you need to apologize to Simone," I told Brooke.

"Sorry," she said, staring at the ground.

"Whatever," Simone said. "I thought I was more than your token black friend. You think I don't hear the shit you say? Whenever we converse, you talk through me, not *to* me. It's like I'm nothing, and I don't matter. I usually don't speak up because I don't want to come across as 'the angry black girl causing problems,' but I'm tired of it."

"Honestly, I've been a real bitch lately, and I've taken it out on you," Brooke said. "Let's just drop it and get over it—"

"It must be nice to be white and have the luxury to tell me to just 'get over it' when you don't walk around in a society where people are always following you in stores and treating you like shit based on the stereotypes regardless of how I conduct myself. You never have to deal with stupid, petty bullshit like white women clutching their purses for dear life when you sit next to them at a public place. Everything you said took me back to feelings of insecurity I had since I was a little kid. If I talk 'hood,' I'm a typical hood rat, but if I engage you in civilized conversation and behavior, then I'm acting 'white.' What's up with all the shit you said?"

"I didn't mean it," Brooke said. "I was just acting stupid because I'm scared I'll never get married. When I see all these guys crowded around you, I get jealous. Can we pretend this didn't happen?"

"I can't. I forgive you, but I can't forget that. It's better this way, because at least, I know where I stand with you."

We walked back inside the club and tried to patch up our damaged night.

Chapter 21

Gabby

Scab

Everywhere I turned, I saw brothas dating white women. It was eight p.m. on a Friday night, and my single ass was listening to music, searching for potential black men on eHarmony. Although there were lots of men I could be compatible with, most of them wanted fucking white girls. I was having terrible luck with men. They were either ugly as hell, gay, only looking for white women, or I just didn't feel that connection that I felt with Ben.

Honestly, I compared everyone I dated to him. My love for him was what kept me finding flaws in every guy that showed an interest in me.

Drake's "Too Good" came on the radio, and I immediately thought about Ben. The lyrics about taking his love for granted were too fitting and reminded me that I'd created this big, life-altering mess that brought him and Becky together.

My relationship with Ben was like a scab that I kept picking at. My actions were what kept it from healing. The conversations I had with him, our inside jokes, our history together—I'd never had that type of connection with anyone else, past or present. Our connection was real and extremely hard to find, which was why I refused to ignore it and let it go. I refused to stop picking at this scab.

When we were kids, I didn't give him the time of day. I figured he was so sprung on me that he'd always be around, but after our night of intimacy, I realized that pushing him away was a mistake. When Ben took me out on that date to Frames Bowling Lounge, what he didn't know was that I spotted Ty there with a white girl. I had a great time with Ben, and the sex was good, but my mind and my heart were on Ty. I questioned why he left me for that white girl and wondered what she had that I didn't.

When I left Ben's place that night, I did a lot of self-inventory. It finally dawned on me that I'd never find another guy who loved me unconditionally the way Ben did. While my aggressiveness scared most brothas away, Ben was never intimidated by me. I went to his apartment to patch things up and work on a relationship with him, but I was too late. Playing too hard to get made him turn to Becky, and she didn't deserve him. Seeing Ben with a white girl after spotting Ty with one pissed me the fuck off.

I wasn't going to lose my best friend—and, in my heart, future husband—to Becky, so I'd been patient. I'd stayed close to him because I needed him in my life. Ben understood me, he listened to me, and, unlike most men, he wanted to do more than just fuck me.

An insult to injury was having to watch Ben and Becky's relationship blossom in front of my face. Seeing him not jump up to please me whenever I called and showing her so much love and attention made me realize that she had replaced my spot in his heart. Jealousy swirled in the pit of my stomach whenever I saw them acting all lovey-dovey.

I was scrolling through the profiles of my matches on the dating site when I came across Terrence's profile. I called him.

"Bitch face? Is that you?" he asked.

I assumed my number showed up on his phone. "Shut up, punk. Why do you have a profile on eHarmony?"

"You wouldn't know that unless you had one too. The question is, why do *you* have one?"

"I'm keeping an open mind. What are you doing?"

"Nothing," he said. "Why? You want some company?"

"Come through."

The truth was Terrence and I had been fucking recreationally for the past four years. Shit, I needed some dick, and he was an excellent maintenance man. At first, it happened as a mistake. One night I invited Terrence over to get drunk with me at my place after Ben canceled plans with me to be with Becky. Things got hot and heavy, and I blamed the first time on the alcohol. I had no excuse for the hundreds of times afterward.

I enjoyed his company, and he was a great fuck, but Ben still had my heart. Terrence and I promised we wouldn't tell Ben about our romps because I'd always felt that, in time, he'd drop Becky, and he and I would start something real. Terrence was a good guy—smart, had a swagger to him, and he was handsome, but he didn't seem like he was ever going to want to settle down, which was why seeing his profile on eHarmony surprised me. What we had was safe and comfortable because we knew where we both stood. He'd never wanted anything more with me, and he knew that when things ended with Ben and Becky, our fling was over.

***

My doorbell rang.

I answered the door, wearing only my robe, and Terrence was dressed in a dark blue suit.

"Nice suit, but where's your tie?"

"I'm too fly to wear a tie. I don't let nothing tie me down," he said, laughing at his corniness.

"Oh my God." I giggled at his line, but his words reinforced in my mind that this was just for fun, while the feelings I had for Ben were real.

Terrence stepped inside and closed my door. He slid one arm around my back and the other behind my knees, scooped me up in his arms, and placed me on my bed.

He sat beside me, but I pushed him on his back, climbed into his lap, and took over the task of undressing him. Terrence lifted his ass, allowing me to pull off his pants and underwear. His cock sprang out. I wrapped my manicured hands firmly around his cock and took him in my mouth. I worked him until he writhed and cursed. I felt him swelling up, but he stopped me. At that point, he laid me on my stomach, his hands glided up and down my back, and he ate me out from behind, his lips tugging gently on my folds.

We both liked to be in control, and it was a sexy game we played to try to outdo each other. There was very little passion in our sessions. There wasn't much kissing. Our sessions were rough, borderline impersonal, which made it easy to not catch feelings for him and fantasize that it was Ben fucking me.

Terrence ripped open the wrapper and rolled the condom on his length swiftly. He flipped me on my back, lowered himself between my spread legs, and sank deep inside me with one swift motion. I felt every stroke. He worked his hips, punishing me with his cock, and it was reminiscent of my first time with Ben. I felt my orgasm building inside me. Terrence increased his pace. I came and had to put major focus on screaming out the right name. Terrence pumped up his fist, celebrating the fact that he made me come first. I turned over and kneeled on all fours, arching my ass in the air.

"Oh damn," Terrence said.

"Give it to me doggie," I said.

I knew the visual of seeing my huge tits bouncing freely and throwing my ass back as he thrusted made him come quick. Terrence hammered me mercilessly from behind. His hands gripped me tightly. I felt his whole body tense up. He moaned and came inside me.

We high-fived each other as he lay next to me. Then Terrence pulled me into his chest and kissed my forehead. I knew this was just a fuck to him, but the affection felt nice.

We showered separately and got dressed. Terrence was hanging out in my living room while I cooked.

"What are you making?" he asked.

"I'm making Ben his favorite, macaroni and cheese. I'm going to surprise him with it in a few minutes and apologize for fighting with Becky."

Terrence gave me a look I couldn't decipher.

"How come you never cook for me?"

"Oh, shut up. I cook for you all the time."

He laughed. "You just use me for my body and don't even have the decency to make me a meal."

"Whatever, punk. We use each other."

His smile dissipated. "It's funny. Ben used to chase you. Now *you're* chasing *him*."

"I chase him because he's worth it. Why do you care? You've been getting a no-strings-attached piece of ass for the past four years. Just enjoy it and mind your own business."

"Ben's not the only successful black man out there. He loves his girl. You need to move on."

"Don't worry about what *I* need to do. Take care of yourself."

"Gabby, I know you love Ben, but eventually, even you have to see that Becky's here to stay," Terrence said.

"You don't know him like I do. When I look him in his eyes, I *know* there's something still there. He knows it too. That's why we talk every day."

"Touching. Well, I'm out. Call me when you want company again."

"Ugh, you're lucky you're cute."

"I know. Bye, bitch face."

"Bye, punk."

Ben opened his door. He stood in the doorway and stared at me.

"Can I come in?" I asked.

"What are you doing here?"

"Don't be like that, Big Head. I made you baked macaroni."

"Uh-huh."

"I'm serious. This is a bona fide peace offering here."

He stepped aside to let me in.

"I see you're still reading up on your case," I said, noticing the files he had on the coffee table.

"Yeah, it's the hardest one I've ever had."

"I believe it. Is Becky here?"

"No, she's out with Simone. I don't know when she'll be back."

"I wanted to say I'm sorry to you—to both of you," I said. "I'm always going to feel a certain way because I love you, but I have to respect that you're with Becky, and even if I don't like her, I can try to be more cordial. You're my best friend. I won't risk losing your friendship because I can't be nice to your girlfriend."

He smiled and hugged me. I just had to be patient. In time, I'd get what I wanted.

Chapter 22

Becky

The Truth Shall Set You Free

"What's up, bestie?"

"Hey, Simone," I said.

"I need to take my fat ass to the gym, and I don't want to go alone. Can you come with me?"

"Ugh, I wasn't trying to go out today."

"Come on, please . . . I'll be your best friend. You know you can't say no to your best friend."

"Oh yeah? Watch me."

"Come on, bestie. I promise we won't stay long. We'll go hard on the weights, do a little cardio, and then be out the door."

I hadn't been as active in the gym as I should lately, so I sighed and said, "All right."

"Cool, can you pick me up? My car's in the shop."

I laughed. "So, the *real* reason for the invite is you needed a ride."

"Nah, that's not the real reason," she said. "Just hurry up."

"I'm on my way."

I put on a sports bra and yoga pants and went to Ben's parents' house to pick up Simone. I texted her to come out to my car. I had no desire to go inside once I saw that

Gabby's Mercedes-Benz was in the driveway next to Mrs. Turner's. I hadn't talked to Gabby since my spat with her in Starbucks last month. When Ben's mom and Gabby were together, their bitchiness was almost unbearable. I wasn't in the mood for that today. Of course, Simone begged me to come inside as she got ready.

I walked to the door, and it swung open before I could ring the doorbell. Simone was dressed in blue jeans and a tight T-shirt.

"You're working out in *that?*" I asked.

"Nope. Come inside for a minute."

I sighed. We passed the living room, and Gabby and Mrs. Turner were laughing and watching the first *Sex and the City* movie.

Simone stopped walking. I waved at Gabby and Ben's mom while they both looked at me like I was crazy.

"Hello, Becky," Gabby said.

"Hi, Rebecca," Mrs. Turner said.

"Do you mind moving from in front of the TV?" Gabby asked Simone.

"Nope," Simone replied. "This is an intervention."

"Oh my God," Gabby said, rolling her eyes.

Mrs. Turner laughed. "Girl, what the hell are you talking about?"

"We all need to talk," Simone said. "It's blatantly obvious that neither of you is fond of Becky and vice versa."

Simone faced Mrs. Turner. "Aunt Mable, you and Uncle Curtis are always telling me that people need closure to move on in life. Well, things won't improve between any of you unless you get everything off your chest."

Mrs. Turner leaned back on the sofa and folded her arms. "OK, but the truth hurts," she said.

"Simone, I don't know if I'm up for a conversation like this right now," I said.

Simone took my hand, and we sat on the opposite couch to Gabby and Mrs. Turner. They looked at me, laughing and whispering to each other.

"What's that about?" I asked.

"Nothing, just an inside joke with us," Gabby said.

I nodded. "I'm ready to have this conversation. I'll start with you, Mrs. Turner. Why do you hate me?"

"I don't hate you, Rebecca," she said. "I just don't feel like you're the right woman for my son. You're weak."

My eyes were teary. She was blunt right out the gate with me. I stood up and was ready to leave when she said, "You see? The first sign of adversity, you run. How do you expect me to respect that?"

I sat back down. "You're right. I need to stop running. Mrs. Turner, I'm not the spoiled, rich girl that you think I am, but you'd never know because instead of getting to know me, you've pushed me away."

"Oh, stop," Gabby said. "You're *not* the victim, although you're really good at playing that role."

"I didn't get to you yet, but since you had to add your two cents, I'll say this: Stay away from my man. I love him, and he loves me. You had your chance, and you didn't appreciate him. I don't care if you or his entire family hate me. It will not stop the feelings we have for each other."

Mrs. Turner nodded.

"Am I supposed to cower because a white woman is demanding something?" Gabby said. "Please. Life has been so easy for you being rich and white—"

"That's what this is really about? Me being white?"

"Too often, in movies and media, black women are portrayed as loud, hostile, and inferior to you white women," Gabby said. "I'd never openly admit it to Ben, but he's a great example of a good black man, and women like you take them. Black men put you on a pedestal, while women like me, who are deserving of a man like him, are left with nothing."

Now I knew how Simone felt when Brooke said similar bullshit. Simone looked at me and shook her head. I faced Gabby.

"All you ever talk about is black and white. I'm not just a color or race—I'm a person."

"We're all people, but you don't care about, understand, or even try understanding the difficulties blacks experience in this world," Mrs. Turner said.

"She doesn't get what we mean when we talk about white privilege," Gabby said. "Her little feelings get hurt, and she catches an attitude."

She faced me. "When we say you're privileged, we're not just talking about financially. It means you see bad things happening, but it doesn't matter to you because it doesn't affect your race or you personally."

"How do you any of you know what I care about or what I understand?" I said. "Neither of you has ever taken the time to get to know me. I don't know what it's like to be black, but that doesn't mean I'm not trying to understand what my man has to deal with. Yes, I'm white, but that doesn't mean I don't care or see that things aren't always fair. What exactly do you want from me? What do you want me to say? What do you expect me to do? I'm sorry, but I refuse to apologize for being white. I haven't done anything to either of you. I haven't owned slaves or downplayed how black people are treated in society. Stop blaming me and holding me responsible for everything wrong that has been done to black people. You're mad at the world and how white people in the past and present have treated you and other black people. You're taking that anger out on me, but I'm *not* one of those people. The same way how you told me countless times in the past that white people shouldn't judge black people by the few that do wrong, you have to apply those same rules to whites."

"Why should we?" Gabby said. "Most white people assume we're all the same. Why shouldn't we return the favor?"

"Because nothing changes if nothing changes. If neither of us is willing to be different, everything stays the same."

"It's easy for you to say that when the world is so perfect for you," Gabby said.

"You think it's easy for me? You think I don't get dirty looks from other white people who think I'm only with Ben for sexual reasons, or fight with my family that thinks I'm just trying to be difficult and rebellious? I fight for my love for Ben every day. It's not easy for me."

Mrs. Turner was surprisingly quiet and just listened to me and Gabby bicker.

"Believe what you want to believe," I continued. "The only thing you need to know is it doesn't matter how much hell you put me through. I love Ben, and I'm going to marry him one day. I don't have to justify or prove my love to anyone. I'm leaving, and I'm not running away. I don't want to waste my time and energy on this anymore."

I stood and headed to the door.

"I'm coming with you," Simone said.

We walked out of the house, and Mrs. Turner followed.

"Rebecca," she called.

I spun around and faced her.

"I've been looking for this type of fight in you for nine years. I know you love my son, but I'll admit I wasn't always the nicest. I promise I'll make more of a conscious effort to get to know you better."

She reached to shake my hand, and I pulled her into an awkward hug. She smiled and walked inside. This didn't fix anything . . . but at least it was a start.

***

Simone and I had just stepped into my doorway when my cell phone buzzed with an unknown number. I answered the call.

"Hello?"

"May I speak with Rebecca Preston, please?"

"This is she."

"This is Maureen Hofer from Legacy Books Publishing. We're very interested in your book and would like to speak with you about it."

I waved Simone over as I put my phone on speaker and laid it on the coffee table. We started preliminary contract talks for a three-book deal, with *Black and White* being my first published book.

"Do you have time to meet with us on Monday?" Maureen asked.

I could barely keep my excitement in as I answered, "Yes, Monday is perfect."

Maureen gave me all the details for Monday. After the call, I jumped up and down in excitement and cried. For the first time in a long time, I was having a good day.

Monday came. I was quiet and kept my meeting from Ben all weekend. His mind was on his case, and I didn't want to jinx myself and have the deal fall through.

I sat in Maureen's office and discussed all the details about the book with her.

"I love the raw honesty of your story. You didn't hold back. Your characters felt authentic, and I feel that's missing in a lot of books these days," Maureen said.

"Thank you," I said, beaming with joy.

The publishing company wasn't a major one, but its distribution would put my book in all the major bookstores.

"With your following from *Cosmo* and our marketing strategy, I believe this book will be a major success," she said.

We discussed the contract, and I had it faxed to my attorney to look over. Once I got the OK from him to sign it, my dream had come true—my novel was finally going to be published.

I shook hands with Maureen and rushed out the door. I wanted to surprise Ben with the news.

Chapter 23

Ebony

Chasing Demons

"Stop it right there," I yelled.

Rashida and I were chasing a teenage boy down Christopher Street for robbing an elderly woman. The boy easily dipped through pedestrians while Rashida and I were bumping into everyone, trying to maneuver through people without dropping all of the equipment on our gun belts.

The boy got stuck at the corner, where a large group of pedestrians was crossing on one side, and traffic was flowing heavily on the other. That little window of time was all Rashida needed to catch him. She grabbed him by the arm. He threw a punch at her, but she ducked and swept him to the ground. I finally caught up with them and helped cuff him.

"This little punk took a swing at me," Rashida said, out of breath.

"Yo, get off me!" he screamed.

People gathered around and filmed us with their cell phones.

"I saw the whole thing. That kid didn't even do shit. The pigs grabbed him for no reason," a woman yelled.

The crowd cursed at us. None of them knew that this kid just robbed an elderly lady. They just assumed that Rashida and I—the police—were the villains. I held on to the boy and advised the radio dispatcher that we'd made an arrest while Rashida ran to get our patrol car.

"The black cops be worse than the white ones," one person said. "All of them be trying to show out to appease their massas. Y'all should be ashamed yourselves, ruining this kid's record."

I closed my eyes and took a deep breath. These people didn't understand that it wasn't my intention to hurt this kid's future. When I looked at the boy, he favored my deceased twin brother so much. He had the same complexion and brown eyes. He was about the same height that Akeem was at that age too. I missed my brother. Since he'd passed, every day felt like a part of myself was missing. The scene of him dying in Billy's arms replayed in my mind countless times and haunted my dreams.

Rashida came to the corner with the car, and I searched the boy before placing him in the back, ignoring the insults from the crowd gathered around me.

We pulled away and headed to the precinct.

"What's your name, kid?" I asked.

"Fuck you," he said.

"Let's try this again. What's your name, kid?"

"I'm not telling you shit," he replied.

"Well, if you want to sit in the cell all day and night, that's up to you, but if you want to go home eventually, you'll listen to me and answer my questions."

"Faizon Jackson," he said.

"How old are you, Faizon?" I asked.

"Fifteen."

He was only a minor.

"Faizon, why did you rob that old woman?" Rashida asked.

"I was hungry, and she was an easy target," he said.

We pulled up to the precinct, and I brought him to the juvenile room. Lucky for him, because he was still a minor, he wouldn't have to sit in the cells with the older criminals.

"Faizon, what's your mom's name and phone number?" Rashida asked.

"I don't have a mom," he answered flatly.

"OK, what's your dad's, then?"

"I don't have a pops neither."

"Who do you stay with?"

"Right now, I stay with Mrs. Janelle Richards. She's my foster mother."

"All right, what's her information so we can reach out to her?"

He told us the number, and I jotted it down. I called Mrs. Richards and let her know what had happened. She said she was on her way to the precinct, but this was becoming an every-week occurrence with Faizon all over the city.

I couldn't get over how much he reminded me of my brother.

"Faizon, Mrs. Richards told me you've been getting picked up by the cops a lot. Why?" Rashida asked.

"Mrs. Richards is nice and all, but she's broke. She barely has money to feed the two of us, so I gotta do what I need to, to survive."

I sighed. "Where are your parents?" I asked.

"My mom's dead, and I don't know where my father is. My brother and sister . . . We all got split up in foster care."

Rashida saw I was getting emotional. She patted my shoulder.

Faizon brought back his tough-guy demeanor. "So, what are y'all charging me wit'? Y'all takin' me to juvie or what? Let's hurry this up."

"I'm trying to help you—" I said.

"Y'all don't care about me. Nobody does. Even Mrs. Richards is full of shit. She only took me in so she could get money from the state to help her with her bills. You're gonna talk shit and load me up with charges, just like all the other cops do."

"That's not true," I said. "I want to help you. I'm not letting you off completely, but I'm not going to add that you tried to assault Officer Harrell."

Faizon rolled his eyes. "Whoopee."

He was arrogant, but I still felt sorry for the boy.

I looked out the small glass window on the juvenile room's door and saw the elderly woman Faizon robbed walk into the precinct. She moved slowly, looking lost and confused at the front desk. She looked like she was in her midsixties, and her salt-and-pepper hair was pulled back into a long ponytail. Rashida and I left Faizon cuffed in the juvenile room and spoke to the woman.

"Thank you for coming," I said. "I'm Sergeant Williams. Officer Harrell is going to help you from here."

"Ma'am, I'm going to need some information from you for the report," Rashida said. "What's your name?"

"Gina Harris," she said softly.

After Rashida gathered everything she needed to start the report, Mrs. Harris tapped me on my shoulder.

"What would make that boy act like that?" she asked.

I explained his sob story, and through her frail appearance, I saw a gentle, sympathetic expression. She felt pity for him also and changed her story for the report.

"Ma'am, you pointed him out earlier and said he punched you numerous times in your face and snatched your purse," Rashida said.

"I know, but now I'm telling you he didn't. I put my bag down, and he grabbed it and ran."

"Are you sure that's what you want in the report? I still see the bruises on your face," Rashida said.

"I'm fine. That's what happened."

I could've easily had Rashida stick with Mrs. Harris's original story, but I understood what she was doing. She didn't want to see another black kid's record ruined. I had Rashida write up the report the way Mrs. Harris said it went, which changed the incident to only petty larceny and possession of stolen property, the equivalent of shoplifting. Since he was a juvenile, his record would be sealed at eighteen, and it wouldn't show up on his record as an adult.

"Thank you, Sergeant Williams," she said. "I'm glad you understand."

I shook her hand.

"If you need anything, don't hesitate to come back and ask for me."

She patted my hand and slowly walked out of the precinct.

There was some mumbling and grumbling around the precinct about me being too soft on him and coaxing her to change her story, but I didn't care. I knew the victim was changing her story up, but I wanted Faizon to realize that Rashida and I cared and wanted to see him succeed in life, not become another negative black male statistic.

Faizon's foster mother, Mrs. Richards, came to the precinct to pick him up. She was a thin, tan woman with curlers in her hair. Rashida explained everything that happened.

"I'm sorry, Officer," Mrs. Richards said. "I try my best to raise him, but I can't control him. Thank you."

"Don't thank me. Thank the complainant," Rashida said. "She's giving him a second chance. He beat up and robbed an old woman. The sergeant is trying to help him, but you need to figure something out quick. The next cops that arrest him might not be as nice as we are."

"Yes, ma'am. Thank you both. Say thank you, Faizon."

He didn't answer . . . just smirked and nodded. They left the precinct. Rashida and I finished our shift and went home. I hoped we'd sparked a change in that boy's life.

The next morning, I walked into the precinct, and Morgan was at the desk.

"You might want to take a look in the juvenile room," he said.

"Why?"

"You'll see. You're not going to be happy about it."

I walked into the juvenile room, and Faizon was sitting there in handcuffs—again.

"What's up, Sergeant Williams?" he said.

"What are you doing in here?"

"They caught me havin' fun," he laughed.

I walked out of the room, and Morgan explained why Faizon got arrested.

"After Faizon left the precinct yesterday afternoon, he ditched his foster mother and met up with his nineteen-year-old friend Devon," Morgan said. "They found an eleven-year-old girl coming from her after-school program, took her to a vacant house that was being remodeled, and raped her repeatedly."

Shocked, I covered my mouth with my hand.

"The people who lived next door to the house heard screaming and yelling late at night. We sent a patrol car to the building. They saw the locks were broken, searched inside, and caught them in the act. The officers arrested them on the spot."

I snatched the arrest sheet off the front desk. I closed my eyes, upset that the sheet confirmed everything Morgan had just said.

The weight of the guilt was crushing me inside. I tried to save Faizon, but he was too caught up in the enticement of the streets. That eleven-year-old girl's life was forever changed, and it made me question if I would've just had Rashida charge him with the robbery and assault and had him detained at the juvenile hall, would things be different? Was this my fault?

Rashida walked up to me and hugged me. She'd gotten the rundown from some other cops about what happened before she even walked into the precinct.

"Don't hug her," Officer Bateman, one of the cops walking around the front desk, said. "If she didn't give the little hoodlum a free pass, he wouldn't have raped that girl."

"Fuck you, Bateman," Rashida said.

"Don't be mad at me. She may want to hold people's hands, be a social worker, but we're cops. Our job is to keep these scumbags off the streets."

"Guess who's going to stand on a foot post all day and guard the location?" Morgan asked him.

"Oh, come on, Sarge—"

"Nope. You want to disrespect a supervisor, you get what you get. Oh, and it doesn't look like you'll be taking a lunch today either."

"This is bullshit," Bateman said.

"A meal is a privilege, not a right in the police department," Morgan stated. "Next time, come correct, and maybe you won't be hit with this cloud of bad luck coming to you."

I appreciated him defending me, but I wondered if he was right. My chest was heaving. I was fighting back tears.

"Boss, maybe you should sit in your car for a minute. You need a minute to calm your nerves," Rashida said.

There was no way I would cry in front of cops in my precinct. I took her advice and pulled myself together in

my car. I felt like the world was crashing down around
me.

"Have a seat, Williams," Inspector Phillips said.

I sat down and looked around his office. I was in awe every time I saw the numerous pictures of him with former
chiefs, mayors, and other politicians. What grabbed my
attention every time was the framed Friedrich Nietzsche
quote that hung above his black leather chair, which
read: *Beware that, when fighting monsters, you yourself
do not become a monster . . . for when you gaze long
into the abyss. The abyss gazes also into you.*

"That's a deep quote you have up there," I said.

"It is. I read it every day. It always helps to center me
throughout my law enforcement career."

I nodded, understood, and agreed on how the quote
was useful and important in our line of work.

"You know what I like about you, Williams? Your
compassion. You see people and still feel empathy, while
a lot of cops I know become cynical and desensitized.
You don't get pressured or take shit from anyone. You're
a fighter. You weren't made that way. It's who you are.
Don't lose that. Keep being who you are."

"Thank you, sir," I said, wondering why he was telling
me this.

"Now for the criticism. Williams, I heard about the kid
in the juvenile room. I know that after you talked to the
victim, she decided to switch up her story about the assault and robbery. As one of my best sergeants, especially
one that's studying for the lieutenants' test, you know
you're not supposed to do that. You've gone through a
lot these last few months. If this were any other time,
I wouldn't hesitate to give you a command discipline.
Instead, I'm going to give you a warning and admonish."

I nodded. I was getting off lucky. "I appreciate it, sir."

"I understand. Your heart was in the right place, but like the old expression says, 'The road to hell is paved with good intentions.' Stick with the protocol. Save people by educating them about the law. Don't lessen the crimes they committed."

"Yes, sir."

He sighed. "You're staying strong, but after the shooting and that kid in the juvenile room, it's been a lot lately, and it's taking a toll on you. Maybe you should take a few days off to recharge."

I didn't fight his recommendation. "I think that's a good idea, sir."

"Good. You're one of my best supervisors. I want to see you back in full form. Head home. Take the rest of the week off, and if anyone asks who authorized it, tell them it came directly from me."

"Thank you, sir."

He smiled. "It's no problem."

Inspector Phillips was right. I needed to clear my mind and recharge.

Chapter 24

Becky

Surprises

"Hi, I'm Rebecca Preston. I was around the area, and I wanted to surprise my boyfriend, Ben Turner," I said to the woman at the reception desk.

"I didn't know he had a girlfriend. Well, it's nice to meet you, Ms. Preston," she said with a smile. "If he's not expecting you, I have to page him on the intercom and tell him you're here."

"OK."

Why wouldn't Ben tell his coworkers about me?

"Mr. Turner said you could head back to his office. It's the third door on the right."

"Thanks."

I walked past a long row of cubicles, down the hallway toward the offices, but I forgot if she said Ben's was on the right or left. I walked into an office and saw one of his coworkers was also in an interracial relationship. The shelves and credenza were loaded with pictures of him and his African American girlfriend, smiling and enjoying life.

"Becky," Ben said.

"Hey, honey," I said, hugging him.

He pulled me toward his office. When I looked around, I saw no pictures of his family or me. There was nothing that told his clients or coworkers anything about his personal life. His office was bland and generic.

"Your office is bare compared to the lawyer next door."

"Yeah, I don't like my coworkers in my business."

He seemed anxious and fidgety, like he was in a rush for me to leave. Between the receptionist not knowing he had a girlfriend, and he not having any pictures of me around like his coworker did, I was getting emotional and felt hurt.

"Are you ashamed of me, Ben?"

He didn't look me in the eyes. "Of course not. I like to keep my personal life private at work."

"Why do you care what these people think? Maybe if they saw you had a family side, they wouldn't overwork you so much."

"I don't want to argue, babe. I'm under a lot of pressure with this case. I'm crazy busy working on this trial strategy. What's up?"

I was taken aback by his impatience with me. "It feels like you're trying to rush me out of here."

Ben sighed and looked at his watch. "I'm not trying to chase you out, but I have to meet Tim in fifteen minutes."

"You don't have to brush me off."

"Babe, I'm not brushing you off, but I'm not trying to come off as unprofessional in front of the partners."

I was hurt, but I wasn't going to cry there. "All you care about lately is the partners and this fucking case," I yelled.

Ben rubbed his hand across his forehead.

All I wanted to do was share my good news with him, but right now, he wouldn't care about it. I was beginning to wonder if he cared about me at all anymore.

"I just wanted to surprise you . . . but I guess I'll leave, since it's obvious you don't want me here."

"Baby, please. It has nothing to do with you, honest. Things will get better after this case, I promise."

I stomped out of his office and headed to the elevator. Ben didn't chase after me. *That* hurt. I couldn't wait until this stupid case was over so I could have back the man I loved.

Chapter 25

Billy

Alternate Reality

"Yo, this trial is gonna do crazy numbers for my reality show," Johnny said. "This bitch's claims are actually makin' me money. My Instagram and Twitter followers have tripled, and my jersey is the number one sold in the NBA since this all started."

"These sons of bitches are either wearing them or burning them," his agent, Paul, said.

He and Johnny laughed together.

Against my wishes, Francis had asked the judge for permission to allow the trial to be televised. The judge agreed, realizing that this high-priority case could help make a bigger name for himself. Johnny was excited about it. His reality show would use some of the footage filmed at the trial.

"Do you think this is a good idea, requesting that the trial be televised?" I asked Francis.

"Once you win this case, the publicity the firm will get from it is going to be huge," he said. "Relax, you got this."

Francis continued to stroke Johnny's supersized ego while I stepped out of my office to escape that madness. Ben's door was open, and I saw him at his desk, high-lighting things in his law books. He looked focused. Even though his case seemed like an automatic loss, I was worried he could pull out a win.

I guessed he felt me staring at him, because he looked up. I gave him an awkward nod. He waved and looked at me curiously. Luckily, my phone rang and ended our awkward encounter.

"Billy, come to Bellevue Hospital. Your mama got admitted again," Ebony's mom, Mrs. Williams, said.

"What's wrong? Is she OK?"

"Doctors are trying to figure everything out now. I'll tell you more when you get here."

I ended the call and let Francis and Johnny know that I had a family emergency to tend to. I wanted to get away from them, but not like this.

My mom slept while I held her hand and read my case files. She'd come down with the stomach flu, and the doctors believed she had experienced a severe relapse of her MS. I was scared that this was it . . . that this time she might not make it out of the hospital alive. She couldn't even feel when she soiled herself anymore. She didn't feel when they did a rectal exam or have the muscle control to clench her buttocks. I hated seeing my mom suffer. Seeing her lying on that hospital bed, my mind was made up. I was going to win my damn case so she could spend the rest of her life living as peacefully as possible.

Chapter 26

Becky

Let's Go Out

I was at home, lying on our bed, crying when I heard the door open. I didn't bother to look up. Over the years Ben and I had been together, it felt nice knowing that for once, I was in love with a man that loved me back. Ben used to be affectionate with me. He used to wake me up by hugging and kissing on me, but lately, all he did was look at files for his stupid case. He hadn't touched me in weeks. I just wanted to feel desired by him again.

"Baby?" Ben said.

"What? You finally noticed me? I'm amazed you left your fucking office to talk to me."

Ben spooned me, leaning close, his lips grazing my earlobe, and said, "I love you. This case just has me stressing, but everything I do, I do for us. Once this is over, everything will be better."

Ben talked to me with a gentleness that I hadn't felt in the months he'd handled this case.

"I hope so."

"I promise. I don't know when it got to this point, but my home life and social life all started to revolve around my work life. This case has me feeling like I'm drowning."

"Well, fuck your case. Let's go out tonight."

I heard Ben's phone vibrate hard on the table. He picked up the phone and squinted at the screen. I lifted his chin and brought his eyes back to mine.

"Put your phone down. This is *my* time," I said.

"I know, babe. I will. The partners want to know every little detail about everything, though."

"Whenever you have an important case, you get consumed by it, and nothing else matters. Sometimes, I feel like I'm not important to you. It's like I don't exist to you when you get like that."

"I promise, once this is over, things will be different."

His phone rang again. He reached for it and snatched it up quickly to hide who it was, but his caller ID showed it was Gabby.

"Just turn it off," I said.

He did it without complaining.

We enjoyed dinner, and for the first time in a long time, I felt like we were "us" again. We laughed and talked, and I enjoyed being with him. He didn't mention his case or Gabby at all, and that made me very happy.

"So, what's next?" I asked.

"I know how much you love Idris Elba, so I figured we'd see his new movie," Ben said.

"I love it!"

We walked hand in hand into the theater. Ben's eyes were focused on another interracial couple. He nodded at the white guy, and the guy nodded back.

"Who's that?" I asked.

"That's Bill, my competition at work."

"He's cute."

Ben frowned at me.

"Aw, don't be jealous. There's only one man that has my heart . . . Idris Elba."

"What?" Ben said, playfully tickling me.

I tried to hold in my laughing. "If you stop tickling me, I'll let you tickle something else later," I said.

"Is that right? I'm down for that."

I cherished our time together. I just hoped we could keep this going from now on.

Chapter 27

Ebony

Date Night

I came home. Billy was sitting on the couch with his head down.

"Baby, what's wrong?" I asked.

"My mom's in the hospital again. I'm so sick of seeing her in pain."

"I know . . ."

"I'm sorry, babe. I'm always talking about my stress with my mom. How was your day?"

I had so much on my mind, but I didn't think he'd understand my stress unless I explained everything to him in detail. Rather than boring him with a drawn-out conversation, I just said, "It was fine."

Internally, all my drama was raging inside me. I was angry. To this day, I hurt from the fact that my brother was dead. I was sad that two of my officers were killed, and I was too late to save them. I was upset that I couldn't save Faizon and that he raped a little girl. I was angry at the protesters that thought I was a sellout. I was worried that I was going to fail the lieutenants' test that I'd been studying so hard for, and I was angry at the fact that I loved Billy more than anything in this world, yet I was attracted to another man.

I tried to push down my emotions. I tried to be tough and hold all my pain inside, but I couldn't. My lips trembled. I closed my eyes tightly and wrapped my arms around myself. My eyes filled with tears, and I cried from the depths of my soul. Billy looked scared and uncomfortable seeing my breakdown.

"Baby, you don't look fine. Are you OK?"

He held me in his arms as I sobbed in his chest. He rocked with me and kissed my forehead.

Skipping over the part about my growing feelings for Morgan, I told him about everything that bothered me.

"Baby, let's forget about my case. Let's forget all that shit that's bothering you and just go out tonight. When's the last time we had a real date? You know, dinner, movie, and you for my dessert."

I laughed. "Let's do it. I need to take a break from my usual bullshit."

Billy handed his keys to the attendant at the parking lot. The lustful looks that he'd been giving me since dinner told me I was slaying in my black leather outfit as we walked hand in hand to the AMC on Forty-Second Street in Manhattan. We drew the attention of a few people on the street, which rarely was positive.

"Whoa-wee! Goddamn, baby. I know that white boy can't handle all that ass," some random brotha smoking a cigarette with his friends commented as we walked down the street. The brotha and his friends licked their lips, catcalled me, and made all types of loud and obnoxious comments to Billy.

Billy's eyes tightened. I squeezed his hand to signal to let it go and not get involved in a pointless argument. The light turned green, and we were stuck waiting at the crosswalk on the same corner with the rude assholes.

"All I need is one night with her." The man with the cigarette grabbed his crotch. "I'd make her love brothas again."

Billy wrapped his arms around me and pulled me closer to him. While I knew he felt threatened by the men heckling him, a part of me enjoyed seeing Billy protective of me.

I looked in his eyes lovingly. Then I kissed him deeply, giving him the reassurance I knew he needed.

"Oh, I get it. You think you're too good for brothas, huh?"

"I love brothas. I'm just not feeling any of y'all," I said, walking away from that nonsense.

Billy and I were standing in the concession line when I saw Morgan holding hands with a sista with a huge ass. She wore a tight black skirt that clung to her booty and a white shirt that had her cleavage spilling out. He saw me and winked. I winked back at him while Billy's back was turned. I felt guilty. I shouldn't be so attracted to him.

The theater was packed, but we managed to get decent seats close to the middle.

A dark-skinned brotha holding the hand of a pretty blonde walked into the theater and sat a couple of seats down from us. Billy and the brotha nodded at each other.

"You know him?" I whispered.

"Yeah, that's Ben, the guy I've been telling you about at work."

Billy looked annoyed when he continued. "You saw how he strutted in here, holding her hand. He probably only sees her as a 'trophy.' Guys like Ben enjoy showing off their success with a pretty girl on their arm."

"You don't think he views you the same way?" I asked.

"What? No, why would he? He doesn't know me."

"And you don't know him, but you're assuming without actually knowing him. Sorry, but that annoys me, because I feel people judge me like that for being a cop. Maybe Ben loves her just as much as you love me."

"Maybe."

After the movie, Morgan smiled at me as he walked past us with his date. I didn't want to acknowledge him. After our earlier drama, I didn't need Billy seeing me making googly eyes with another guy.

"I'm gonna go to the bathroom before we head out," Billy said.

"OK, I'll be right here."

I stood across from the bathrooms, staring down at my phone, texting with my mom when I felt hands slowly wrap around me. I turned around and saw it was Morgan.

"Hey," I said.

"Hey yourself, sexy."

I held in my smile and asked, "Where's your date?"

"She's in the bathroom. Where's your white boy?"

"He's in the bathroom too. How's your date going?"

"She's fine and all, but she's lame."

I laughed. "Why is she lame?"

"She just doesn't have ambition." Morgan held my hand, stared me in the eyes, and said, "At least not like you."

I blushed and giggled.

Billy cleared his throat and nearly scared me to death. It dawned on me that Morgan was still holding my hand. I quickly dropped it. Billy stood there, sizing Morgan up.

"Baby, who is this?" Billy asked. I could see in his eyes that he was jealous.

I couldn't bring my eyes to his. I felt ashamed of myself for getting caught flirting with another man. I tried to clear the awkwardness.

"This is Morgan St. Clair, my study partner for the lieutenants' test. He's one of the sergeants that works with me at my precinct. I've told you about him."

Morgan extended his hand. "Nice to meet you, Billy."

Billy shook his hand but stared him down. "It looks like you're trying to do more than just study for a test with Ebony."

"Billy!" I yelled.

Morgan waved the comment off. "I'm sorry if things looked inappropriate, but I'm not trying to push up on your lady. My lady is coming out of the bathroom too—see?"

Morgan pointed to his date, who smiled at him and walked over. He introduced us to her, and we all exchanged pleasantries. Then we said our goodbyes and went our separate ways.

Billy was silent on the car ride home.

"You all right?" I asked.

"Say what you want, but that guy wants to fuck you."

"Billy—"

"Nah, I saw how he looked at you. I saw how he held you when he didn't know I was looking. He wants to be more than friends. Apparently, everyone wants to take you away from me."

"Pull over for a second."

"Why?"

"Just pull over."

Billy did as I asked, and I turned and faced him. I looked him squarely in the eyes and said, "Look at me. In our relationship, I'm all in. Do you hear me? No one is going to take me away from you. I'm committed to only you."

He looked back at the road and pulled off.

"C'mon, Billy, I got enough going on," I said. "Are you gonna be salty with me the rest of the night?"

"Nope."

We walked into our bedroom. He was still mad. I knew I had to do anything I could to boost his ego.

"Does this mean you're not going to have me for dessert?"

He smirked at that.

I took off my clothes, unhooked my bra, and shimmied my panties down my legs.

Billy fumbled with his belt, tugged his pants off, and pulled his shirt over his head. He shoved his briefs down his legs, kicking them off to the side.

Billy positioned me to face the mirror on the dresser. He pushed my legs wide apart and rammed his cock inside me. Then he gripped my waist. My breasts bounced and swayed as he plunged deep inside my tightness. The feeling of his strong hands circling my waist as he pulled me possessively against his body drove me wild.

"Yes!" I said breathlessly.

My mind drifted to Morgan. I envisioned his chocolate skin radiating with a sexy glow, him fucking me from behind, hearing the loud slap of his muscular thighs as he pounded me with sensual ferocity.

"Don't stop, Mor—"

My eyes widened. I'd almost slipped and said Morgan's name.

"What?"

"Don't stop . . . More! I want to feel *more* of you."

With each thrust, I felt his anger, his fears, and his frustrations. The speed of his thrusting caused me to come quickly. I screamed.

"Oh God, keep doing that."

My powerful orgasm seized me. My pussy pulsated and clamped down on Billy's cock. His fingers pressed into the sides of my ass, and I felt him spew his come inside me. He pulled out of me, and I faced him. We panted and rested our foreheads on each other.

"I love you, Ebony."

"I love you too."

We held hands and bathed each other in the bathroom, which led to another romp session before we made it to bed.

I opened my eyes.

Billy pulled me into his chest and kissed my forehead. "Hey," he said.

I smiled. "Hey. What are you doing?"

I didn't realize I had drifted off to sleep in his arms.

"Watching you sleep," he said.

I chuckled. "That's so creepy."

He held my hand and said, "I'm sorry I get so jealous. Every time someone makes a stupid-ass negative comment about us, it puts the fear back in my head that I could somehow lose you. Seeing that guy at the movies tonight amplified that fear."

"Baby, my heart is with you. You're not going to lose me."

Billy smiled. He closed his eyes and gradually drifted off to sleep peacefully. I felt terrible for thinking of another man while being intimate with him. I lay in his arms and quietly cried myself back to sleep.

Chapter 28

Bill

Consequences

"Billy, are you even *listening* to me?" Ebony asked.

We were sitting in the living room, eating dinner. Ebony was telling me about her day, but I was bothered by my own stress at work. I hated watching Johnny smile in front of the cameras that followed him around twenty-four-seven and acted like he was a role model, when I knew for a fact that he'd raped that woman.

"I'm sorry, baby. This case is stressing me out," I said.

"I knew something had to be on your mind. You've been spacing out for, like, ten minutes. You worried that guy Ben is going to win his case?"

"Nah, it's not that. I'm sure I can win, but I don't know if I should."

Shit! I didn't mean to say that last part. It slipped out.

"Huh? Why wouldn't you want to win?" Ebony asked.

I sighed. I questioned if I should tell her the truth, but I figured she'd understand.

"Johnny's a dick. He acts like he's from the street, but he lived in the fucking suburbs and went to private schools. He thought because he's into black women that he and I were the same, and admitted to me that he raped the stripper."

Ebony dropped her head and went quiet.

"I can win the case, but I hate knowing that he's guilty."

"What? Are you telling me you *know* he did it?" she asked.

I didn't answer. I stared at the floor, realizing telling her wasn't a good idea after all.

Ebony sighed. "You not saying something speaks volumes, Billy. Wow."

I rubbed my face and tried to find the right words to say.

"Billy, I know this is part of your dream, but is it worth your soul? Here's some food for thought. If he rapes her and gets away with it, do you think he'll stop or keep doing it?"

I didn't answer.

"If he gets away with this, he'll rape more black women, and every time he does, he'll come back to you to help get him off. That girl might not be smart, she might have picked the wrong profession, but she's still a black woman. That could've easily been me in her predicament. What would you say if someone violated me and had a lawyer like you that set him free?"

I reached for her, but she recoiled at my touch.

"Come on, baby," I said. "I'm having a hard time dealing with this as it is. I just need you to understand and give me a little support."

"Well, you're not going to get it from me," Ebony said, turning away from me.

I touched her shoulder. She faced me, and at that moment, it took one look in her eyes to understand what her mouth wouldn't say: she felt betrayed by me.

"From what you told me about Ben, I expected this from him, but not you," she said. "Do you want to know why this hurts me so much? It hurts because you *know* better. You've seen firsthand how white men with power abuse it and prey on black people. You saw my brother lose his life because of a racist monster. You swore you'd be a lawyer to fight against guys like that, but now you're defending one. This whole situation makes me see you in an entirely new light."

I couldn't bring my eyes to hers. I felt ashamed of myself.

"Look, I'm doing this for us," I said. "I'm trying to get my mom into a home that can take care of her full-time, so she's not a burden on your mom and Mrs. Wilson. I'm trying to put the money together so I can marry you and give you the wedding you deserve."

"You ever heard the verse, 'Everything is permissible, but not everything is beneficial'? You should apply that to your life."

"Where is that from?"

"I'm paraphrasing the Bible, 1 Corinthians 10:23, you heathen. You need to keep it in mind when you try to justify your stance on defending that asshole. You know damn well your momma wouldn't want to go to a cushy place knowing what you'd have to do to pay for it, and if it means ruining another black woman's life to get my dream wedding, I don't want it either. I'd rather go to city hall and marry you there, but I don't know if I could do that now that I see you're selling your soul to the devil."

"I'm still gathering all the facts. For all I know, she might've had this shit planned too."

"Stop trying to justify it, Billy. You *know*."

"I don't know for sure," I said.

"Even if you try to convince yourself she's faking it, your conscience is telling you that you're wrong."

"I'm constantly getting flack at work, and when I come home, I don't want to argue about it with you. I don't need this shit right now. Yes, I know he's guilty. Yes, I know morally it's wrong to defend him, but this is my job, and winning this case can open a lot of doors for us when I make partner."

There was nothing left to say. No words could improve this situation.

Ebony stood up.

I reached for her hand, but she recoiled and pulled it back.

"Don't touch me."

"Where are you going?" I asked.

"You need some time to get yourself together, and I need to figure out if I can live with myself being with you after you crucify that poor black woman. Some food for thought for you. Is this case and your career worth losing me? I know how I am, and if you win, you might fool the world, but I'd always know, and I'd blame you like it was your fault. I'd eventually grow to hate you because of it. Would you be OK with that?"

I shook my head.

"I didn't think so."

Ebony walked out the door. I hoped this wasn't the beginning of her walking out of my life.

Chapter 29

Ebony

Deal Breaker

I was speeding, but I didn't know where I was going. I thought about that boy Faizon and that girl he'd raped. I felt powerless then, and I felt powerless now. I couldn't image Billy protecting anyone that would do that to a black woman.

I thought about going to my mom's place but figured if I went there distraught the way I was, she'd only question me, and I wasn't ready to answer the questions I knew she'd ask.

I called Rashida, but she wasn't answering her phone, so I reached out to Morgan. He invited me to his place and answered the door wearing black basketball shorts with no shirt, showing off his sculpted arms and chest. The next thing I knew, I was crying on his couch, telling him everything about Billy and me.

Morgan sat behind me. He massaged and kneaded into my tight shoulders to calm me down.

"Ebony, it's cool. We all go through rough patches," he said.

He kissed a path down my neck and slid his hands down my body. I slowly pulled away from him.

He pulled me closer. I didn't resist. He leaned in to kiss me, but I pulled away slightly, looked up in his face, and said softly, "What are you doing?"

"I want you. I know you want me too. I know you feel our chemistry."

"I can't."

"You can't, or you won't?"

"Both. I love Billy . . . I shouldn't be here right now. I'm too emotional."

"You're right where you need to be," he said. "Fate brought you here for a reason."

I broke out of his embrace, turned away, and headed to the door.

"Where are you going?" he asked.

"I have to get out of here before I make a mistake."

"Who said it would be a mistake?"

"I gotta go. I can't make decisions when I'm in this state of mind."

I walked out of his condo without looking back.

"Well, isn't this a surprise," my mom said.

I gave her a kiss on the cheek. "Hey, Mom."

"What brings you here today? I haven't seen you in at least a month. You barely even sent me a text after you were involved in that arrest with that crazy rapper that killed all those people. You only stop by unexpected like this when something is wrong. So, what's wrong?"

"That's not true, and please, don't ask, Ma."

"Oh, this has to do with you and Billy," she said. "What's going on? Y'all had a fight?"

"Something like that. I just need a place to cool off."

"Well, you know I'm not gonna stop until you talk about it."

I sighed. I knew I shouldn't have come here, but she was right. I knew she wouldn't stop asking me what was wrong until I gave in and told her, and it was true . . . I usually stopped by unexpectedly like this when I had a problem and wanted her advice without actually telling her I wanted it.

"Be honest. Do you sometimes wish Billy were black?" I asked.

"I won't lie. Sometimes, but I love him. What's got you asking that question?"

I told her about my stress with Morgan, and Billy's case. She nodded as she took in every word.

"Baby girl, listen and listen good. Billy loves you. He treats you like a queen, and you've both been bringing out the best in each other since you were kids. When I see the way he looks at you, I think back, and I've never had a man look at me with the same passion I see in his eyes for you. When I was young, I turned down a lot of good men who were going places for your father. Don't get me wrong. The best thing to come out of that relationship was you and your brother, may he rest in peace, but I put off those good men because I was excited and curious about being with a bad boy. The only thing that curiosity got me was him deserting us. Don't let go of something good to chase something that's uncertain."

"I understand that, Mom, but what about Bill representing that rapist?" I asked.

"I can't defend that, but you have to put the shoe on the other foot. With your job, haven't there been times when you had to do things you didn't totally agree with?"

I mostly fought against things I didn't believe in, whether it be in work or life in general, but I could admit there were some times early in my career when I questioned some of the things I was ordered to do.

"I guess—"

"You might not have wanted to do what was asked, but it was your job, right?"

"Yeah, but I never did anything that could ruin someone's life. I have integrity. That woman could've been you or me. That lady's life is forever changed because of that guy who raped her, and now, Billy is going to get him off?"

Mama looked at me with sad eyes.

"Say I stay with him, and he wins this case. My thoughts would always take me back to that woman. I know how I am, and I'd end up hating Billy for it. I love Billy, Mama, but this, to me, is a deal breaker."

"What do you plan on doing?"

"I wanted to stay with you at least until the trial is over so I can think."

"And then what?"

"If he loses, I think he and I can work it out, but if he wins . . . Hopefully, I'm strong enough to end things quickly."

"You know this is always home for you, but I hope you and Billy can get through this."

"Me too, Mama. Me too."

Chapter 30

Bill

Crushing Evidence

"You wanna hear me say it, fine. I fucking raped her, and I'm not sorry about it, either."

I couldn't sleep. I kept thinking about Johnny admitting to me that he raped Sophia. I rolled over on my back and stared up at the ceiling.

Ebony walked into the bedroom. I sat up against the headboard.

"What's the matter? You can't sleep?" she asked.

"No."

"That's your conscience eating you."

She opened drawers and started packing clothes.

"What are you doing? Where are you going?" I asked.

"I'm staying with my mom until I figure out where our relationship is going."

"Ebony—"

"No, Billy. I can't stay here and sleep next to you every night knowing that you're working hard to defend a rapist."

"Are you leaving me?"

"I don't know. I have too much shit going on right now. Once your case is over, we'll talk."

"That's a month away," I said.

"We're not broken up. We'll still see each other and speak every day, but I can't stay here with you."

"Who are you staying with, again?"

"My mom."

"Shit, she knows?"

"She's rooting for us to stay together."

"Are you rooting for that too?"

"Of course, I am, but it all depends on how your case turns out. How long did you know he was guilty? How long have you kept this from me?"

I poured all of my feelings of regret into my gaze. "Baby, I didn't know—"

"Don't bullshit me. How long, Billy?"

"About a month. Look, I'm not sure—"

"Stop. Just stop." Ebony shook her head. "You're going to try to manipulate the jury by using technicalities to make her look bad to disguise the truth that he raped that black woman. You *need* to lose sleep over that."

She finished packing her bag and left me to my thoughts again.

"It's good to see y'all could make it," Jerrod, the strip club owner, said.

We exchanged pleasantries.

"You said you had something to show us," Francis replied, cutting straight to the chase.

"Yeah, follow me. The bitch's head was getting too big. I told her dumb ass to stop fuckin' around," Jerrod said.

My phone buzzed. I glance at it quickly. It was a call from Ebony's mom, Mrs. Williams. I sent it to voicemail.

He took us to his office, which had close to thirty high-definition cameras on the two huge screens mounted on his wall. He walked over to the DVR behind his desk and pulled up the search bar on the screen. Then he typed in a date, and the screen showed Sophia going down on a white man in the VIP room.

"Look at the date. Sophia is still fucking people. Don't get me wrong. I love the attention she's bringing. It's drawing more people to my club, but I don't need her skanky ass bringing the heat back on my business. Once the jury realizes that she's lying and the media attention dies down, I want the cops to know I did everything to cooperate with you and tried to stop her. That police raid two years ago almost ended things for me. I can't have that shit again."

"You're doing the right thing." Francis smiled. He faced me. "With this video, we got this case in the bag."

My phone buzzed again.

"You need to get that, Bill?" Francis asked.

"Sorry, I'll be quick." I smiled.

"Mrs. Williams, I'm a little busy right now," I answered. "I got to call you—"

"Billy, your momma's gone," she said.

"What?"

"I'm sorry, baby. She just passed a few minutes ago."

I dropped my phone. My hands trembled. I felt the tears welling up in my eyes. I never wanted my mom to die alone. I knew Mrs. Wilson and Mrs. Williams were taking care of her, but I felt like I should've been there. I was so close to winning this case, getting the partnership, and moving her to get better care . . . but I was too late.

Chapter 31

Ebony

Drama Build-up

"Momma, what's up? I'm working," I said.

Rashida and I had just broken up a big street fight between a group of teenagers. Now we were driving to a domestic incident.

"Billy's mom died."

That stopped me in my tracks.

"What?"

"She passed a few minutes ago while I was reading to her at the hospital."

I signaled to Rashida to pull over. "Does Billy know yet?" I asked.

"Yeah, I told him. Ebony, I know you two are going through something, but he needs you right now. Put your fighting aside and be there for your man."

"I will, Momma, but I'm not moving back in with him yet. Not until this case is over."

"I understand, but worry about all of that later."

She encouraged me to work things out some more before we ended the call. I finished up things at work and left early. I needed to comfort my man.

***

"Billy?" I called, taking my shoes off at I entered our place. My feet were killing me, and I'd been sitting in traffic for the past two hours.

He didn't answer, but I was sure he was home because his Range Rover was parked outside. I got a text from Morgan.

Morgan: Where'd you go? Are we still studying tonight?

Me: Billy's mom died. I had to go home.

Morgan: Is that a no? I wanted to drill you tonight.

I shook my head. I bet he did. He sent another text immediately after.

Morgan: Our test is two weeks away. We got to stay focused. Plus, I want to see you.

Me: You see me every day.

Morgan: I want you to myself.

He was getting too blunt. I cut the conversation short.

Me: I gotta go. Talk to you later.

I walked into our living room, feeling guilty. Billy was sitting on the couch holding his face in his hands.

"I heard about your mom. I'm sorry."

His lips trembled. He cried hysterically, and I held him in my arms.

Seeing Billy weeping made me feel like an asshole for the way I'd been treating him. I was mostly taking my anger out on him, but the truth was, I had other issues going on that his situation only amplified.

"Are you here to stay?" he asked.

"Billy, I love you, and I'm going to be here for you, but nothing's changed. I'm not coming home yet."

"Why?"

I wanted to ask him how his case was going defending a rapist, but I knew that would only lead to an argument. He was stressed as it was, so I just dropped it.

"I don't want to fight with you. Let's just get through this, and we'll work on 'us' later."

"If you're with me out of pity, don't worry about it. I'll be fine."

"You know it's not out of pity. I loved your mama as much as you love mine."

"I'm sorry . . . for everything. I can't lose you too."

I didn't respond. I held him, and we cried together. I questioned if I could really let him go if he won his case.

The firm paid for a decent flower arrangement to give off the façade that they gave a shit about Billy's mom passing, but during the week he took off to get her funeral arrangements in order, all the partners did was call him to make sure his head was still in the game for the case. They didn't care that he was in mourning. They wanted to make sure the firm looked good and won the case.

I stayed by his side the whole time, but I didn't stay overnight at our home. When he wasn't organizing things for the funeral, he would help me study for my test. We joked and laughed, and it felt so comfortable, but every time I saw him prepping for his case or talking on the phone with one of the partners, it brought me back to reality and pissed me off all over again. I studied with Morgan often, but I kept our study sessions at the academy. I didn't trust myself to be alone with him while I was vulnerable.

The test was finally here. I looked at the test packet and pencil in front of me. I stared at all the other sergeants in the classroom, and they seemed confident, but doubt was creeping into my mind. I kept feeling like I wasn't ready. I closed my eyes, and the thoughts of my cops being murdered, protestors' negative comments toward me, the guilt of not putting Faizon in juvenile detention, and my budding feelings for Morgan flooded my mind. I thought about Billy and how we used to study together as kids, and even though his momma passed, he still took the time to help me study and get ready for this. That memory gave me the strength and motivation I needed. I opened my eyes and opened my test.

I was ready.

Chapter 32

Billy

Lights, Camera, Drama

The day was finally here. CNN, the E! channel, and local stations were in the courtroom ready to film the case.

"All rise," the bailiff called.

The courtroom was packed. Cameras flashed as Judge Norris quickly walked into the courtroom through a side door. He sat down and instructed everyone to be seated.

"Please introduce yourselves to the court," Judge Norris said.

"Bronx County District Attorney Anthony Rodriguez and Assistant District Attorney Kenneth Ellis for the City of New York."

Francis and I stood. "William O'Neil and Francis Lincoln of Wayne, Rothstein, and Lincoln," Francis said.

It felt uncomfortable having a television crew filming the trial. I tried to ignore the cameras and focus on the task at hand.

The jury had seven women and five men. Eight of the jury were black—six of whom were women—one female Hispanic, two black males, one Asian male, and two white men.

Francis explained to Johnny that the first few days of the trial would be the hardest, but we had everything under control.

One by one, the DA had four dancers from the strip club go up on the witness stand to testify on Sophia's behalf, explaining how distraught she was that night.

I observed the DA's strategy and saw the direction he was going, but with no DNA evidence, he didn't have a leg to stand on. The only things he had in his favor were the video and Sophia's testimony.

"Court is adjourned for today and will resume at nine a.m. tomorrow morning," Judge Norris said. The courtroom was buzzing, and the television cameras were taking in everyone's reactions. Johnny didn't seem to give a shit about the women's testimonies. He was more concerned about if he looked "hot" for the cameras. I left it to his entourage to assure him that he did.

Chapter 33

Ebony

True Colors

"Congratulations, boss lady," Rashida said.

After Rashida and I had hit the mall for some much-needed therapeutic shopping, we stopped by my townhouse. I checked the mail while Rashida sat in the living room and turned on the TV. I saw that I had a letter from the police department. I held the letter with teary eyes and trembling hands and read that I'd passed the lieutenants' test. I jumped up and down with Rashida and pumped my fists in the air, elated that I was one step along in my goal of climbing the ranks. I wanted to call Billy and share the good news with him, like I'd always done . . . until I saw his case on TV. Seeing Billy's client slumped in his chair, unmoved by the women's testimonies, made my happiness wane.

My phone buzzed with a call from Morgan. I turned my phone away from Rashida so she wouldn't see who it was and lecture me.

"I'm gonna head out. Osborne just texted me, and she wants to come over for some servicing," Rashida said.

I laughed, rolled my eyes, and waved, then answered the phone.

"What's up? Did you get your results today?" Morgan asked.

"Yup. I got 97 percent. What did you get?"

"I got an 86. We should celebrate."

"What did you have in mind?"

"Come to my place, and I'll show you."

"Morgan, I'm still with Billy—"

"I know," he said. "I'm not going to push up on you, trust me. We'll just hang out. I'll order us dinner, and we'll have a good time."

I knew I shouldn't, but somehow, Morgan convinced me to come over.

We sat on his couch, ate Chinese food, drank wine, and laughed about the latest precinct dramas. I wasn't drunk, but I knew I was reaching my limit. Morgan moved closer to me and wrapped his arms around me. I tried to avert my eyes from his hard-on that was poking through his black jeans. He grabbed my hand and placed it on his cock.

"Do you see what you do to me?" he said.

I moved my hand, but I couldn't help noticing that he was huge. "What the fuck, Morgan? You know I have a man," I said.

"I know, but I thought maybe you'd want to try something better."

I shook my head and glared at him. I felt stupid. I knew this was coming, and I didn't listen to my gut.

"Say we did fuck, what happens afterward? Are we going to start a relationship?" I asked.

"I'm not the relationship type, but we'd be friendly."

I shook my head again. I heard my mother's words in my head. *"Don't let go of something good to chase something that's uncertain."* Morgan had played with my head to get me to let my guard down. He used my deeply hidden insecurity about being with Billy against me to make me vulnerable enough where he felt comfortable to try to get me in his bed.

"I'm not going to be another woman you brag about fucking in our precinct," I said.

He held my hand and looked me in the eyes. "I haven't fucked anyone in the precinct."

I snatched my hand from him. "Gossip says otherwise."

"Well, your gossip is misinformed. There are rumors and shit about me, but they're all bullshit. I'm feeling *you*. I want you, Ebony."

"But you don't want a relationship with me."

"I don't like labels."

"And I don't like liars."

Morgan rubbed his hand down his face, visibly frustrated. "Spend the night with me. We'll never know what it can blossom into."

The feelings I thought I had for him were quickly evaporating. I realized he was just persistent with me because I was a challenge. This was all a game to him.

I got up and walked to the door. "All you want to do is fuck me. You don't give a shit about me," I said.

Morgan threw up his hands. "You're staying faithful to a fucking white boy who defends men who rape black women, but you're judging *me?* Get the fuck out. I wasted enough time on you, fucking tease."

I finally saw the true side of him. Before this conversation, he was always gentle and patient with me, and now he was kicking me out of his condo.

I walked out, my head down as I strolled to my car, sat inside, and wept. For months, I'd been fantasizing over Morgan, believing he was a decent brotha—but he wasn't shit. He was just another manipulative asshole that wanted to prey on me. I needed Billy. I wanted to make love to the only man in my life that cared about me, and secretly apologize to him for the thoughts he would never know about or understand. Instead, I thought about his case, drove to my mom's, and went straight to my old room to think. Then I texted Rashida and filled her in on the drama.

Me: Sorry if I'm interrupting your romp.

Rashida: It's cool. After I had serviced her something proper, I kicked her out. Back to you. I told you he was a playa. I knew he wasn't shit.

Me: Well, I have to work with this asshole now.

Rashida: Word around the precinct is he might be a daddy soon.

Reading that shit, I had to call her. I couldn't discuss that over text.

"Hello," Rashida said.

"You lyin'."

"Nope. She's been throwing up all week. I thought she just had the flu, but during our brief pillow talk, Osborne told me what was going down."

"You're sure? Suzan Gibbs? The white girl?" I asked.

"Yup. Apparently, they've been hooking up on the low."

"Isn't she married?"

"Uh-huh. Osborne said Gibbs took a couple of pregnancy tests and told some of the girls in the locker room that if she's pregnant, she's keeping it. I think she's scheduled to see her doctor tomorrow to find out if it's official."

All this time, Morgan had made me believe I wasn't true to myself or my people by dating someone white, and his ass was fucking a white girl. I felt so stupid. I was smarter than that. What should've been a good day for me had turned out to be a nightmare.

"Where the fuck is St. Clair?" Officer Gibbs's husband asked.

He was tall and muscular. His face was fire-truck red, and he had veins popping out of his neck and bald head.

Officers Mendez and Mahoney tried to calm him down, but he kept calling for Morgan.

"Tell St. Clair to come down and face me like a man. He needs to stop hiding behind these cops like a bitch."

Rashida and I stood by the desk and enjoyed the show. Morgan was upstairs in the locker room.

When we came in this morning, we didn't acknowledge each other. I was fine with that. This morning, Gibbs walked into the precinct and confirmed that she was pregnant and keeping it.

"Morgan, we need to talk," Gibbs said.

Her green eyes were red-rimmed. It looked like she was stressed out.

Morgan and I both walked behind the front desk to sign in for the day. He waved her off.

"Go on, girl. I just walked in the door. I don't got time for your shit right now," he said.

I pretended to check the attendance sheet so I could eavesdrop on their conversation.

"You know I always wanted children," Gibbs said. "Mike has a fertility problem. This is my only chance."

"That's not my fucking problem. Stop talking to me about this shit. The kid could be anyone's."

"Really? You fuck me, and after you got what you wanted, you treat me like this?"

He stormed around the desk, grabbed her by the arm, and took her into the juvenile room. Everyone else in earshot and I ran to the juvenile room to try to listen to their yelling through the door.

"Mike is unemployed," she said. "Between your salary and mine, we could have a good family life."

"You're not grasping the type of relationship we had," Morgan said. "Fuck buddies don't start families together. You need to take care of your problem and get out of my face with that bullshit."

"No. You're not going to treat me like some fucking thot. I'm *keeping* this baby. Regardless of whether you're with me, you're going to *pay* to take care of it."

"We'll see about that after the paternity test."

"You're a fucking asshole. Mike is on his way here right now."

"For what?"

"What do you think?"

"Fuck that. I'm not losing my job over you."

Morgan opened the door. Everyone scattered and tried to act busy, but Rashida and I didn't.

He held the elevator open before going up, looked at me, and said, "If anyone asks, I'm changing into my uniform."

I rolled my eyes. Two minutes later, Gibbs's husband stormed in ready to beat his ass.

"That motherfucker knocked up my wife. I'm going to kill him," Mike said.

Officers and other supervisors were texting Morgan not to come down. Inspector Phillips walked off the elevator.

"Mendez, Mahoney, get him out of here now," the inspector ordered.

"Yes, sir," they said in unison.

"Sir, if we see you around this precinct again, you *will* be arrested," Phillips told him.

"Come on, buddy. Let's go," Mahoney said, taking Mike by the arm.

The inspector looked at me and said, "Have St. Clair and Gibbs come to my office—immediately."

"Yes, sir."

Rashida messaged both of them for me. I watched them enter the office and wondered what was in store for them.

Inspector Phillips had both Morgan and Gibbs transferred to different precincts. I watched as Morgan cleared out his locker, walked to the parking lot, and loaded everything into his car to take to his new precinct. We stared at each other. Then I walked back inside the precinct, glad that I hadn't become another conquest for him.

Chapter 34

Billy

Villain

I was lonely, sitting in my living room, flipping through channels. *The Dark Knight* was on HBO, so I settled on that. One line that the character Harvey Dent said kept eating at my already-destroyed conscience: *"You either die a hero or live long enough to see yourself become the villain."* I felt like a villain. The moment I stepped in that courtroom and defended that fucking rapist, I felt like a failure.

I hadn't heard from Ebony today. I felt empty. I didn't have the responsibility of taking care of my mom to help get my mind off Ebony not being here anymore. The movie quote kept echoing in my head. I felt like everything I was fighting for didn't matter anymore. My mom was dead, so I didn't need money to take care of her now. Ebony was still giving me the cold shoulder. Winning this case and making partner didn't mean shit if I wasn't going to marry Ebony. I felt lost.

The next morning, the trial resumed. The cameras were set up and ready to film Sophia's testimony.

Sophia walked up to the witness stand and took the oath. She was wearing a tight tan business suit that clung to her chest, hips, and ass. She wore a white blouse that had her cleavage spilling out.

"Ms. Winters, I know it's uncomfortable, but could you please tell us what happened during your encounter with Mr. Alfieri?" the DA said.

Sophia took a deep breath as she prepared herself to relive the whole ordeal from beginning to end.

Johnny slouched in his chair, deliberately displaying how unmoved he was by her testimony with his nonchalant attitude. Tears streamed down her face. She wiped her tears with the back of her hand and took a deep breath, attempting to pull herself together as the memory faded.

I turned to face Johnny. I watched as he licked his lips and swallowed hard at her testimony. The bastard looked like he was getting off hearing her recap the experience.

Sophia continued, lost in her story. When she was finished, many of the jurors were wiping away tears and frowning at Johnny.

"I have no further questions, Your Honor," the DA said.

I stood up to cross-examine Sophia, handing her a tissue for her tears. Sophia dabbed her eyes. She smiled and said, "Thank you."

"It's no problem," I said, smiling back.

I started off aggressive because I wanted to make her slip up.

"Ms. Winters, you work at J's Gentlemen's Quarters, is that correct?" I asked.

"Yeah."

"What kind of business is that?"

"It's a gentlemen's club."

"Is it safe to say another name for a gentlemen's club would be a strip club?"

She hesitated. "Uh . . . I guess some people would call it that."

"And what's your occupation there?"

"I'm a dancer."

"When you are dancing, are you usually naked?"

". . . Yes."

"Is it safe to say, you are an erotic dancer?"

". . . Yes."

"Would another term for an erotic dancer be considered a stripper?"

"Objection, Your Honor. He's leading the witness."

"Overruled. Ms. Winters, please answer the question."

Sophia sighed. "Yes. Another name for an erotic dancer would be a stripper."

"Was business good for you before the incident with Mr. Alfieri?"

"It was OK, I guess. I was getting by."

"How has business been going recently?"

She looked like she was trying to pick her words carefully. "It's been steady," she said.

"Is it true that since you made the accusations against my client, business has more than tripled for you?"

"Objection!" the DA said.

"I'll withdraw and rephrase the question," I said. "Ms. Winters, has your career been prosperous since this case began?"

"Yes, but—"

"Is it safe to believe that you're using this case to propel your career, that you're risking the reputation, livelihood, and freedom of my client with your allegations for your own benefit?"

"No—"

"Isn't it true that you've been made the headliner of the club and have been receiving more requests than ever to meet clients in the VIP section?"

"Yeah, I have, but—"

I walked near the jury box when I said, "Ms. Winters, answer this question truthfully, and remember, you're under oath. Have you engaged in sexual activity with customers at the strip club after your allegations against my client?"

Sophia slowly nodded. Her lips began to tremble. "Yes."

Everyone in the courtroom was whispering and shaking their heads.

"Ms. Winters, do you enjoy sex?" I asked.

"Wh-what?" she replied, fidgeting in her chair.

"Do you enjoy having sex with a charming, handsome man?"

"Objection," the DA said. "These comments and claims are irrelevant to these proceedings, Your Honor."

"Your Honor, the question is leading to the motive of the complainant," I said.

"Overruled. Ms. Winters, please answer the question," the judge stated.

"Yeah, I enjoy sex," Sophia said softly.

"Did you engage in sexual intimacy with Mr. Alfieri on May third?"

"You know I did."

"Did you enjoy the intimacy?"

"No, I didn't."

"When Mr. Alfieri paid you for your time with him in the VIP room, what did you do with the money he left you?"

She shook her head. Tears formed in her eyes. "I took it," she said, a little above a whisper.

"I'm sorry, Ms. Winters, what did you say?"

"I said I kept the money."

"Uh-huh. Isn't it true that Mr. Alfieri informed you that he was a famous basketball player?"

"Yes."

"Isn't it true that you didn't agree to go to the VIP room with him until *after* he informed you of his profession?"

"Yes, but—"

Tears were freely flowing from her eyes now. She was stammering and flustered. I knew I needed to keep throwing questions at her to trip her up.

"Isn't it true that you willingly took off your clothes when you first entered that room?"

"Yes."

"And knew that there were cameras in the VIP room?"

"I did know about the cameras, and I did take off my clothes, but—"

"Did you not encourage him during the sex to ejaculate inside of you?"

"I did."

"You enjoyed sex with him, didn't you?"

"I did—No! I mean, I didn't."

Sophia shook her head and looked desperately to the jury. "I swear to God, I didn't enjoy it," she said.

I knew the damage was done. The jury was already giving her halfhearted looks.

"Ms. Winters, have you ever been arrested?"

"Yeah," she said, her voice shaky.

"What charges have you been arrested for in the past?"

She was hesitant and looked fearfully at the district attorney.

"I'll repeat the question. Ms. Winters, *what* have you been arrested for in the past?"

Sophia shook her head but didn't answer.

"Will the witness please answer the question," the judge said.

"Prostitution and soliciting prostitution," Sophia responded shamefully. She dropped her head. She looked defeated.

I cleared my throat and asked, "How many times have you been arrested for those charges?

"Four times."

The jury and crowd talked amongst themselves. The judge banged her gavel to gain order.

"Weren't you arrested two years ago for prostitution?"

"Yes."

"Be honest. You knew claiming that a major NBA star raping you would gain you a lot of press and boost your popularity in your career, right?"

"No . . ."

"This man's career and life are on the line—"

"That man raped me. Yeah, I've fucked some guys at the club after I made the charges, but I relapsed because I felt that was all I was good for. He ruined me."

Sophia wailed and broke down on the stand, sobbing while holding her face in her hands.

"We'll take a fifteen-minute recess," the judge announced.

Francis was smiling and laughing with Johnny and his crew. Sophia was sitting with the DA trying to pull herself together. I felt like an asshole. I stood up and rushed toward the men's room.

Quickly, I walked inside and threw tap water on my face, then stared and cursed at my reflection. How could I do that to that woman? She'd poured her heart out to that jury, and I made her look like she was nothing more than a whore, when I knew for a fact Johnny had raped her and enjoyed it. What type of man was I becoming?

Francis strolled into the bathroom and walked up to the urinal. "You had that girl on the ropes." He laughed while pissing. "I loved how you played on her last arrest. It left her speechless. I think the jury sees now that she's just a money-grubbing whore that's looking for her ten seconds of fame." He walked to the sink and washed his hands.

I held on to the sink and continued to look at my disgusted expression in the mirror.

"He's guilty," I said. "I know he's guilty. He told me he raped her, and he doesn't give a shit about it. This isn't like other cases where my clients were just using a loophole in the system, or I had an idea they might be guilty but didn't know for sure. I know the truth, and he raped that girl."

"Calm down, Bill," he said. "You're getting yourself all worked up over nothing. So what if he's guilty? You're a lawyer. It's never been about if our clients are right or wrong, lying or telling the truth. The truth is not as important as what you can persuade the jury to believe, and the secret to disguising a lie to the jury is to mirror it with the truth."

His response was emotionless and detached.

"How can I defend that man knowing the truth?" I asked.

"Are you fucking kidding me right now?" Francis said. "Are you *really* asking that question? This is your fucking job—that's how. You don't sound like partner material right now, and the way you're acting under pressure, you're making me question if you're competent enough to continue working at this firm in general. Suck it up and man up, because we're expecting you to win this case for the firm."

I squeezed my eyes shut and took a deep breath. "I went into law to do the right thing and defend those who really needed it."

"Oh, spare me the bullshit. It's one thing to lie to me, but if you believe in the lie you're telling yourself and can't see it's a lie, that's a damn shame, and you're delusional. You want to be some fucking hero? Quit the firm and become a public defender. Go ahead and help all the little niggers and spics with their legal problems and make crumbs for a living. Be my guest. You work for a major law firm for a reason: to make money. Don't act all self-righteous now because this case hit a sore spot with you and you developed a conscience. Now, pull yourself together, put a smile on your face, march in that courtroom, and do your fucking job."

I walked out of the bathroom, feeling like a villain.

"The defense would like to call Mr. Jerrod Jefferson to the stand," I said.

Jerrod walked to the witness stand and was sworn in.

"Mr. Jefferson, were you working on the night in question?" I asked.

"Yeah, I was there."

"Do you remember seeing Ms. Winters that night?"

"Yeah, she was working."

"After the incident, how was Ms. Winters's behavior?"

"She wasn't happy, but most women aren't after fucking guys for money."

The courtroom laughed.

"Order!" the judge said, banging her gavel. "Mr. Jefferson, refrain from using that language in my courtroom or you'll be placed in contempt."

"Sorry. She wasn't happy," Jerrod said.

"Did she seem sad or distraught?" I asked.

"If she was, she got over it quickly, because she was giving lap dances later that night."

"Why did you decide to place cameras all around your business?"

"To try to stop these bit—girls from sleeping with the customers."

"Other than the night in question, do you know if Ms. Winters slept with customers after her allegations against my client?"

"Objection, Your Honor," the DA protested.

"Your Honor, again, this shows motive," I said.

"Overruled," the judge stated.

"Yup, she slept with close to ten guys afterward. I'm not trying to get in trouble for her bull . . . actions, so I made sure to document it and report it."

Tears streamed down Sophia's face. I knew her will was broken.

"I have no further questions, Your Honor," I said.

The DA cross-examined.

"Mr. Jefferson, two years ago, was your business raided?" he asked.

"Yeah."

"Were arrests made in this raid?"

"You know there was. What's your point?"

"Were you included in those arrests on that date?"

"Yes."

"So, it's safe to say you knew then about the sexual acts being performed in your club the same way you do now."

"No, I'm trying to put an end to it by documenting and talking to y'all now," Jerrod said. "I want to run a legit business."

"So why not fire her if she is going against your club policy? Isn't it true that you are still benefiting from her sleeping with clients?"

"She's a decent worker, and in my business, that's hard to find. I've given her warnings, and I videotape every inch of my club, so you can see I get no money from her sleeping with these guys."

The DA was reaching. He had nothing, but he had to show he was still fighting.

Chapter 35

Bill

The Last Straw

We were back at the firm. I stood up from the conference table, looked out of the window, and watched Johnny's camera crew finishing loading their equipment in the trucks. Francis, Johnny, and his entourage were seated at the conference table, laughing and celebrating as if the case were already won. However, I didn't celebrate victories until the win was official.

"Tomorrow, we'll put Johnny on the stand to testify, and that'll put the nail in the coffin for her. Bill crushed her today," Francis said to Johnny's agent.

"I don't think we should put him on the stand," I told Francis. I didn't give a shit that Johnny, his agent, and publicist were in the conference room when I said it. They all needed to hear the truth. I glared at Johnny, and I didn't give a shit that he saw it. I'd never pretended to like him.

"I don't like the way your boy looks at me," Johnny said.

Francis patted him on the shoulder. "Don't mind him. He just has his game face on. Let's hear him out." Francis faced me and asked, "Why not?"

"His cockiness is going to be his downfall," I said. "Just looking at the jury's faces when they see him at the defense table, I already know they're not fond of him. All it takes is for Johnny to slip up and say one bad thing, and it will undo everything we did today. There's nothing more we need to do. We gave the jury enough to get the verdict."

"You worry too much," Francis said. "Once we tell the jury about all of his community service and charity work, they'll be eating out of his hand."

Francis went back to laughing with Johnny's people, explaining how they wanted the commercial of Johnny surrounded by minority children on heavy rotation.

Johnny stepped to me. He grabbed me by the forearm, leaned close to my ear so only I could hear him, and whispered, "After I beat this case, maybe I'll pay *your* girl a visit. I'll give her the same treatment I gave this bitch."

I lost my temper and punched him in the jaw. "Fuck you, you son of a bitch," I shouted.

Francis's eyes grew wide with shock. He rushed toward me, jabbed his index finger in my chest, and said, "Are you fucking crazy? What the hell is the matter with you? You never assault a client."

Francis turned to Johnny, who was still holding his jaw. "Are you all right, Mr. Alfieri? I apologize for this—"

"He's fucking done," Johnny said. "I want him gone. There's no way he's representing me anymore."

Francis stuttered and stammered. "That's no problem, sir. We'll find you another attorney right away, Mr. Alfieri."

Francis stomped over to me and yelled loud enough so Johnny could hear, "Clear out your fucking office. You're fired. You better hope and pray you didn't ruin everything and I can convince him to stick with our firm."

Francis turned to Johnny. "Again, I'm so sorry about this. Do you want to press charges?"

"Nah, fuck him. I don't need this shit leaking out that he sucker-punched me. It'll hurt my reputation."

Francis turned back to me. "You're lucky he's not asking to have you fucking arrested. He ought to sue your ass for assault. Get out of my fucking sight."

The eavesdroppers around the office scattered and acted busy as I opened the door of the conference room and stormed toward my office. I heard the other associates whispering and laughing at their desks. Mrs. Wilson rushed toward me.

"Billy, what happened? Why are you so mad?" she asked.

"Walk with me to my office while we talk."

She nodded.

"I found out that scumbag I was defending really *did* rape that girl. When he said after I win the case and clear him, he'd visit Ebony and give her the 'same treatment' he gave the stripper, I lost it and punched him in the face."

Mrs. Wilson covered her mouth in shock, her eyes teary, and hugged me. "I'm so sorry, Billy. The bastard got what he deserved, but what are you going to do now?"

"I don't know. I'll figure something out, but don't hang around me. Go back to your desk. I don't want the partners to take their aggravation for me out on you. I'm going to pack up my things."

She nodded, kissed me on the cheek, and headed back to her desk. Ben stepped out of his office and stared at me.

"Good luck to you," I said. "I'm no longer in the running for partner."

I didn't have the energy to answer his questions or watch him gloat. I kept it moving, grabbed some boxes, and got started on clearing my office. I looked at the ring I'd bought for Ebony and cursed everything I'd lost while handling this case. Now that this case was over, I hoped I could get my woman back.

Chapter 36

Ben

Understanding

Mark opened my office door and walked in without knocking. "Did you hear about your boy Billy's meltdown?" he asked.

"What?"

"Billy punched his basketball star client in the face in front of his agent and Francis."

"You got to be kidding me," I said.

"Nope. Francis fired him on the spot," Mark said. "Billy is in his office right now, clearing out his things. I just got assigned the Alfieri case. I've been following it. He had this case won already. Between me winning all the cases I got from you and inheriting this gem of a case from him, you guys are making me look like a superstar."

The bastard couldn't even try to mask the happiness in his voice. I gave him a very noticeable frown, which made him laugh.

"Look, do me a favor. Your case sounds like a dead end. Don't go punching your client in the face now. I have a good winning streak going on, and I don't want to ruin it. Later." He laughed, walked out of my office, and didn't bother shutting my door.

I walked out of my office to, to confirm with other people if the gossip he told me were true. Mrs. Wilson was in the hallway, shaking her head in tears as she released Billy from a hug. Billy looked at me and said, "Good luck to you. I'm no longer in the running for partner."

He went to his office and started packing up boxes with his belongings.

"What's going on?" I asked Mrs. Wilson.

She wiped her tears with the back of her hand.

"Bill just got fired by the firm. That basketball player he was representing said something sick about doing the same thing he did to that stripper to Billy's girlfriend Ebony, and Billy punched him."

I was in shock. I couldn't believe Alfieri would say something like that, and after everything Billy had gone through the last couple of months with this case, prepping for this case and the death of his mom, I was surprised he'd react that way and lose his job.

While his firing increased the odds of me getting the partnership, I still felt sorry for him.

"Mrs. Wilson?"

"Yes, Mr. Turner," she said, dabbing her eyes with a tissue.

"If you don't mind me asking, why are you so close with Bill? I see you guys chatting every morning, and you're emotional about his firing. What's that about?"

She gave a soft laugh. "Billy is like a son to me. I've known him since he was a little boy. He grew up in my neighborhood and went to school with my oldest son. They're still best friends to this day."

I'd heard her in passing have conversations about her neighborhood and knew she lived in Queensbridge. I knew there were next to no white people that lived in those developments, so I had to reconfirm what she was saying.

"Bill lived in Queensbridge?" I asked.

"Yes. His mom still lived there. He visited almost every day." Mrs. Wilson smiled at me.

"I know you probably thought he was some privileged white man that thought minorities were beneath him, but he's not. Billy is a good guy. I've watched him grow up, and he never changed. Once he finished law school and won a decent number of cases, I convinced Mr. Rothstein to consider him for the firm. He was impressed and took Billy in."

"You got him his job here?"

"Yes. I've been here for years, and let's just say . . . The partners owed me one."

It all made sense now. I thought about her comment and felt like shit. She was right. I did to Bill what I assumed white people did to me: I assumed the worst. I had already pegged him as just another bigoted asshole without even knowing him. The person who really acted like minorities were beneath them . . . was me. The conversation I'd just had with Mrs. Wilson had to be the longest conversation we'd had in the eight years I worked here. How many times had I walked past her or any other minority employee that wasn't a lawyer and not even acknowledged them?

"I feel sorry for him," I said.

"Billy's tough. He'll land on his feet."

"I'm going to invite him out to lunch today. Thank you."

"For what, Mr. Turner?" she asked, confused.

"For helping me see that I was close-minded and prejudiced toward him."

"Well, you're welcome. I used to be the same way toward his mom, Debbie, before I got to know her. Back then, my husband had passed away, and my youngest son, Jerami, had leukemia. Struggling to care for him was causing me to miss a lot of time at work. Paying for all my family's bills alone on top of Jerami's hospital bills was draining me financially. I was close to being fired, but Debbie babysat Jerami at no charge to me. On top of that, Jerami needed an expensive treatment that wasn't covered by insurance, and I had no way of paying for it at the time. If he didn't get that treatment, there was a big chance that he would've died. When things looked bleak, and I thought I was going to have to bury my son, Debbie gave me the money to save his life. She had her own health problems and debt too. For years, I've tried to pay her back, but she didn't want money or anything in return."

Mrs. Wilson nodded at the fond memory and continued. "She did it just to be nice. She helped me when I was at my lowest, and I'm forever grateful to her for that. Well, let me get back to work. We should talk like this more often, Mr. Turner."

"I'd like that, Mrs. Wilson."

She smiled and went back to work.

I walked to my office and stood in my doorway. Since his office was across from mine, I watched Bill finish up boxing his things. I thought about treating him to lunch since this was his last day at the firm and getting to know him personally.

The other associates shook their heads and averted their eyes as Bill walked past them, holding his stuff. Everyone was whispering about who was going to take his place. I raced up the hall to catch Bill before he left.

"Bill, wait up," I said, lightly jogging up to him.

"Look, if you came to gloat, save it. Good luck with your case, man," he said.

"I'm not here to heckle you. I wanted to let you know Mrs. Wilson told me what happened, and I'm sorry you got let go."

Bill looked at me skeptically. "Thanks . . ."

"I need a break from everything. Would you want to come with me to lunch? It's on me."

"Why are you acting nice all of a sudden? We've worked together for, like, eight years, and we've rarely ever talked."

"Between this case, things going in my life, and talking to Mrs. Wilson today, I realized I need to stop judging people before I get to know them. I thought you were an elitist who acted like he cared for minorities but really didn't. I was wrong, and I apologize."

He smiled. "It's cool. I thought you were a boujie douche bag."

We laughed.

"I'll take you up on that offer for lunch," he said.

We ate at the Metro Diner. At first, we talked about our cases, but our conversation evolved. We had a lot of differences, but we also had a lot in common.

"I've heard the fucked-up jokes the partners say to you about not being 'black enough,'" he said. "I used to get it too. They used to say I talked like I'm black. A lot of people think it's all an act, but they don't know who I am or where I came from. I'm not pretending to be anyone else, and I'm not trying to imitate black culture. I'm just being me."

I sat back in my chair and slowly nodded. Bill's words mirrored how I'd always felt but never put into words.

"Seriously, I wish I never got this case. I lost my mom, I lost my job, and I probably lost my girl," Billy said.

"Sorry again about your mom. I know how you feel, man. I'm always fighting with Becky because she feels like I'm neglecting her."

"I'd rather have my girl feel like I'm neglecting her than to think I'm a secret racist," he said. "Ebony felt like I betrayed her by defending a guy I knew raped a black woman. I didn't want to defend that dickhead, but I was trying to make a better life for her and my mom. I hope I didn't lose her too."

I was curious to understand his relationship with his girl. "What do you love about Ebony?" I asked.

"Since day one, I always felt like we were a team. We've been together since we were kids."

He leaned in close.

"Real talk: she's the only woman I've had sex with, and she's the only woman I want. To this day, I still think she's gorgeous, but it's more than looks with her. She's smart, determined, and when she puts her mind to something, she can do anything. She makes me step my game up and pushes me to want to be the same way."

The way his face lit up when he talked about her, I knew his words were genuine. Before I got to know him, I thought he was like the countless guys that dated Simone—just a white guy that loved fucking black women because it gave him a sense of power—but I was wrong. Hearing him talk about how much he loved his girl made me think about Becky.

"What about you? What do you love about your girl?" he asked.

"With Becky and me, it's always been us against the world. Her parents hate me. My parents aren't too fond of her, either. At times, it feels like no one wants to see us together, but we fight for each other. Truthfully, she balances me out. She still surprises me with the things she does. I couldn't picture my life without her."

Billy nodded. "I feel the same way about Ebony."

We bonded over that lunch. We exchanged numbers and promised to keep in touch and have a couples' night before we went our separate ways. One thing was for sure: after talking to him, I knew exactly what I needed to do next.

Chapter 37

Bill

The Future

My lunch with Ben put everything into perspective. I was tired of fighting with Ebony, and with everything that happened today, I'd do anything I needed to have her in my life again completely. I toyed with the ring.

I went to Mrs. Williams's house.

"Hey, Billy. How are you, baby?"

"I'm good. Is Ebony here?"

"No. She's not here. She's been really depressed lately, and I don't know where she goes when she gets like that."

"I think I know where she is. I'll find her."

"I hope you two work everything out."

"Me too."

The sun was setting. I searched through Queensbridge Park for Ebony. She always loved this park because she used to come here with Akeem and enjoy seeing the entire city skyline in the distance and the glow of the lights at night.

I found her sitting on a park bench by the water.

"Hey," I said.

"How did you know I'd be here?" Ebony asked.

"I've known you since we were kids. You and Akeem would always come here when you needed to think. What are you thinking about today?"

She didn't answer, just stared at me in silence.

"I'm sorry about everything," I said.

She sighed. "I'm sorry too. I had a lot of things going on. Between studying for my test and shit going on at work, your situation amplified everything that was pissing me off and stressing me out."

"I know that feeling. Did you pass your test?"

"Yeah. I'm going to be a lieutenant."

"See, I knew you would."

"You always believe in me."

"Of course. I love you."

"So, how did your case go?" she asked. "Did you get him off?"

"I got removed from the case. I could've won, but I lost it when he whispered in my ear that he wanted to do the same thing he did to Sophia to you. I finally realized I couldn't live with myself if I helped him get away with raping that girl."

"Well, that's good. I'm proud of you. You stuck to your morals."

"I got fired today, Ebony."

"Why? What about everything you wanted?"

"If I stayed there, I would be right back to handling cases I didn't agree with, and that isn't why I got into law. Most importantly, working there would've pushed you further away from me. You're my world, and I couldn't risk losing you."

Ebony stood up and hugged and kissed me.

"I'm sorry. I know how hard you worked to rise in that firm. What are you going to do about everything?"

"I honestly don't know. I'm sure I can find another firm, but before I do anything, I need to ask you a question."

"What's the question?"

I got down on one knee and opened the black ring box and showed her the ring that sat neatly on the velvet fold. Tears streamed down her face. I looked up at her and asked, "Ebony, will you marry me?"

She nodded rapidly. "Yes!"

We kissed long and deep. I wasn't sure what the future held for us, but I knew I could face anything as long as I had her in my life.

Despite not being on the case anymore, I did watch Johnny's trial on TV and enjoyed every minute of it. As I thought, instead of just going straight to closing arguments, Francis and Mark were too confident and put Johnny on the stand—which was a *huge* mistake.

Johnny puffed up his chest as he strutted to the witness stand. Things went south really quickly when he made several slipups during his testimony.

"This bitch—"

"Objection, Your Honor," the DA said.

"Mr. Alfieri, I advise you to refrain from calling Ms. Winters derogatory names," the judge said. "If you do it again, I'll hold you in contempt."

"I gotcha," Johnny said. "Anyway, she wanted me. I had to push her around a bit at first—"

"I'm sorry, did you say you 'pushed her around'?" the DA asked.

"Yeah, she was trying to pull away at first, but I wanted her to hear me out. After we had handled our business, I paid her. If I'm guilty of anything, it's getting a prostitute in the first place. I didn't rape her."

There was nothing but questioning glances and whispered voices from everyone in the courtroom.

Francis and Mark were animatedly trying to get Johnny to stop talking, but he wasn't paying them any attention.

"So, Ms. Winters was trying to leave, and you wouldn't let her go until she heard you out and complied with what you wanted?" the DA asked with a huge grin on his face.

"You know how black people can be. They're stubborn."

The crowd collectively gasped at that statement. The TV camera zoomed in on Mark's and Francis's faces. The looks on their faces showed they knew they had just lost this case because of his testimony.

When the verdict came down, Johnny couldn't believe his ears when the jury found him guilty on all charges. He pulled away from the court officers and squirmed to prevent them from grabbing his hands.

"You can't do this to me!" he yelled.

"It's OK, Johnny," Francis said. "We'll appeal. Just keep quiet. We'll work this out."

The court officers were trying to talk him into complying, but Johnny wasn't having it. Sophia was crying and just observed his outburst.

Johnny broke out of the court officers' grips and walked toward her. "Come here, bitch. You wanna ruin people's lives? I got something for you."

The courtroom was raucous. The judge continuously banged her gavel for order. "Get him out of here now."

Four court officers wrestled Johnny to the ground. He was on his stomach with his arms being wrenched behind his back. Then the officers yanked him up.

"Fuck this. I'm Johnny Alfieri. Y'all can't convict me because of this nigger bitch's lies. I didn't rape her. She wanted it. I paid the bitch, and this is what I get? I shouldn't have given her shit. Back in the day, guys like me used to take the pussy for free."

Johnny was dragged away, fighting with the officers in the small hallway going toward the holding cells.
While the door was open, the film crews craned their
necks to see what was going on back there.

Francis and Mark walked out of the courthouse. Mark
warded off reporters' questions about the loss as they
entered the limo with Johnny's agent and publicist. I
laughed to myself. Johnny better not drop the soap when
he showered in prison. I hoped the prick got what he
deserved, and the inmates gave him the same treatment
he gave Sophia.

Chapter 38

Ben

Sacrifice

We walked up to Becky's parents' door.

"Ugh, I hate these parties," she said. "My mom only throws this party every year so she can show off to New York's high society and give off the illusion that we live the perfect life."

"Maybe this year's party will be different," I said, ringing the doorbell.

"I highly doubt that. I'm just happy you decided to come with me this year. Usually, you have me make up some lame excuse for you, so you don't have to meet my parents' rich, racist friends."

"I want you to see that I meant what I said. I want to make you happy, even if it means spending a night in hell with you tonight."

Becky smiled and held my hand.

Bernard opened the door and welcomed us. He took us to the dining room.

"Rebecca, darling, you made it," Susan said. She turned to her guest. "My incredibly talented daughter was recently offered a lucrative publishing deal for one of her novels. It should be in bookstores all around the country by . . ." She faced Rebecca. "I'm sorry, when, dear?"

"In two weeks, on Valentine's Day," Becky said.

"What is your book about, Rebecca?" an older white woman wearing a huge pearl necklace and flowered dress, asked.

"Uh, it's a fictional story about the trials and tribulations of being in a relationship," Becky said.

"Who is this handsome young man?" a woman who looked like she was in her midfifties asked. The way her eyes flirtatiously roamed my body, she looked like she was *definitely* interested in getting to know me.

"This is . . . Rebecca's, uh . . . boyfriend, Ben," Susan said. "He graduated from Columbia University with Rebecca, and he's been a lawyer with Wayne, Rothstein, and Lincoln for the past nine years. He's being considered for a partnership with the firm, and he's handling that big case about the rapper that murdered those four people."

Her guests smiled and nodded, showing they were impressed. To some, it probably looked as if Susan were bragging about me, but I knew the truth. Susan was rattling off my accomplishments as a means of justifying why it was OK for Becky to date me. She wanted her guests to know that I wasn't the stereotypical black man that they probably thought I was.

I picked up a wine goblet and tapped it with a fork. The dining room fell silent. Everyone stopped what they were doing and faced me.

"Everyone, I have something I need to do, and I would like everyone's attention." Then I turned to Rebecca.

"Babe, what are you doing?" she asked.

I got down on one knee, pulling the ring I bought after talking to Bill from my pants pocket. Becky covered her mouth and nodded.

"Rebecca, you've been supportive, loyal, and honest with me since we started dating. We've faced a lot of obstacles, but like you told me when we first made things official, 'I love you, and you're worth fighting for.'"

I cleared my throat before I continued.

"Will you continue to fight with me for our love forever? Will you make me the luckiest man in the world and marry me?"

Becky never stopped nodding when she yelled, "Yes!" with tears streaming down her face. I pulled the ring out of its velvet box and placed it on her finger.

She cupped my face with her hands and kissed me.

Mr. Preston stood up quickly, his face beet red, his hands balled up into fists as he slammed them down on the table.

"Enough."

All heads turned to his direction.

"You've embarrassed this family enough by turning my daughter into a damn nigger lover, and I won't let this go any further."

Spittle flew out of his mouth with every bigoted word as he continued. "I already told you there'd be no way in fucking hell I'd let you marry my daughter."

"Daddy!" Becky screamed.

"Rebecca, your mother and I love you, but this shit ends tonight. You have to choose right now. If you marry him, you'll be dead to your mother and me. You'll never see another dime from us. If you leave him now, I promise we'll always take care of you, but you have to make a choice now!"

"Dad, this isn't funny. You can't be serious," Becky said.

"I'm not kidding. If you say yes to him, your trust fund will be cut off first thing tomorrow morning. That I promise you."

"That's not fair. I love him. If you force me to make that decision, you know I'll choose Ben," she fired back.

"Can you take this conversation to the study?" Mrs. Preston said. "I think we've embarrassed our family enough in front of our company."

Mr. Preston pointed. "My study—now!" he said through gritted teeth.

There was a chorus of gasps and murmurs from the guests. Becky faced her mother, who had tears in her eyes. Her hands were clasped together as if she were praying Becky would choose to leave me.

Becky and I followed Mr. Preston to his study. He slammed the door behind us. Then he came nose to nose with me.

"I'm so sick of your people trying to take everything. I will *not* allow you to take my daughter. You will *never* be a part of my family."

Becky wedged herself between her father and me to prevent us from getting physical. It was killing her, seeing her dad and me fighting. I couldn't be selfish. Becky had way more to lose than I did.

"Becky, I think it would be best if we broke up," I said.

She froze at my words. "What? Baby, you don't mean that," she said, grabbing my hand.

There was no going back at this point. I couldn't take back what I said. The damage was done. I lowered my eyes before I spoke.

"I do. I never wanted to put you in a position where you'd have to choose between your family and me. They're important to you, and I can't do that to you. I won't be the cause of you losing your family. I love you, and I know you love me, but I have to make this decision for you. We can't be together anymore, Becky. I'm sorry."

I let go of her hand. Her lips quivered, and tears filled her eyes and spilled down her cheeks. I wanted to go to her, to hold her and tell her that I didn't mean it, but this was for the best. I turned my head. I couldn't look at her anymore. I hated seeing that heartbroken expression on her face. Mr. Preston stared me down.

"I'm going to go home," I said.

"I think that would be for the best, Ben," he said with a smirk.

It took every bit of strength I had to push past her as she wept.

"Ben . . . Ben . . ." Becky cried.

She called my name over and over, but I didn't answer. I needed to go home as fast as I could to be alone and think.

Chapter 39

Becky

Sorrow

I wanted to crawl into a hole and die as I leaned against my old bedroom window and sobbed.

"Let him go, Rebecca. You're better off without him," Dad said.

I didn't respond. I held myself and watched sadly through the window as Ben drove off.

"What's done is done. Give me your cell phone and take off that damn ring," Dad ordered.

I handed him my phone but placed my ring on my dresser.

Dad powered off my phone and snatched my engagement ring and my keys off the top of the dresser.

"You don't need these anymore. Tomorrow, I'll go with some movers to his place to get your things and give him back this ring."

I continued to cry hysterically. "Are you happy now? Do you feel good about yourself now that you finally drove him away?"

"Honey, I don't like seeing you in pain, but I did this for your own good," he said, closing the door behind him.

In his bigoted mind, I knew he believed he was doing what was best for me. It pissed me off that my parents always felt they needed to "fix me." Thinking of that sent me into a deeper depression. I spent the rest of the night crying myself to sleep on the floor.

The next morning, I sat balled up on the living room floor surrounded by empty liquor bottles, eating ice cream and crying off and on. My depression led me to drink everything straight from the bottle.

Mom walked into the living room and rolled her eyes. "Jesus, Rebecca, you look ghastly. Stop being so dramatically pathetic and pull yourself together."

I stuck my ice-cream-covered tongue at her.

"I'm off to my tennis lesson. Enjoy wallowing in your sorrow." As she was leaving, my dad came home. He looked extrachipper.

"I had the movers take all your things from his place, so you'll never have to go there again," he said.

"Was he there when you got them?" I asked.

"No."

"Where's my ring?"

"I left it on the counter with your keys. Rebecca, stop worrying about that stupid ring. That nightmare of a relationship with Ben is over. Do yourself a favor and move on."

I had no intention of moving on. I loved Ben. I pulled out my cell phone. My fingers hovered over his name on my iPhone. Even though I wanted to hit call, just to hear his voice, I couldn't call him. I wanted him to reach out to me. I wanted to know that he needed me as much as I needed him.

Chapter 40

Ben

I Want My Becky Back

It'd been two weeks since my breakup with Becky. I hadn't seen or spoken to her since that night, and neither of us had made an attempt to get back together.

Coming home the day after our breakup, seeing her keys and engagement ring on the counter, and discovering all her things were gone from our townhouse, confirmed that our relationship was truly over. Although I didn't want her to lose her family because of me, I thought she would've at least put up more of a fight, but I guessed that was asking for too much. I drowned myself in my work. I ran five miles every day to clear my head, but the only thing that did was make me think about her more. As much as I wanted to completely forget about her, as much as it would make my life so much easier, I couldn't. I missed her. I loved her.

I stared aimlessly at the ceiling, but I couldn't sleep. I tried reading my case files, but I found myself scanning the same page repeatedly. I couldn't concentrate on anything I was reading. I threw my folder to the side and attempted to go to sleep again.

It was only nine p.m., but I tried to force myself to sleep. I tossed and turned in my bed, constantly changing

positions, trying desperately to fall asleep, but I couldn't.
My mind wouldn't stop thinking about Becky.

Suddenly, my phone vibrated on my nightstand. I saw
it was Gabby and debated not answering but picked it up
before it went to voicemail.

"What's up, Big Head? What are you doing? You mop-
ing around at home having a pity party?"

"Bye, Gabby."

"Wait. I'm sorry. I didn't mean to sound so insensitive.
I'm trying to work on that. I know you're down. Do you
want me to come over?"

"Nah, I'm going to look over this case some more and
watch TV."

"Come on, Big Head. We can watch the recap of the
Knicks game while you vent."

Gabby wasn't the best choice to vent to, but I really
didn't want to be alone.

"So, am I coming over or nah?" she asked.

"Yeah, come over."

I was running a highlighter on some documents I was
reading when the doorbell rang.

"Hey, Big Head," Gabby said as I opened the door.

"Hey."

We hugged, then walked toward the living room,
where I had documents spread out all over the couch and
coffee table.

"You're at this nonstop, huh?" she asked.

"I need this win."

"I feel you, but give it a break for now."

I turned on the TV and flipped to the game. Gabby
tried to stir up a conversation, but I barely listened.

"Stop looking so sad," she said.

"It's hard to stop when I feel sad."

"Ugh, I'm sick of you harping over fucking Becky. Get over it."

I shook my head, picked up the TV remote, and flipped through the channels. Gabby took the remote from me.

"First off, you need to drop this whole woe-is-me bullshit. I'm here. You don't need to be thinking about another woman. Think about back in the day when it used to be just you and me. We used to hang out alone like this all the time."

We started reminiscing about old times. Gabby chuckled. "Remember when we were kids, and you used to write me love letters?"

"Yup. You used to correct the grammar in them and hand them back to me."

We laughed. I thought about how far I'd come since then, how my life had changed for the better. All of those thoughts made me even more depressed that Becky wasn't in my life anymore.

Gabby rested her head on my shoulder and said, "You ever wonder how things would've turned out if we gave 'us' a try back in college?"

I didn't really know how to answer that question. "Time has changed us. We're not the same people we were back then. It's not healthy wondering about the what-ifs with us." I chuckled. "Besides, we would've fought all the time in a relationship."

"That's a shitty thing to say," she said.

"That sounded worse than I meant it to, but it's true. Your tongue can be real sharp and hurtful sometimes."

"Sorry, but I'm not Willy Wonka. I don't sugarcoat shit. I'm not the coddling type. I don't cry at weddings or sappy movies, and I damn sure don't tell people they're good when they suck. With me, at least you know I'm always straight with you. Wouldn't you want a woman that is going to be honest with you?"

"You can be honest without being brutal."

"I don't have time to stroke egos. If a man is too weak to handle me being real, that's on him."

"And that's your fucking problem, Gabby," I said. "I'm not asking you to be fake or to baby a man, but you should have some tact. You're not uplifting, and if you want to have a lasting relationship, you need to work on that."

"Who says I have a problem or need to work on anything?"

"Your dating history does. No one is ever good enough for you. You find faults in everything. You block yourself from being happy. I'm going to tell you something not to be mean, but as your best friend who cares. I'm not telling you to lower your standards, but if you don't get it through your head that no guy is ever going to meet every expectation you have, you're going to end up a lonely, bitter old woman."

Gabby scowled at me. I thought she was on the verge of cursing me out, but she didn't. Her face softened, and she nodded, sat back, and looked like she was really thinking about what I'd said.

Then Gabby kissed me on the cheek.

"I had a long day. Make me a drink, Big Head."

"I think I got some Captain Morgan in the kitchen. You want a rum and Coke?"

She nodded.

After making the drinks, I walked out of my kitchen and saw a trail of clothing sprawled out on my floor. I followed the jeans, shirt, and lace bra and panties set that led to my bedroom and picked them up while juggling her drink in my hand. Gabby was naked on my bed.

"Why don't you come over here and let me relieve some of that stress you have?" she said seductively.

I licked my lips and gulped down her drink. She looked so damn good, but I couldn't sleep with her. Not yet, anyway. I tossed her clothes to her.

"I can't, Gabby. It's too soon."

She sat up. "What? I know you're not gonna pass this up, pining over some silly white girl," she said, looking deeply insulted.

I stood in my doorway in silence.

"Becky is gone," Gabby said. "She made her choice, and like I've always told you, when it came time for her to choose between you and her cushy life, she wanted her life."

"She didn't choose. I made the choice for her."

"You did, but where is she, Ben? You told me yourself, she left her key and engagement ring on the coffee table, right?" Gabby shook her head, stood up, and got dressed.

"I don't get it, Ben. What does she have that I don't? I'm practically throwing myself at you, and you're dismissing me like I'm not shit."

I took a deep breath and exhaled slowly. "Gabby, I'm very attracted to you. You're gorgeous, sexy, and smart, everything I want in a woman, but I'm still dealing with my breakup. My feelings for her have nothing to do with race. I don't think she's better than you, but while I love you and always will, I'm *in love* with Becky. If we're ever intimate again, I want it to mean something special, not just a rebound thing, like our first time was for you. Until my feelings for her fade, it wouldn't be right for me to fuck you if my heart isn't fully in it. You mean more to me than that, and you know this already."

Gabby's lips trembled. She didn't look at me as she got dressed.

"You going to be OK?" I asked.

She put on her shades, adjusted her clothes, hiked her purse on her shoulder, and said, "Of course. Why wouldn't I be?"

"Wait."

"No. I'm not going to play myself and accept being treated like I'm second best anymore."

She walked out of my house without a goodbye. I hoped that wasn't another relationship I'd fucked up.

Chapter 41

Becky

Mourning

I couldn't help myself. I needed to see Ben. I drove to our place, but when I got there, I saw Gabby pulling off in her car. I couldn't bring myself to knock on his door and have it confirmed that he fucked her . . . or worse. That would break my heart. I was sure once she heard I was out of the picture, she'd try to replace me. I decided to go back home. Maybe she already had.

The editor of *Cosmopolitan,* Harriot, was pissed that I didn't show up to our weekly staff meeting or hand in my article this week. I told her I was sick with the flu. In reality, I wasn't in the mood to be around people yet, and in my mind, heartache totally counted as an illness. I needed to have my article ready by five—and I had nothing on my computer screen.

Ugh! I couldn't focus. I needed to get out of the house and take my mind off of Ben. I pulled myself together and forced myself to go to work.

After breaking down and crying in my cubicle several times, I finished the article I was working on, but even I knew it was shitty. Brooke tried to console me, but it wasn't helping. I told her everything that led to my breakup with Ben.

"I know you love him, but the best way to get over a broken heart is to find someone new," she said.

"I don't want anyone else. I love him."

"Was he that good?"

"What do you mean?"

"In the sack."

"This has nothing to do with sex. Is that the only reason you think I'm with him?"

"Well, why are you so hung up on him?" Brooke said. "Gabby's not around. You can be honest. He's black. Besides him fucking you silly, I can't see why you couldn't easily find a quality white guy to be serious with."

I looked at Brooke in shock. This time, she couldn't blame her words on the alcohol. This was how she honestly felt. I couldn't hold back my anger.

"Fuck you! You can't find a decent guy because you're not even a decent person. People are more than just their race."

"Oh, don't start saying shit you don't mean," Brooke said.

"I mean it. You're an ugly person inside."

"And you're a pathetic person inside *and* out. I don't need your white-guilt-having ass in my life. Do you want to know why your book wasn't getting picked up? Because *no one* wants to read about a stupid white woman struggling with her nappy-headed nigger. Your book is going to flop, and you won't have me to be your shoulder to cry on anymore. Enjoy your life."

I had to get out of there. I'd lost my man, and now I'd lost one of my best friends. I couldn't take any more negativity for the day.

Chapter 42

Ben

D-Day

"You're up, kid," Francis said. "We need you to pull off a miracle. After that Alfieri case disaster, we don't need another big negative blow to our firm."

Francis was seated with the public directly behind the defense table.

"No pressure," I said sarcastically.

Tim waved off Francis's comment and turned to Reggie.

"Today's the first day of the trial. Things might not look pretty, but don't get discouraged," he said to Reggie.

"I'm cool," Reggie said.

Reggie leaned over to me. "I'm alone here. None of the executives from my record label are here, not even my manager and agent. I haven't heard from anyone from the label in two months. I guess they figure I'm finished."

I patted his shoulder. "I'm here with you, and I'm going to do my best to make sure you're acquitted."

"All rise for the Honorable Judge Brewer," the bailiff said.

The judge stepped up to the bench and looked over the courtroom before sitting. "Please be seated."

The jury had eight men and four women. Six were white, four black, and two Hispanic. I didn't even know if a balanced jury of minorities would be advantageous for the case. I was fucking nervous. With all the information and images that were shown on the news, there was no way this jury would be impartial. They were already looking at Reggie as if he were guilty.

After the defense and prosecution teams introduced themselves, we went into our opening statements.

I stood up and looked at Reggie. Fear was in his eyes. I turned around and faced the jury. I took a deep breath and told myself, "I can do this."

I began, "Ladies and Gentlemen of the jury, during this case, I want you to think."

I paraphrased a line that I'd once heard Becky say. "It's easy to just look at the world in black and white, but life isn't that simple. Life is in color, and sometimes things aren't what they seem at first. Right now, I want you to imagine you're driving and another car is zigzagging through traffic. The driver cuts you off, and you have words with that driver. Now, imagine you and that same car, later on, get into an accident. Despite being in that dispute, did you want to be in an accident? Did you want to hurt yourself or that other driver? I'm sure pretty much all of you are saying no. My point is, in that situation, you had no intent to harm anyone. You were just in the wrong place at the wrong time."

I took another deep breath.

"My client Reginald Brown did argue with two of the victims, but murder them—he did not. He was at the wrong place at the wrong time, and during this trial, I will prove to you that the wrong man was arrested. The killer is still out there, and once I prove that to this jury, I hope everyone does the right thing and acquits Mr. Brown. Thank you."

I sat down and felt relieved getting the opening statement out of the way, but I knew this was just the tip of the iceberg. Seeing the solemn look on the jury's faces, it was hard to read their moods and whether I sparked their curiosity about another man committing the murders. DA Torres stood up from the prosecution table and winked at me. He walked around the courtroom with a swagger of a man who knew he had this case won.

"Ladies and Gentlemen of the jury, the evidence clearly shows the defendant holding the murder weapon with the victims' blood on him. The evidence also shows the defendant's DNA on the trigger, the slide, and the grip on the murder weapon. Ladies and Gentlemen, this case is open and shut. This isn't the movie *The Fugitive*. There is no one-armed man that committed these grisly murders."

DA Torres stopped walking in front of the jury and pointed at Reggie.

"It was *that* man, Reginald Brown, who did these crimes. The evidence goes on to show that when the first set of police arrived at the crime scene, they were ambushed by the defendant before they could even exit their patrol vehicle."

The DA walked over to the evidence table and grabbed the gun that was encased in a plastic baggie. He walked to the jury box and continued.

"The defendant used this weapon to end the lives of two police officers and a happy couple. If convicted of these heinous crimes, we are asking that Mr. Brown receive a life sentence without the possibility of parole."

The first day was disastrous. The 911 operator, medical examiner, crime scene unit, cops, and witnesses were all set to testify.

First, the DA called up the emergency operator, who played the chilling 911 calls on the night of the murders. Next, the medical examiner explained how the victims suffered when they died. When the crime scene unit testified, photos from the crime scene of Reggie holding the gun, photos of the slain officers, and the couple's bullet-riddled bodies were displayed.

I stood and cross-examined the CSU detective.

"Detective Harbor, were my client's fingerprints found on the murder weapon?" I asked.

"The gun is ridged, so that makes it extremely difficult to get a fingerprint off it, so to answer your question, no, his fingerprints weren't on it," she answered.

"Can you please explain to the court the process with which you examined the gun?"

"We examined the gun for DNA, and we found Mr. Brown's DNA on the grip and trigger. We used another technique called 'fuming' on the magazine, because sometimes, we can find a fingerprint on the magazine."

"And were my client's fingerprints or any other person's fingerprints or DNA found on the weapon?"

"Mr. Brown's fingerprints weren't found on the magazine, but his DNA was on the trigger and grip. Another man named Kuwuan Mitchell's fingerprints were found on the magazine, and his DNA was also found on the trigger and grip."

The jury and courtroom were all talking after hearing that.

"Order," the judge said, calming down the courtroom.

"Do we have a description of Kuwuan Mitchell?" I asked.

"He's a dark-skinned black male. Approximately six feet and 200 pounds."

"So, it's safe to say that Kuwuan's description is identical to my client's?" I asked.

"Your client was at the scene with blood on him, holding the smoking gun," Harbor said. "Kuwuan Mitchell has never been arrested for killing people. He's a small-time gun dealer from Harlem."

"That's not what I asked you, Detective Harbor. Now, please, stop tiptoeing around the question."

"Yes, they look similar."

"Do we know Mr. Kuwuan Mitchell's whereabouts on the night of the murders?"

"No."

"Has he been labeled a suspect or questioned about the incident?"

"No. No one has seen him around lately," she said.

"So, we have someone who was potentially involved, seeing that his fingerprints and DNA were found on the weapon. Yet, he hasn't been labeled a suspect, questioned, or searched for?"

"No."

"Could it be that my client's statement is true, and he didn't kill those people, but you and your colleagues want him to take the fall for these murders because it's easier to handle?" I asked.

"Objection, Your Honor," the DA said.

"Sustained," the judge said.

"I'll rephrase," I said. "Could it be that my client's statement is true about being at the wrong place at the wrong time?"

"I highly doubt it," Harbor said.

"This looks like a good place to stop for today. We will reconvene bright and early tomorrow morning at nine. Court is adjourned," the judge, Brewer, said, banging his gavel.

I sighed.

"Ben, relax," Francis said. "We knew the first day would be brutal. Being a successful lawyer is like being a great chess player. You have to study your opponent and use the right strategy. Ben, I have nothing but faith in you to make us all proud and pull out a win for this case."

I couldn't tell if he meant that or if he was just trying to keep my spirits up.

The second day of the trial was just as bad as the first. Officer Mendez, the first police officer on the scene that night, was up first on the witness stand, followed by his partner, Officer Mahoney. Bill's girl, Sergeant Ebony Williams, took the stand and told the jury the gruesome details about discovering the victims, and the items on the scene that were vouchered. When she was done, I had no questions to ask her. It just didn't seem right. I could've fired off questions to try to trip her up and make her and the officers seem incompetent, but I couldn't bring myself to do that.

Ebony exited the witness stand and cut her eyes at me. I figured she saw me as the devil for representing the guy that had allegedly killed her colleagues.

When the DA put on the videos from the incident, I knew I had to start being aggressive. I asked the witnesses question after question to trip them up and contradict themselves.

"Ms. Taylor, are you certain the man you saw that night was my client?" I asked.

"Absolutely," she answered.

She looked like a party girl. She wore tight tan pants, and there was a blond streak in her brown hair.

"How far would you say you were from Mr. Brown when you witnessed what he allegedly did?"

"He was about a block away from me."

"After watching the videos from the incident a few minutes ago, what was the perpetrator wearing?"

"Objection, Your Honor," the DA said.

I faced the judge.

"Overruled," the judge said.

"All black, I think," Ms. Taylor replied.

The video showed the killer wearing a black and red hat and sneakers, but Ms. Taylor had failed to mention that.

"Did you noticed anything specific the defendant was wearing?"

"Nope."

"Was the killer wearing boots or sneakers?"

"I don't know. I don't remember."

"Was he wearing a hat or not?"

"I don't know. I don't remember."

"You just watched numerous videos showing the incident a few minutes ago. You can't remember if he wore a hat or what type of shoes he was wearing?"

"Nope."

The room fell silent. I walked over to the projector and played the grainy video again. I paused it on the clip that showed the killer had on a hat and sneakers.

"Ladies and Gentlemen, as you can clearly see from the video, the killer was wearing a black and red Chicago Bulls hat with matching sneakers."

I walked over to a clear picture of Reggie holding the murder weapon and faced the jury.

"In this picture, it's clear that my client doesn't have a hat on, and he was wearing all-black Tims. How is it possible that in a matter of seconds, Mr. Brown was able to change his shoes and ditch his hat?"

I turned back to Ms. Taylor.

"I'll ask you again, Ms. Taylor. We watched the video again, and you just looked at the picture. Are you certain the man you saw that night was my client?"

She looked confused. "I-I don't know."

I nodded and said, "No further questions."

This case was far from won, but I felt like I was at least getting the jury and everyone in the courtroom to start thinking.

The second day of the trial was now over. The angry faces on the jury showed that, despite my arguments, none of them believed for a second that he was innocent. I rubbed my hand over my face. Reggie slumped in his chair.

"Man, these people think I did it," he said. "I swear on my life I didn't kill anybody."

"I know you didn't, Reggie, but we need to prove that to the jury."

"So, what are you waiting for?"

"I'm going to talk to you in a few minutes."

He looked at me with uncertainty. "A'ight."

Reggie sulked as the court officer walked over to take him back to the holding cells. He didn't look in Tim's or my direction when they hauled him off. I didn't know how I was going to break it to him that we might lose this case.

"Hey," I said, feeling deflated.

"What's wrong? You don't look like your usual corny self," Reggie joked.

"Listen, is there anything else you can tell me about that night? I'm trying to attack this case from every angle, but I'm running out of ammunition."

"What? What are you saying?"

"I'm saying if we don't come up with something big to help prove your innocence, it doesn't look good for us."

"Us? What do you mean *us?* They're gonna lock *my* black ass up for life." Reggie shook his head. Anger was all over his face.

"You really had me buggin', believing I had a legit chance to be free of this shit. I should've never let you put those bullshit thoughts in my head. It's over for me."

"That's not true, Reggie. I'm trying to help you."

"Nah, you don't give a shit about me," he said. "You just want to prolong this shit to get paid. I get it. Just let the hood nigga rot in jail for the rest of his life while the Oreo lives the high life, huh? I can't believe you. You knew you couldn't win this from the beginning, and you played me. You made me think I could have a normal life when this was all over, and I'm the real sucker because I believed you. I've dealt with a lot of hustlers in the street, and none of them got me to buy the shit they were selling like you. You're the smoothest hustler I ever met."

"Reggie, it's not like that," I said. "I'm trying to help."

"Cut the bullshit. From now on, don't talk to me. I got nothing else to say to you. I'll sit there in court and wait to hear my guilty verdict."

Reggie stood up fast, letting his chair fall behind him. He gave me the finger with both hands as he walked away backward. Then he faced the door and called for the guards to let him out.

The clock was ticking. I needed to find a way to win this case.

Usually, after a rough day in court, I had Becky and Gabby to comfort me, but since neither of them was talking to me, I was alone. I went to my parents' place for advice and support.

I opened the door to their place and loosened my tie. As I walked around the house, I saw Dad sitting in his office playing himself at chess.

"Hey, Dad."

"How was the trial today, son?"

"Terrible. Where's Mom?"

"She's out shopping with Simone," he said. "I told them both that I did some investigating on your aunt Joan and found out that Simone's sister lives in the Bronx and has a successful photography business. They went to the mall to think on whether Simone should go to the business and meet her. I say yes. It's always good to meet your family. But anyway, why was your trial so terrible?"

I explained what went down.

"Son, no one ever said this trial was going to be easy. You're going to have to weather the storm and stay strong."

"It's not just the fear of losing the case," I said. "Reggie thinks I'm not putting my all into defending him, and I'm going to let him rot in prison for life. He believes I'm some boujie Oreo that only dates white women and doesn't care about our people. Every black person I meet seems to think the same thing. All my life, I've been either too black for white people or not black enough for our people."

"Do you feel you're that way?" Dad asked.

"No."

"Son, James Brown once said, '*A man can't get himself together until he knows who he is, and be proud of what and who he is and where he comes from.*' I watched you struggle for years, trying to figure out if you're black enough and hoping to be accepted. Until you love yourself for who you are and what you're about, you'll never find peace."

I slowly nodded as he continued.

"You can never forget black history, because it's a part of who you are, and the world will always remind you that you're a black man, but if you make a conscious effort to improve the world and the lives of our people, if you understand the plight that less fortunate people in our race face on a regular basis and seek positive change, then you know in your heart you're 'black enough.' You won't ever have to worry about proving it to another brotha or sista again."

And just like that, I finally fully understood what the purpose of those trips to his old neighborhood were about. My dad knew that some people viewed him as a sellout. He was aware that there were some that were just using him, but in his heart, he knew that his purpose for going down to that neighborhood was right, so he didn't need validation from the community on whether he was "black enough"—he knew it.

I hugged my father.

"Thanks, Dad. You don't know how badly I needed to hear this today."

"Anytime, son."

I closed my eyes and pressed my fingertips to my temples, slowly massaging them as I sat in my office, thinking about my next move.

Cardboard file boxes were piled all over my desk. I was in full panic mode. Unless I came up with something immediately, I was going to lose this case, and Reggie would spend the rest of his life in prison for no reason. The thought did cross my mind that maybe he was lying and all of this stress and aggravation was for nothing, but his story never changed.

I looked through the various videos of the outside cameras, briefs, and witness testimonies, but I couldn't find anything that would prove Reggie's innocence. I rewatched all the videos. Sometimes lawyers and cops could get so focused on a particular person that they developed tunnel vision and failed to see other minute details and possible scenarios around them. However, I found nothing.

As a last resort, I went back to the crime scene. I walked around all the nearby businesses in the vicinity that might've caught the incident. I needed anything that could help prove there was another person involved.

I sat inside Hector's Café and Diner after I failed to find anything new. While paying the cashier, I noticed the TV screen with the diner's surveillance cameras on it. I noticed the camera angled on the registers.

"Excuse me. Are these cameras new?"

"No, we've always had them," the cashier said.

I'd overlooked this angle because it was an inside camera, but the way it was situated, if it was on the video files the cops gave me, it could've caught a direct view of the murders in the background.

I quickly paid my bill, pulled out my cell phone, and called Tim.

"What's up, Ben?" he asked.

"I think I found what was missing to win this case."

"What do you mean?"

"I was at the diner across from the crime scene. If we have all the camera angles like the detectives say we do, we might be able to prove that there was another person present."

"We need to see that video."

"I'm rushing back to the firm now."

"Right there—freeze that frame," Tim said.

On the screen was the image of an unidentified, dark-skinned, black man wearing similar clothes to Reggie—but with a red and black hat and matching sneakers—murdering the gay couple and then rushing toward the cop car and killing the policemen.

"Oh my God, I can't believe you're really going to pull this off. You did it, Ben," Tim said.

I smiled and pulled up the video from the club where Reggie was. Sure enough, it showed him leaving the club at the exact time the couple was being murdered. The camera from the diner showed the blind spot that we didn't have before of Reggie and the real killer colliding. Reggie was telling the truth all along, and this video had been in our possession the entire time. I rushed to make a clip and sent a copy to the district attorney.

The commotion and chatter from the jury and spectators after watching the clip caused the judge to bang his gavel down heavily.

"Order. Order in the court! Will the defendant please rise?"

Everyone was stunned at the video. I was certain they would've found Reggie guilty without it. The jury's demeanor previously gave the impression that they didn't believe there was another shooter, after all the evidence pointed to Reggie. This cleared him and kept an innocent man from going to prison for life.

"Your Honor, due to the newly found evidence that has been presented to us, our office declines to prosecute further and moves to dismiss all charges against the defendant," the district attorney said.

Reggie was crying. He couldn't stop thanking me.

I smiled.

"You're welcome, but face the judge," I said.

The judge cleared his throat. "It's the court's decision to grant the prosecution's motion to dismiss. All charges against the defendant Reginald Brown are hereby dismissed with prejudice. You're free to go, Mr. Brown."

We walked out of the courtroom and were engulfed by a sea of the press and spectators. CNN, FOX, CBS, and other news vans were parked outside. Camera flashes went off all around Reggie as thousands of fans and spectators reached out and called for him. Reporters stuck microphones in front of him. Tears streamed down Reggie's face as reporters asked him questions.

"Co-Kayne, how does it feel to be proven innocent?"

"Yo, I just want to say thank you to my lawyer Ben Turner," he said. "He had my back from day one and never gave up on me. When everyone thought I was guilty, Ben was the only person that believed me when I said I didn't do it. I figured I was finished. I thought my life was over, but Ben wouldn't stop trying to show the world that I was innocent. He saved my life, and I can't thank him enough."

Reggie turned and faced me. He pushed through the dozens of microphones and cameras being shoved in his way.

"Come here, man," Reggie said.

He hugged me and whispered, "Thank you. Thank you for not giving up on me when I had already given up on myself."

Chapter 43

Becky

Disowned

I was dispiritedly eating dinner with my parents at home. I should be ecstatic with my novel being number two on the New York Times bestsellers list. My novel was getting rave reviews, and the sales numbers were the largest for any novel published by Legacy Books nationally, but I missed Ben. Having my book released on Valentine's Day and Ben not being around to help me celebrate broke my heart. I spent that entire day in my bedroom crying and wondering what Ben was doing. Not getting any type of communication from him on Valentine's Day confirmed that we were over. I wondered if he'd spent it with Gabby.

"You know, your father and I are used to seeing you quit everything you do," Mom said. "It's good to see you stuck with your writing. I always thought it was a silly hobby, but your book is doing very well. We're proud of you, Rebecca."

"Thanks," I said, poking my steak with my fork.

"Yes, Becky Bear. It looks like your life is finally turning around," Dad said.

I didn't respond. He grabbed the television remote and changed the channel on the TV mounted on the wall from FOX Business to FOX News. I saw Ben standing next to his client doing a press conference. The headline read: *Rapper acquitted on all murder charges after surveillance video cleared him.*

"Ha. It looks like your loser ex pulled it off," Dad said.

I was so happy for Ben. No one deserved the win or the partnership more than he did. He'd worked his ass off for years, and it was nice to see all that hard work had paid off. Seeing Ben on TV only confirmed that I needed to talk to him. My book's success, my parents—nothing mattered if I didn't have him in my life.

"I have to see him," I said, pushing away from the table.

"Rebecca, leave him be," Dad said. "You're doing fine without him. This is all for the best."

"It's not fine. I love him."

"Rebecca, you made your choice, and he made his. You know what you'll lose if you marry him," Dad threatened.

I didn't care about the money or what everyone else thought. My heart was with Ben, and I wanted to be with him even if it meant giving up everything.

"I don't care about the money, Dad. You can't control me with that anymore. I make my own money."

"So, you're willing to give up your family to chase some nigger?" Dad said. "Let him take care of you. Pack two bags with as much as you can carry. Whatever you leave here with are the last things you'll ever get from your mother and me. Oh, and while you're at it, hand me your house and car keys."

"You would really disown me?" I said, staring at him.

"Without hesitation," he said sharply.

"Mom, you're going to let this happen?"

She didn't answer. I saw the pained expression on her face as she turned her head. I was sure she wanted to say something on my behalf, but she was a kept woman, and I knew she didn't want to risk ruining that.

"Fine. I'll start packing," I said.

"I'll have Bernard get the car ready so that he can drop you off," Dad said. "Once you step out of these doors and go to him, you're dead to us. You better hope your nigger takes you back."

Tears streamed down my face. I couldn't believe my father would talk to his only child like this.

I packed my bags and walked to the door. Dad was in his study. Mom was standing by the front door with Bernard.

"Becky, please don't do this," she said. "Just go upstairs and let's pretend this never happened."

I shook my head.

"Rebecca, can you stop fighting me and listen for once? Life doesn't have to be so hard. You're making this situation harder than it needs to be. Forget about Ben."

"Mom, I'm not like you," I said. "I'm not prim and proper, and I'm not going to stop fighting for something I love because Daddy wants to control me. I'm going to live my life and be happy. He's kicking me out of his life, but both of you will always have a place in mine."

Mom hugged me one last time, wiped her eyes, and walked upstairs.

"Are you ready, Ms. Rebecca?" Bernard asked.

"I'm as ready as I'll ever be."

Bernard dropped me off.

"For what it's worth, Ms. Rebecca, I think what you're doing is noble and brave. You're a strong, young woman, and I wish you nothing but the best."

I smiled through my tears. "Thank you, Bernard."

"I'm sure your father will want me to dispose of your things. When you patch things up with your fiancé, I will have everything stored for you so you can pick them up when you're ready."

I hugged him.

"Well, goodbye, Ms. Rebecca."

"Goodbye, Bernard, and thank you."

We hugged again, and he wished me well. I sat on the stairs in front of my old townhouse and texted Simone, letting her know what happened.

Me: Well, it's official. My parents disowned me and kicked me out. I'm sitting on the stoop in front of Ben's townhouse, hoping he'll take me back. I gave up everything for him.

Simone: What? I can't believe it, and, of course, he'll take you back. He drowned himself with work, but I know for a fact he was just as miserable as you were. I'm on my way. At least you can sit in the car with me until Ben comes home to let you in.

Me: You're the best.

Simone: I know this.

A huge raindrop landed on my forehead. It started to drizzle, and I prayed this wasn't a bad sign.

Chapter 44

Ben

Disappointment

"How do you feel?" Richard asked me.

We were back at the firm. Mrs. Wilson placed champagne and glasses in the conference room to celebrate the victory.

I gave Richard a faux smile.

"I feel good. I'm just happy this is all over, and I'm excited to embrace my lifelong goal of becoming a partner."

Richard, Tim, and Francis exchanged looks. Tim reeled back in his black executive chair. He looked uncomfortable before he spoke.

"About that . . . Well, it might be awhile before you become a partner, buddy," Tim said.

My smile quickly faded. "What do you mean, Tim? I sat with the three of you, right here in this conference room, and all of you assured me that if I did the impossible and pulled out a victory for this case, I'd make partner."

Tim couldn't look me in the eyes. Richard stood, turned his back to me, and stared out the window.

"Now, Ben, we never *promised* you that you'd be a partner," Francis said. "We said you'd be *considered,* and we did consider you, but we decided to go another route."

I willed myself to calm down and shook my head. "May I ask who the worthy one was that beat me out of the partnership?"

"We went with Mark Cruz," Richard said over his shoulder without turning to look at me.

I nodded slowly. "And you felt that he contributed to this firm more than I have in his short time here? I've been with this firm for nine years. He's been here for two."

"Now, Ben, there is no doubt you work hard for this firm," Francis said. "You're a strong, competent lawyer, and everyone in this room likes you. We've trusted you with a lot of high-profile cases, and today, you pulled off a miracle, but there's always room for growth. We gave you the incentive to grow with our consideration, and look at how well you did. In time, if you keep working hard for us, you'll make partner someday."

I curled my lips and exhaled slowly. I didn't want to say something I'd regret, but I was having a hard time holding my tongue.

"Sir, if not now, then when? Mark is a decent lawyer, but I put my heart and soul into working for that position. Dangling the possibility of one day making partner in my face feels like I'm being strung along and used. You haven't given him half of the responsibilities or difficult cases that I've been given. He took over the Alfieri case and lost. I've given this firm nine years of devotion, time away from my fiancée, my family, and my friends, because that's how much making partner meant to me, and to see it go to someone who hasn't been here as long as I have or who has put in as much work as I do . . . I'm sorry, but it isn't right."

Tim lowered his eyes to his hands resting on the table. I could see in his face that he knew everything I said was the truth, and this situation was wrong. Francis and Richard were fuming. Their red cheeks were telltale signs that they were pissed with my comment.

"Now, don't get cocky, Ben," Richard said. "It's true, we've given you a lot of difficult cases, but you've risen relatively quickly in this firm. You aren't too big where we couldn't put you right back to handling all of the grunt work—don't forget that. Mark hasn't been here long, but we felt he was well suited for the position. I and the rest of the partners' decision on the matter is final. We don't have to explain our reasoning. You're lucky we're even having this discussion with you. We're grateful for what you bring to this firm, but don't let it go to your head. There are thousands of lawyers out there that would kill to be in your shoes and could easily take your place. You're good, but you're *not* irreplaceable. Remember that."

I stared blankly at the shiny conference room table, stunned at the bullshit they were telling me.

"Look at it like this, Ben: we motivated you," Francis said.

"Motivated me?" I said. "Why couldn't you motivate Mark? My win record is way better than his, yet all of you feel he's better suited to make partner?"

"You need to watch your tone, Ben," Francis said. "If you don't end this conversation right now, we'll no longer have a place for you in this firm."

"After everything I've done for this firm, *that's* what you're telling me?"

"That's *exactly* what we're telling you," Richard said.

I shook my head. "None of you have respect or appreciation for me or what I do here, so expect my letter of resignation within the hour. All of you made it very apparent that I have no real future here at Wayne, Rothstein, and Lincoln."

"Ben, please don't—" Tim said before Richard cut him short.

"Let him go. He's nothing special. He's a dime a dozen."

His words reminded me of what Reggie once said to me on one of my visits to Rikers. He'd said once I was no longer useful, they'd view me as just another nigger, and he was right. That was exactly how I felt now.

"That's where you're wrong," I said. "I just won a major case. My client publicly told the world my name. I'm sure I'll have plenty of calls from other firms. Maybe I'll even start my own practice."

"Good luck. Hurry up and clear out your office," Francis stated coldly.

I walked my last box of things to my car. I was physically, emotionally, and mentally exhausted. After I sat behind the wheel, I cried. My chest heaved as I tried to release everything—the stress, the drama, all the shit I had gone through over these last few months. Then I drove home.

I parked my car in front of my townhouse. Becky was sitting on the front stoop with her head down, face buried in her hands as her elbows rested on her knees.

All the negative emotions dissipated the moment I saw her sitting on the stoop. Between my case, her book, and our family dramas, it felt like we were in an emotional hurricane, but seeing her now was proof that we'd weathered the storm.

I held my arms out, and Becky dove right into them. I kissed her and said, "Baby, what are you doing here?"

"I left my family. I gave up everything. I told you from day one, I love you, and you're worth fighting for."

I choked back tears and pulled her deeper into my arms. Gently, I lifted her chin to look in her eyes. "I'm sorry I hurt you. I love you, Becky."

Epilogue

Gabby

Leaving Ben's place after our argument, I needed time away from him. Two weeks later, I called Terrence over for our regular fuck-buddy sex session, and instead of doing our usual, I ended up venting and telling him everything that had happened between Ben and me.

"Why don't we give us a try?" Terrence asked.

I looked at him, surprised. "What?"

"You and me. We have chemistry. We've known each other forever, we have great sex together, and we're friends. Why don't we give it a try?"

I thought about it, and he was right. I needed to move on from Ben. I'd kept trying to preserve feelings that we had in the past that were faded. As much as I knew I'd always love him and his family, his heart wasn't with me anymore, and I had to accept that.

"Let's start off slow and see where we go from there," I said.

After that day, Terrence and I went on real dates beyond just meeting to have sex, and I felt my heart opening up to him. Since he and I had been single for so long, it took some getting used to when it came to being in an actual relationship, but I enjoyed his company. Before we made things official, we told Ben about us dating at one of our usual coffee dates.

"I'm very happy for both of you," he said. "Besides myself, I can't think of a better guy for you, Gabby." He hugged and kissed me. Then he turned to Terrence.

"I look at you like a brother, but if you hurt her, I'll kick your ass," Ben said.

They laughed and hugged. I was happy that I was dating a man who loved me. I didn't get the man I wanted, but life gave me the man I needed.

Ebony

"Oh, that looks good on you, boss lady," Rashida said.

I twisted side to side and admired my figure in the wedding dress. We were at Lotus Bridal on Avenue U in Brooklyn.

I was enjoying planning my wedding. Billy and I had made cutbacks to help save for it, but I wasn't worried about having an extravagant wedding. I was just happy that I was marrying Billy. I knew my brother was smiling down on us from heaven.

My drama with Morgan had made me face my guilt that I was silly enough to let my curiosity and inexperience with men manipulate me into lusting after another. Morgan and I never talked again. I heard rumors that Gibbs and her husband worked things out after she had the baby, but Morgan still had to pay child support. He wasn't thrilled about that. I was lucky. I could've easily been another statistic like Gibbs.

Going through my drama only made my relationship with Billy stronger. I continued doing my community events, but I didn't worry about how people perceived me when I took Billy with me to them anymore. I realized that the same way that I made it my goal to show communities that cops weren't all the same, I had to do the same thing for my relationship with Billy. When he went with me to my events, I proudly introduced him as my fiancé. I wasn't ashamed of him, and if I'd learned anything from these past months, it had been that you could still love your people and marry outside your race.

I turned and faced Rashida. "I think this is the one," I said. "It suits you."

"It's expensive."

"You got the money. You're getting promoted in a few months."

I laughed.

The past months had shown me that I didn't need to sleep with a hundred guys to know that I was happy. It didn't matter what people thought of me being with someone white. I couldn't let their opinion affect my goal of making a difference and uplifting my people.

Bill

After the Alfieri case, Wayne, Rothstein, and Lincoln blacklisted me with other firms. I wasn't a fan of going back to being a public defender, but it looked like I had no choice. Luckily for me, Ben called me up out of the blue and asked me if I wanted to become a partner with him in a new firm he was building with his best friend, Terrence. I'd never been the type for idleness, and with being unemployed for over two months, I jumped at his offer. After dealing with the Alfieri case, I was done with practicing criminal defense law. As a partner in our new firm, I decided to focus on civil, commercial, and environmental litigation. I never wanted to be put in a situation similar to Johnny's again.

Ben and I became good friends. After Ebony realized that Ben's client didn't kill those cops and couple, she cut Bill some slack, and we'd been hanging out, having couples' nights on the regular. It was nice seeing Ebony becoming close to Ben's girl, Becky. Ebony, Becky, and Ben's cousin, Simone, made it a ritual to go once a week to get mani/pedis done.

I missed my mom every day. I hoped if she could see me now that I'd make her proud. Life for me had never been easy, but everything worked out for the best.

Ben

Months passed. Reggie became an even bigger star after the case and sent me tickets to all of his concerts whenever he was on tour. Lots of firms wanted me after my big win with Reggie, but after a lot of thought, I decided to listen to Terrence and start a practice with him. To help out our firm, I suggested we pick up another partner, and I knew just the person. It was a win for all of us when Bill joined us to form our own firm, Jensen, Turner, and O'Neil. Thanks to Reggie, all types of celebrities came to our firm for legal advice and services.

Becky and I were still going strong. Her book, *Black and White,* reached number one on the New York and LA Times bestseller lists. Her book was being considered for a movie adaptation, and she was working on her next novel, *Wounded.* Becky's parents kept their promise and disowned her. She reached out to them on numerous occasions, but they wanted nothing to do with her. It took her awhile to adjust, but after giving up her family for me, my parents were extraloving toward her. Becky continued to surprise me. She planned a trip for us to go to Washington, D.C., and see the National Museum of African American History and Culture. It made me happy to see that she wanted to and was willing to learn more about my culture. With Gabby dating Terrence, Becky didn't look at her as a threat anymore. I knew they'd never be friendly or hang out alone together, but it was nice seeing Gabby, Simone, and Becky cooking with my mom in the kitchen on my birthday. They'd promised to make me a feast. My dad and Terrence were setting the table.

"Look at the most important women in my life working hard in the kitchen," I said.

"Gabby is showing me how to make macaroni and cheese, and your mom is teaching me how to make the chocolate chip cookies you like," Becky said.

"*That's* what I'm talking about," I replied.

Dinner was great, and Becky handed me a box of cookies with a note in it.

"What's the note say?" I asked.

"Read it and find out, Big Head," Gabby said.

I opened the note.

Eat all the cookies. I don't want to be the only one with a huge belly. Love, all of us.

It took me a second, but then it hit me. I was going to be a father!

"Really?" I asked.

Becky nodded.

I hugged and kissed her.

"Congratulations," Gabby said.

She didn't look like she was holding in anger—she genuinely smiled as if she were happy for me.

My dad and Terrence hugged me, and I was excited to start a family with Becky. Like life, our relationship was a beautiful struggle, but together, we made it worth the fight.

Simone decided she would be more open-minded, and dated men of every race instead of limiting herself to the white ones. She wanted to improve her life and felt the next step to doing that was by meeting her sister.

Simone and I walked into S&S studios in the Bronx. No one was at the counter.

"Give me a second. I'll be right out," a female said from the back room.

When the woman stepped out, she had the same green eyes, complexion, and cheekbones as Simone.

"Can I help you?" the woman asked us.

"I-I-I'm Simone Miller. Are you Samantha?"

The woman looked taken aback by her question.

"I am. Why?"

"I'm not trying to cause any trouble, but I'm your sister."

"Excuse me?" Samantha said. "I think you have the wrong person. I'm an only child."

"Was your mother named Joan?" Simone asked.

"Who are you? Who's this guy with you? I don't know what shit you two are trying to pull, but it needs to stop."

"No. Please, I'm not trying to get anything from you. This is my . . . our cousin. He's here for support because I wanted to meet you finally."

Samantha balled up her fist. She looked like she was about to start swinging and cursing us out. Simone quickly kept talking.

"Your father's name was Sam Miller. Our mother's name was Joan. She had me seven years before you were born, but her half brother, Curtis, took me in because she couldn't stop using."

Samantha's face softened. "What do y'all want from me?" she asked.

"Nothing. I just want to get to know you," Simone said.

Their relationship wasn't built overnight, but over time, Simone and Samantha became close. Samantha even gave Simone a management job at the studio.

Every year, Simone, Samantha, Becky, and I went with my dad down to the old neighborhood and helped him hand out food to the community. I finally understood the reasoning and purpose of why we did it.

My case with Reggie helped me gain a strong sense of who I was. I was just me. Regardless of whether people thought I "acted white," I didn't let idiotic statements by some people faze me anymore. I was secure with being the strong black man that I was, and I didn't need anyone's validation.